A Casualty of Hope

Marguerite Mooers

Books by Marguerite Mooers

Take My Hand (2014)

The Shelter of Darkness (2015)

A Casualty of Hope (2016)

The Girl in the Woods (2017)

The Life That He Lived (2018)

The Lies That He Told (2019)

Praise for Marguerite Mooers' novels

"**Take My Hand** is a very good read--a well constructed mystery with an appealing detective reconstructing the scene and possible suspects of a 'cold case' child abduction. Mooers constructs the pieces of her puzzle nicely with an ultimately persuasive but not immediately obvious solution." Amazon review.

"The tension of '**Take My Hand**' really builds from the moment the detectives start investigating and does not let up---no easy feat for a procedural like this. Lorna is a great secondary character, with a well-developed emotional arc and compelling relationships that make her involvement in the case even more tense and dangerous." Writers Digest 23rd Self-Published Book Awards

For **The Shelter of Darkness** "The character of Al brought great tension to the story and when they found his body, well, it only got better until ending on a wonderful, heartwarming note. A wonderful book. I thoroughly enjoyed it." Goodreads Review

"Marguerite Mooers is a talented writer whose characters will send your heart pounding with fear and your palms sweating with suspense. Overall I loved this novel. **A Casualty of Hope** is everything readers will want and ask for in a fictional piece. Brilliantly well written and told for readers worldwide to enjoy. I highly recommend this book to all" Universal Creativity Inc14 review

"A deftly crafted and riveting novel. **A Casualty of Hope** is a compelling page-turner from beginning to end. Very highly recommended." Midwest Book Review

For **The Girl in the Woods**. "*I loved this book right from the beginning, it grabs at you, making you keep turning the pages. I would highly recommend this book!*" Amazon review

For **The Girl in the Woods** "*Being a northern New Yorker myself, I plucked this murder mystery off my to-read pile, figuring to spend a few spare minutes looking into it, only to find that I couldn't put it down, ending up reading it in one setting, something I almost never do. Ms. Mooers, an Adirondack '46'r' is a marvelous storyteller, a crafter of mystery plotting whose intricacies will keep you guessing right up to the jaw-dropping ending. If you're ever camping in the Adirondacks, Ms. Mooers is just the yarn-spinner you'll want around the midnight campfire.*" Amazon review

For **The Life That He Lived**: " (I) *Would like to say I loved this book and would refer it to everyone that reads. The book only took me 3 days to read. I couldn't put down.*" Amazon review.

"Hope is the last thing ever lost."
Italian Proverb

"When the world says "Give up,' hope whispers '
Try it one more time'."
Anonymous

Chapter One

"Why are you here, Mrs. Robertson?"

I looked at Dr. Swartz, a slender middle-aged man with graying temples and bright blue eyes partly hidden by glasses. His right hand held a pen poised over a yellow legal pad, waiting.

"Call me Bernie," I said. "It's short for Bernice, although I know no one names their kid Bernice these days, but my mother thought I ought to have a family name and so that's what I got..." I was foaming at the mouth like a landed fish, something I'm prone to do when nervous. I looked at Dr. Swartz who had crossed his legs and was flexing the hand not holding the pen, waiting for me to get over my attack. I shifted in my chair, trying to see if he wore a wedding ring. Did it really matter if he were married or single? I needed to concentrate on why I was here.

"My mother sent me," I blurted, which, although true, makes me seem like I'm twelve, when in fact, I am twenty-six, almost divorced and supporting myself and my child. Even though my mother had pushed me into making the appointment and was paying the bill, I had agreed to this.

"At least, she suggested it," I added. Dr. Swartz had turned toward the window, where outside I could hear a bird singing. *Come on, Bernie. Tell him why you're here.*

"I have a recurring nightmare that terrifies me so much that I'm afraid to go to sleep."

He began to scribble on his pad.

"I'm in the desert. It's night and snowing hard. I can hear the person behind me who is so

1

close I feel his breath on my neck. When I try to go faster, I keep slipping on the snow. Someone has hold of my hand and is urging me to go faster, but I can't."

"You've had this dream more than once?"

"I have. I wake and feel like I'm still locked in this scary dream bubble, in a world that I can't break away from. I don't know why I'm in the desert, or why someone is chasing me. All I know is that I have to get away."

"Dreams aren't always rational Bernie, but a recurring nightmare like this could be a response to stress." He smiled at me. "Tell me what's going on in your life."

"I'm divorcing my husband Charlie," I said. "And I'm single-handedly raising an eighteen-month old daughter, Miranda." I could have told him that I lived in a crappy two bedroom apartment and that Charlie was never going to pay me alimony, no matter what the courts said, and I'd probably be as poor as I was now for the rest of my life.

"Do you have a lot of stress at your job. You said you were..." He glanced at the pad on his lap.

"I'm a secretary in the Anthropology department of Tyndale college. It's not a really stressful job and the boss is great. I was all set to go to Cornell on a scholarship before I graduated from high school."

I don't really know why I said that bit about my early acceptance. I didn't want this kindly man to see me as a woman with only a high school diploma. I wanted him to know that once, before I married Charlie, I'd had a promising future.

"How do you feel when you wake up from one of these dreams?"

"Shaky, tense. My heart is beating fast and my hands are wet. I'm struggling across the desert, slipping in the snow and I have to hurry because the person with the gun..."

"The gun?"

"He has a gun and he's getting closer, yelling at me to stop, but my mother is pulling me along, telling me to hurry."

"Your mother is in this dream?"

"It's not the mother who adopted me when I was little. It feels like this woman is my birth mother."

"Have you ever met your birth mother?"

"Never."

"Do you have a good relationship with your adoptive mother?"

"The best. She really loves my daughter, Miranda, which is a good thing, because Charlie, my almost-ex, wants nothing to do with her."

"Dreams are the body's way of processing things that have happened in your life," Dr. Swartz said. "Your feeling of being chased could be triggered by the stress of the divorce."

"My dream is always the same. If it were just stress, wouldn't the scenario change?"

He was silent, looking down at the pad resting on his lap. "The other possibility is that this recurring nightmare reflects something that happened in the past, but that you have forgotten. Sometimes people's minds push aside events because those things are too terrifying to remember, being sexually assaulted as a child, for instance. Do you think this was the case Bernie?"

I thought back to my father, a large quiet man, who was always working, but made time to be at every school play, concert, baseball game or junior high science project that I'd ever participated in. Had he been a different person than I remembered?

"My father was a good man. He died three years ago of a heart attack and I miss him. If he had done that kind of thing, wouldn't I feel differently about him?"

"What about your birth father? You said the woman in the dream felt like your birth mother. Could you have been running from your birth father?"

"I suppose. But why am I remembering this now?"

"Sometimes repressed memories can be triggered by something related to the event. In this case, divorcing your husband makes you feel powerless. The events in the dream may be different, but the emotion is the same."

"On the other hand, if the dream is the repressed memory of an actual event, you might begin to remember other details surrounding it. What initially emerged in the safety of your dreams now begins to speak to you directly. Do you remember when these dreams began, and can you recall anything that might have triggered them? Was there something frightening that made you feel at the mercy of someone else?"

I thought for a while. It was now September and the dreams had started in midsummer, possibly July. What had happened then?

"It was about eight o'clock at night, and I was crossing the parking lot of the grocery store, pushing my cart with Miranda in it. Suddenly an SUV roared into the parking lot, coming to a stop about two feet from me, its headlights blazing. The driver, who was a woman, got out and apologized, but my heart was pounding and all I could think of was that I had to get away. I raced to the car, strapped Miranda in, loaded the groceries and sped out of there. I think it took me two hours at home to finally calm down and later that night, I had the dream for the first time."

"Could there be a connection between the SUV in the parking lot, and your dream of being chased through the desert?"

"I guess so."

"Let me give you some relaxation exercises to try," Dr. Swartz said. "I'd also like you to keep a dream journal, writing down everything you can remember immediately on waking, and putting down events of the previous day that might have triggered those dreams. If you have a strange reaction to what should be an ordinary event, write that down too."

"When Charlie and I moved into our apartment, I made him help me remove the doors to every closet in the place."

"Why was that?"

"I was afraid of getting trapped inside."

"Have you ever been trapped inside a closet?"

"No. Do you think I'm crazy? Charlie thought I was."

"How do you feel when you are inside a closet with the door closed?"

"Panicked, like I can't breathe. It's like there is someone outside who is threatening me and I have nowhere to run."

He was writing in his notebook again. I glanced at my watch and realized that our time was up. I had only a few minutes to get to Little Tots Daycare and pick up my daughter.

"Bernie, would you consider hypnotism? It might help you with your anxiety, and we could possibly get to the root of your dream."

"You won't make me dance naked on the desk?"

"Promise," he said and smiled. "See you next week?"

I nodded. Grabbing my purse, I raced toward the door.

When I got to Little Tots and saw the empty lot, I realized that I was seriously late. I raced toward the toddler room where my daughter was sitting alone on the floor. Seeing me, she got up, cried "Mama" and waddled toward me, grasping me firmly around the legs. Miss Mary, a fifty-something matron with badly dyed hair and false teeth was glaring at me. Miss Hazel, the other caretaker was busy flipping off lights

"It's late, Mrs. Robertson," Miss Mary said. "We close at five-thirty."

It was now almost six. "I'm sorry. I just couldn't get out of the meeting any sooner. I promise it won't happen again."

Miss Mary wasn't buying any of it. She thrust Mira's bag at me and handed me the clipboard to sign. Struggling to put on Mira's coat in the darkened room, I silently cursed the two women, especially Miss Mary, who would be better off working as a prison warden. With Miss Mary and Miss Hazel close behind, I hustled my daughter to the car. "OK, princess," I said, when we were strapped in, "Shall we have pizza for supper?"

"Piza, piza," Mira shouted.

Normally we eat out only on Friday night. This was Wednesday and if I had been a good mother, I would have taken my child home to a supper of pasture- raised beef and free-range vegetables. Instead we would dine on three of the standard American food groups: white flour, fat and salt. Mira loved pizza, and would eat it twenty-four seven. Some things were just easier at the end of a long day.

On Saturday, we would be at my mother's house and Mom would cook us something healthful and delicious. Bliss.

We stopped at Angelo's Pizza to pick up our order. Angelo himself stood behind the counter, greeting us enthusiastically as we entered.

"Miss Bernie, Miss Miranda. How are you guys?"

Angelo had moved to Tyndale, New York from Brooklyn twenty years ago to get away from the city. You can take the boy, or in this case, the balding, overweight, voluble Italian man out of Brooklyn, but you can never take Brooklyn out of the man.

"You want the usual ?" he asked, turning to take a pizza box from behind him.

We'd been buying one small cheese pizza, and one small pepperoni pizza every week for a year now. Why make life complicated? Mira was behind me, mauling an incredibly patient cat that lay on the tile floor. Mira loved animals and was always begging for a cat or dog, but the closest we'd ever gotten to a pet, was when we took in a neighbor's hamster for a week, and after seven days I was eager to give it back. I had only enough energy to care for myself and one other living being.

"Your husband Charlie, he came lookin' for a job," Angelo said. "Told me he needed the money so he could support his two angels."

What a load of crap. If Charlie had thought of us as his 'angels' he would have worked harder to keep a job while I was still married to him.

"Did you hire him?"

"Nah. I ain't got but one person to work with me. I don't need more. Charlie said he was lookin' to move up to management. What's management? I'm the management. Ain't no one else." He handed me the pizzas and I paid him. Mira reluctantly released the cat, and we went to the car.

Driving home, I thought about Charlie. If my ex-husband was going to be in the area, I might see him at a restaurant, the local hardware store or the Feed and Grain. He might end up fixing my car, or mowing lawns in my neighborhood. Charlie was never going to be management, much as he might think so. I wished he would just move away.

I got to our building and muscled the baby and all of our stuff out of the car and up the stairs to the second floor apartment. Putting Mira down, I unlocked the door and pushed the pizzas, my purse and Mira's things inside. I flipped on the light and we went in.

Since Charlie and I had split a year ago, I'd made some changes. I'd painted the walls, replaced an elderly couch with a sprightlier one, and put some of my own pen-and-ink drawings on the walls in place of Charlie's rock star posters. But I had to face it. The place was still a dump.

I pulled off our coats, hung them on the hook, and turned on the TV, pushing a DVD into the player.

"Piza," Mira said.

"It's coming. Let's get you some milk and a drink for Mommy."

I know. In addition to picking their children up at daycare on time, good mommies take the time to entertain their children with uplifting educational experiences, treasuring every minute with the little ones. Bad mommies plunk them in front of the TV, so they can get supper and have a glass of wine, not necessarily in that order.

When I got back to the living room with the food, Mira was glued to the set. I put the pizzas on the coffee table and sat on the couch sipping at my wine. Picking up the crumpled paper Miss Mary had handed me, I read about Mira's day. "Snack at 8:30. Ate everything." I'm afraid my daughter has my genes, and if she's not careful, she'll have a weight issue. But at eighteen months none of that matters. *Eat up sweetie, this is your chance.* I went back to the list. "Ten o'clock used the potty." Good girl. She still wore diapers, but soon, soon, she might even go without those.

"Horsie Mommy," Mira said, pointing to the TV where a horse was galloping across the screen.

"Yes, a horse," I said. "Come on, honey. Don't just eat the cheese and the sauce. Eat the whole pizza."

Mira made a face. Two cut up crusts sat on the table in front of her, nakedly accusing. She'd be hungry at midnight and then we'd both be up.

I had just taken a bite of my own pizza when my cell phone rang. It was my mother. I turned on the speaker phone.

"Hi, honey. How are you doing?" Her voice was riddled with static and hard to hear.

"Just a minute Mom, my phone's giving me trouble." I moved it away from the TV and the static died down.

"What's wrong with your phone?"

"I don't know. I need to trade it in for a new one, but I just haven't had the money. Sometimes the line is all staticky, or the battery goes dead for no reason or the light comes on. I need to spend more money the next time."

"How did it go with Dr. Swartz?"

"OK. He thinks the dream might be a response to my divorcing Charlie."

"I could have told you that for free. What are you guys doing?"

"Eating pizza and watching a DVD. Mira only eats the cheese and sauce. She's covered with it right now, but she's happy. Want to say hi?"

I put down the phone. "It's Grammy, Mira."

Mira turned her attention from the TV and grabbed the phone with sauce-covered hands. She began to relate a long, convoluted story that seemed to be mostly about what was happening in the movie.

"Did you understand any of that?" I asked when I got the phone back.

"Not much, but it's wonderful that she'll talk to me."

"She adores you, Mom. You still want us on Saturday?"

"Of course, come by at ten. I'll have a nice brunch , and I have someone to tell you about."

"Someone? Like a male someone?"

"His name is Clint Morrison. I met him on line. Oh Bernie, I feel like I'm twenty years old again."

A wave of jealousy swept over me. Why should my fifty-five year old mother have a boyfriend, when I, an eligible twenty-six year old, hadn't had a date since God was in diapers? I rung off and stood, flipping off the TV. Mira looked at me, her face crumpling.

"Bed time sweetie." In fact it was almost eight-thirty, way past Mira's bed-time.

"No." she said. In the last few months this had become her favorite word.

Tomorrow was a work day, which meant early reveille for both of us.

I picked up my ornery daughter, who was struggling against me. "No." she said again.

I wiped her face and hands of pizza sauce, then I said. "We'll get into our PJ's, and have a story. How about *The Bear Who Flew*?"

"No." Mira said. I went to her bookshelf and pulled out three of her favorites, *The Giving Tree*, *You Are My Sunshine*, and *Baby's First One Hundred Words*. When I was putting on her pajamas, she asked. "Where's Grammy?"

"She's at her house. We will see her on Saturday."

"Sataday."

We snuggled together in our story chair, Miranda's favorite book in front of us, the bottle in her mouth. "The little bear was really sad," I read. "He missed his mommy and daddy, and especially his pet elephant, Burt. " I stopped reading and looked over at Miranda who was fighting sleep. *Come on, honey, go to sleep I want some time to myself tonight.*

Mira opened her eyes. "Mommy?"

"What, sweetie?"

I waited, watching Mira's eyes closing. The question hung in the air unspoken. I stroked Mira's fine hair, feeling the softness under my hand and hearing her breathing became regular. When she started to snore, I put her in her crib and made my way quietly out of the room.

In the living room, I wiped up the pizza stains from the coffee table, the television, and the cell phone. I gathered up Mira's dirty clothes and put them in the hamper and washed out her snack container, and our dishes. Then I poured myself another glass of wine and sat on the couch.

Glancing around me, I remembered how exciting this small apartment had been when I was seventeen and newly married. I'd never lived with anyone but my parents, and being a new wife, and mother-to-be made the drab place fun. Every day, during those first few months, I would spend hours teaching myself to make exotic recipes, some of them even edible, and each night I would set the table with candles and wait for Charlie to come home.

When I was seventeen, I thought that Charlie wanted what I wanted: children and a home. I thought he would work his way up to be the director of a local company, or start his own firm. I never occurred to me until after we lost our first baby how unhappy Charlie was.

In the years that he was employed, Charlie complained that his co-workers disliked him, that his boss didn't understand him, or that the work didn't give him a chance to show what he could do. Even with all my encouragement, he couldn't find his niche. And then, belatedly, I realized that there never would be a niche for Charlie.

Several months after our seventh anniversary, I came home to find Charlie in our bed with the babysitter. After I got over my anger, I realized that even though we had a daughter together, we would never be happy, and I filed for divorce. Since then, Charlie seemed to have no interest in seeing his daughter, and had contributed nothing to her support. Well, I said to myself, that was his loss.

It was getting late. I got up from the chair and gulped down the rest of the wine. It was almost eleven, and with luck I would sleep without any dreams at all.

Chapter Two

On Saturday morning, Mira and I drove east to my mother's lakefront home. After my father died, my mother sold the house in Tyndale and moved to a place on Little Beaver Lake. She said she wanted live theatre, an art center where she could paint, a fitness center and unlike Tyndale's only big box store, Wal-Mart, she wanted quality shopping. Although Mom had no interest in water activities, she did like the view, which today as we went up the driveway was spectacular. Carmine and gold trees glowed against the blue sky. A group of geese were swimming across the water, and as we watched, they become airborne moving into the V formation as they traveled.

Mom was standing in the front hallway when we arrived, and as we got closer, Mira rushed toward her grandmother and they hugged eagerly. Mom took Mira up and kissed her loudly all over her fat little cheeks. Then she tickled her, which left Mira breathless with laughter. Whatever neglect Charlie showed toward Miranda is more than made up for by my mother's enthusiasm for her grand-daughter. Maybe in the end, unconditional love from someone is all a child needs really needs.

I followed my mother into the kitchen which smelled deliciously of newly-brewed coffee. If you saw my mother and me together, you would know immediately that we're not blood relatives. My mother is five foot six with blonde hair, blue eyes, and a perfectly sculpted face. Some of this is good genes, but a lot of it is plastic surgery, a strict diet and Jazzercise. She loads her arms up with silver

13

bangles that jingle as she cooks or drinks a cup of coffee, something she's doing now.

I, on the other hand, am five feet in my stockings with brown eyes and straight dark hair. I tend toward plumpness, and have no money for fancy jewelry, silver or any other kind.

When the enthusiastic greeting had quieted down, Mom offered me coffee while Mira got milk. We sat at the table while Mom served up hash browns, scrambled eggs and apple muffins. A bowl of cut-up fruit went on the table, as well as a pitcher of orange juice.

"I love this restaurant," I said.

"It's great to have you here."

We ate in silence. I'd been trying to work out why the particular scenario of the dream should be in my head. I'd lived my whole life in northern New York and snow wasn't a surprise. But why should I dream about a desert?

"Mom, when you adopted me, was it anywhere near a desert?"

"Of course," she said, "The orphanage was in Laredo, Texas, right on the border of Mexico. The Chihuahuan desert is on both sides of the border."

"How old was I?"

"Three or four. No one had a birth certificate for you, so we had to take a guess. And you were so tiny." And then she launched into a story I've heard many times before, the one I call "How I Found You."

"Your father was working for Anadarco and we were living in San Antonio. We'd been married for five years, and I was beginning to wonder why we couldn't get pregnant. One day, I was visiting Laredo and I saw this gaggle of little boys and girls, all about three, four, and five and wearing some kind of uniform. I followed them. They were so cute, and I had nothing better to do. They went to a park and played, under the supervision of two nuns. At first I thought it was a play group, but then I realized, because of the nuns, that it was a Parochial pre-school. I sat on a bench, watching the children run around and for the first time, I realized how much I wanted to be a mother."

"And you followed the group back to the building," I said. I knew this story by heart, but my mother never tired of telling it.

"When the children went inside, I followed them."

"And you learned that it wasn't a school, but an orphanage. What did they call it?"

"The Sacred Heart Children's Home. It was run by nuns called The Servants of the Sacred Heart of Jesus."

She walked back to the stove. "More eggs or hash browns?" I shook my head turning toward Mira. "In the orphanage, Grammy saw this little girl who was called Grace. That was me."

My mother came over to me and gave me a hug. Then she pushed up the sleeve of my sweater and gave the little birthmark heart on my arm a kiss. "You were my little darling," she said.

I knew that my birth mother had left me at the orphanage and then had disappeared, and in April of the following year, I'd been found wandering by myself in Laredo. In 1994, after giving up the search for my parents, the orphanage allowed me to be adopted by Ralph and Cyndi Sorengard.

I knew this story by heart, but I had no answer to the question that was stuck squarely in the middle of the tale, and which I'd thought about over and over since I was a child. Had my birth mother abandoned me at the orphanage because I was an inconvenience, or had she done it for some other reason? And what had happened to cause me, a toddler, to wander out onto the darkened streets of Laredo, Texas alone?

"You said I didn't talk when they found me?"

My mother nodded. "When the police took you to the orphanage in Laredo, the nuns recognized you as Grace Morales. Because you didn't talk, we didn't know anything else about you."

"But they tried to find my birth parents didn't they?"

A look passed over my mother's face. "Of course they did," she said. "They tried everything."

"How long was I in the orphanage?"

"Six months, I think. Let me show you something."

She left the room and returned a few minutes later with a cardboard box that once held shoes. "I thought this had been lost, but it was with a box of stuff from our Texas days." She opened the box and pulled out a folded garment.

"This was yours," she said, holding up a child's dress. A piece of paper fluttered to the ground. My mother picked it up and shoved it into her pocket before handing me the dress.

"What was that?" I asked.

"What was what?"

"The paper that fell to the floor. You stuck it in your pocket."

"Nothing. An old newspaper ad. Look at how small you were."

I looked at the dress which was covered with a faded pattern of roses. It was made of cotton, washed to a thin, soft remnant of its earlier self. There were little puff sleeves and a tiny collar.

"You were wearing this dress when they found you. And this was pinned to the dress. " She handed me a thin silver medal. "It's called a *milagro*. A good luck charm."

The charm was made of thin metal, oval in shape with the image of the Virgin Mary. Her cloak covered her head, and around her head and body were incised rays.

I studied the little dress, trying to imagine myself wandering in a strange town and being picked up by a stranger. I had no memory of who my birth parents were, and no memory of the first few years of my life. Nothing except the nightmare of running through the desert in the snow, pursued by a man with a gun. A nightmare that might be just a figment of my stressed-out brain.

"What shall we do today?" my mother asked, looking at Miranda. "How about the zoo?"

"Tigaas," Miranda said.

"And monkeys," I said. "We love the monkeys don't we?"

Miranda nodded enthusiastically.

"We could go to the mall, too." My mother said. "I noticed how small Mira's winter coat is."

"I should have bought one last August when the coats were on sale at Wal-Mart" I said. "Now, in September, there are none left."

"I want to buy you a new coat too, Bernie."

"You don't need to, Mom. I can eke out another season with the one I have."

"I'd like to get you a coat, honey. Someone on her way up in the business world needs proper clothing."

I'm not exactly "on my way up in the business world," but I appreciated my mother's faith in me, and her willingness to front the bills.

By the end of the day, Mira had run her little legs off at the zoo and crashed as we cruised the mall looking for winter coats. The speed at which my child outgrows clothing staggers me. I need one of those swap thingies where you hand off one used garment your kid has outgrown in favor of another used garment someone else's kid has outgrown. When I was first married, I had a group of friends from high school who would meet regularly and chat. Since then, most of those girls have gone to places larger than Tyndale, or found jobs that paid more than secretarial work, or had married husbands who didn't cheat on them. I was so embarrassed by my crappy apartment, that I didn't invite former friends over, and as a result my back closet was filling up with Mira's old stuff.

I had just come into the living room after putting a tired toddler to bed. Mom was sitting at the couch with a bowl of popcorn and two glasses of wine. Did I say she paid attention to what she ate? Sometimes.

She flicked on the TV and pushed in a DVD. *Jane Eyre* popped up on the screen.

"How many times have you seen this movie, Mom?"

"This version? About six times. There are about four or five other versions, but this one is the best."

"I love that line where she says 'Do you think because I am poor, obscure, plain and little, I am soul-less and heartless. I have as much soul as you, and fully as much heart.'"

"And then she says, 'It is my spirit that addresses your spirit, just as if we'd passed through the grave and stood at God's feet equal— as we are.'"

"He's a bastard. But she loves him." I sat down beside my mother on the couch, ready to do what women love to do, find a good sappy movie and cry their hearts out.

We got to the part of the movie where Jane is sent to the work house, one of those grim Dickensian places where underfed children shiver in their beds and get whipped if they ask for 'more, please.' As the camera panned to an entry shot of the work house. I could feel a Tsunami of grief welling up inside me, and the tears starting. "Mama," I said.

"Bernie, what's the matter honey?" my mother asked, putting her arms around me. "Tell me."

I couldn't speak. I didn't know why I was crying, just that some image in the movie had cracked my heart open.

"Let me turn this off," my mother said, rushing to shut off the video. We sat on the couch together, my mother with her arm around me as I sobbed into her shoulder.

"Tell me what is it," she said.

I shook my head. I didn't know what had happened, only that something on the screen had triggered a deep sadness inside me.

"Well," my mother said, finally. "I'm going to make an exception to one of my own rules about food. How about ginger ale with ice cream and no *Jane Eyre* for a while."

"Mom," I asked. "Do you remember what the orphanage in Laredo was like? The one where you found me?"

"Hmmm. Let me think. A yellow two story building with a huge entrance way. We only saw the public rooms where prospective parents met the kids, never the bedrooms or the dining room."

"People in uniforms?"

"Nuns. They were very nice to us. But then we were there to adopt a child."

"Thanks."

"OK to start it up?"

I nodded, wondering what had caused that flotsam of memory to rise to the surface? Before my dream of running through the desert in the snow, I'd been blissfully ignorant of a former life, but now something was rumbling deep inside me, not yet ready to erupt, but present and waiting.

We watched the rest of the movie without any more incidents, but that night I dreamed of a large building with huge windows. I was standing in an entryway, and a nun was reaching for my hand while my mother stood beside me. I clutched at my mother's legs, begging her not to go, tears streaming down my face, but she slowly disengaged herself, gave me a kiss and was gone.

I woke to darkness and quiet in the house. Finding my robe, I wandered into the kitchen, thinking I'd make a cup of something that might help me sleep.

Beside the kitchen is a little nook that holds a washer and dryer. A load of dirty clothes lay in a basket on top of the washing machine, and in the basket were Mom's jeans. A tiny slip of paper was sticking out of one of the pockets. Had this been what she'd plucked up from the floor when she was showing me the dress?

I snatched the paper from the pocket and went back to the kitchen, unfolding it on the table. It was a personal ad from *The Laredo Morning Times*, dated October 29, 1994 and read:

"Looking for my little girl. Graciela has dark curly hair and a heart shaped birthmark on her arm. Reward offered. If you find, please call L. Morales."

Listed was a phone number and a reward for information.

My mother said I was called Grace Morales. Had she lied when she told me she had no knowledge of my birth parents? L. Morales might be my birth mother or my birth father. I wondered if my mother had ever made that call.

"You're up," It was my mother's voice. She was standing in the doorway to the kitchen wearing a pink terrycloth robe over cotton pajamas.

I held up the newspaper. "Why didn't you tell me Mom?"

My mother said nothing. I walked toward her. "This might have been my birth mother or my father. Someone was trying to find me."

"Bernie, listen to me, please." She took me by the hand but I shook her away.

"I found that ad three weeks after your adoption was finalized. We were passing through Laredo on our way to go shopping. I don't know why I bought the paper. Wait. Yes, I remember. We were looking for furniture for the house. I pulled out the personals because sometimes people advertise cheap stuff in them and there it was. When I read it, I felt like someone had taken a sharpened stick to my heart."

She walked toward the stove and stood facing me. "I couldn't give you back, Bernie. We had waited so long for a baby and I wanted you so much. How did I know that the person advertising in the paper wasn't some psycho who wanted a child for slave labor? I hid the paper and forgot about it. I never even told your father." She took the coffee pot to the sink and poured water into the carafe and then went about putting in grounds and turning on the machine. I watched her. This woman was the only mother I had ever known, but at that moment she was a stranger.

When the coffee had begun to brew she turned to me again. "I love you, honey. Please don't hate me. Your father and I wanted to give you the best life we could, and we did didn't we?"

I nodded. I had been lucky in my adoptive parents, but the thought that all this time there had been someone searching for me was haunting.

"I should have thrown the paper away," my mother said. "It would have been easier."

"You wouldn't have done that, would you?"

She shook her head. "I thought about it. But it was your history I would have been destroying, and I realized that someday you might want to know who your birth parents were. This was the only clue I had."

She poured two cups of coffee from the carafe and brought them to the table, where I was sitting. Pushing a cup toward me, she said, "You are entitled to your own history, Bernie, and if you choose to go back and find where you came from, I can't stop you. As much as I wish I were the mother that gave birth to you, that isn't the reality, but I do love you very much."

She wiped a tear away with a tissue and took a sip of her coffee. I leaned over and kissed her. "You're my mother," I said. "Always will be."

Chapter Three

When I got back to the apartment on Sunday afternoon there was a familiar truck
waiting in the parking lot. *Damn,* it was late and I was tired. I had no energy for wrangling with Charlie.

"Hiya Bernie," he said. He was leaning against the side of the building, just outside my front door. I hadn't seen him since the day after Mira's birthday when he'd arrived with a toy that scared the pants off her. His hair needed cutting and his jeans were torn and dirty. If he was with someone, she wasn't taking very good care of him.

"I don't have time for this, Charlie. I've got work tomorrow." I set Mira down on the ground and fished for the keys. Mira clung to my pant leg, looking at her father with apprehension.

"She doesn't like me much, does she?"

"Children live in the present, Charlie. She hasn't seen you since you moved out. If you'd come around more often, she might warm up."

"I wouldn't have been a stranger to Jimmy."

It was such an off-the-wall thing to say that I stopped and stared at him. Jimmy or James Carter Robertson had been our baby that died. He'd been born full term, with lots of dark hair and a lusty cry that could be heard down the block.

One morning when Jimmy was two months old, I'd gone to his crib to wake him. It was later than he usually woke, but I thought a growth spurt might have prompted his desire to sleep in. It wasn't until I touched his skin, and found it cold that I realized Jimmy would never wake or cry again. I would never see him learn to walk, hear his first words, watch him graduate from high school, or get married. Jimmy was gone. The doctor diagnosed SIDS, which was really no diagnosis at all. As much as I loved Miranda, some deep part of me still grieved for the loss of my little boy.

"Are you telling me that if Mira were a boy, you would come see her more often?"

Charlie stared at the wall, not willing to look me in the eye. "A man needs a son, Bernie, someone to carry on the family name."

"Carry on what family name? It's not like we're royalty or anything. And what noble attributes would you have your son carry on? You haven't held a job for more than a month in all the years we were married. You want a son that will be as shiftless as you are?"

I could see him stiffen in anger, but he tried to control it. "I didn't come here to argue, Bernie. I just wanted to talk."

"The only thing I want to talk about, Charlie, is money. We have a daughter that I'm raising on my own. It would be nice to have some help with that."

We were standing in front of the open door to the apartment. He pushed past me and I followed him inside. "Charlie," I said. "In less than two months we will be divorced and when that happens, I don't want you here. If you come again, I'll call the police and have you thrown out."

"Don't do that Bern. Please. I just want to talk for a minute. I know I was a shitty husband and a bad father. I can't change any of that. Will you just give me five minutes?"

"I need to get supper for Miranda and me. Sit there and don't touch anything."

He was walking around, admiring the books in the bookcase, the drawings on the wall. "You got anything to drink, Bernie?"

I said nothing. If I gave him a drink, he'd just stay longer. "Let me feed Miranda," I said aloud, thinking *will you just leave.*

I put the baby in her high chair and heated up some chicken in the microwave. I cut up some vegetables and put them on the tray next to the chicken. I filled her sippy cup with milk. All the while, Charlie was watching me. I didn't want to eat while he was here because that, too, would delay his leaving. Miranda ate some of her supper, but her eyes were drooping. I fixed a bottle and then took her to the bedroom where I sat in the rocker and fed her until she went to sleep.

When I got back to the living room, Charlie had made himself comfortable on the couch with wine he'd found in the refrigerator and some peanuts. I sat down on a chair opposite him and poured myself a glass.

"OK, what is this all about?"

"I need to borrow some money, Bernie. I have no one else to turn to."

"I don't have any extra cash, Charlie. I can barely pay the rent and buy food."

"What about your mother?"

"What about her?"

"She was willing to give us money for a house when we married. What happened to that?"

"You didn't want to take any money from my parents, don't you remember? We got this apartment because it was all we could afford."

"But they bought you a car."

"Because I needed to go to work and all we had was your old pickup."

"What if I got a job where I made enough money to buy you a house. Maybe we could start over."

"You've had your chance to buy me a house, Charlie. You think I love living in this place? I hate it, but it's what I can afford. I don't think you're ever going to make enough money to buy me anything."

"Let's say, I buy into a franchise. Would your mother give me the money as an investment?"

Not on your life. "How much money do you need for this franchise?"

"Six thousand. No, make that ten."

"Ten thousand dollars? That's an awful lot of money. What's the name of the company you're investing in?"

"It's only for a short time. A couple of months, then I promise, *promise*, I will pay back every cent."

I shook my head. "My mother is too smart to fork over ten thousand dollars for something she knows nothing about." *And in a little while, you will no longer be her son- in- law.*

"Bernie, this is a great chance for me. If I just can get this one little break, I know I can make it. "

I shook my head again. "I'm not asking my mother for money."

"I want to make it up to you Bernie, help you out with the baby. I could get you some nice furniture. Heck, you could even quit your job and go back to school if you wanted to. Please, give me a chance at this."

"OK, I'll talk to her. But she's a pretty savvy investor. She'll need the name of the company that's giving you the franchise. She'll need to know the expected rate of return, how long she has to wait before she gets the interest on her money and how long before she gets the principal. That sort of thing."

I took paper and pen from a drawer and handed them over.

"She knows me, Bernie. Won't she just trust me?"

I wanted to say that Charlie was a man my mother would especially *not* trust, but I kept my mouth shut.

"Your mom and dad did pretty well, didn't they?"

I stared at him. My parents had worked hard, and had been financially secure. They had never done anything illegal or even immoral. They had been good parents to me, and good children to their own parents. I didn't begrudge them the success they had made of their lives; they'd earned it. The only sad thing for me was that my father had died before knowing his grand-daughter.

"How much do you think you'll get when your mother dies?"

"That's a terrible question."

"When your father died, it all went to your mother. When your mother dies, it will all go to you. You and Miranda. Do you think any of it will come to me?"

"I don't like where this is going, Charlie. My father never showed me his will, and Mom never talks to me about how much money she has. They were always generous to both of us. I don't want to think about her dying."

"They were generous to you. Me, they couldn't stand."

I glanced at the clock, which showed almost seven p.m. "Mira will be up at five-thirty tomorrow, Charlie. I need to get my own supper, then get ready for Monday."

"So, you'll talk to your mother?"

I glanced at the paper sitting on the table between us. It was blank. "Not without more information."

He stood up abruptly. "You know I'm trying, Bernie. But I can't do this all by myself." He walked toward the door.

"You remember the first time I asked you out, Bernie?"

"Of course. You asked me out twice. The first time I said no. I couldn't understand why someone like you, who always had these cheerleaders hanging on your arm, asked me for a date. But you asked me again."

"Do you know why?"

I thought back to my senior year in high school. "You said I was cute. You told me I'd be fun to go out with. I didn't think about why you were asking me."

He had perched himself on the arm of the chair and was swinging his leg back and forth. "So why do you think I asked you out?"

Charlie and I had been married for almost eight years. We'd had two children together, and now I felt as though I'd fallen into a hole that I couldn't crawl out of. "Why did you ask me out, Charlie?"

"Bill Grainger and I had a bet."

"A bet?"

"Yeah. Bill bet me that I couldn't sleep with the worst dog in the school."

"The worst dog?"

"Come on Bernie. You must have known why no one ever asked you on a date. You were short and dumpy and you wore those shapeless sweaters and long skirts with black high tops. You never smiled or laughed. All you did was study. Bill and I sat down and rated all the girls in the senior class by how hot they were. You were number twenty-five out of twenty-six. Barbara Ferris was number twenty-six. I absolutely refused to go out with Barbara Ferris."

"Barbara Ferris had a speech impediment that made her spit when she talked."

"And she lurched from side to side when she walked."

"But I had an early acceptance to Cornell."

He shrugged.

So my getting pregnant on the first date, and then having Charlie ignore me. The tense meeting with our parents, and the wedding, where the minister called me Bennie, and Charlie's father got drunk and made a speech implying that Charlie could have done better. All of it because of a bet?

"You must have felt incredibly....." I searched for the word.

"Screwed? For sure. In a nanosecond I went from being the coolest guy in the class to the class clown. Didn't you ever wonder why I stopped going to school? Don't get me wrong. You weren't bad, but it wasn't like you were someone I would have chosen myself."

"Not like Amy Lincoln, the cheerleader."

"Yeah. She was super hot and great in the sack. But after a while I thought. What does my marriage matter? I can have a son that will look like me, have my name. Someone I can teach to play football and take fishing and ..." his voice trailed off.

"And then Jimmy died."

"Yeah," he said. "My son died." He got up from where he was sitting and, without another word, he left.

When the door had closed behind him, I locked it from the inside. Then I went to the bedroom mirror and took a long look. I had a pretty face, and my dark hair shone. OK, I was a little on the plump side, but when I smiled, my teeth were straight and my eyes sparkled. How could I have been the twenty- fifth least desirable girl in the school? What about Evelyn Armstrong, who never wore a bra and whose double E breasts bounced all over the place? What about Tina Brancusi, who had thick hair all over her body. When she went swimming, she looked like a gorilla in a bathing suit. Susan Clayton had braces and inch-thick glasses. Muriel Bentley's front teeth stuck out at a ninety degree angle. You'd risk serious lip damage if you kissed her. Were all those girls hotter than I was?

I thought of the words Jane Eyre says to Mr. Rochester. I might be short. I might be plump. I might be the twenty fifth least sexy girl in my senior class, but I had a brain and a heart equal to anyone. And I had something Charlie Robertson could never take away. I had daughter named Miranda who loved me. With her I would always come first.

Chapter Four

That night I dreamed I was locked inside a closet. I could hear voices outside talking, but as much as I called and rattled the doorknob they would not let me out. I woke in a sweat, trying to get my heartbeat to return to normal. The alarm sounded and I glanced at the clock. Miranda would be awake in half an hour. Groggily, I got out of bed and padded to the kitchen for coffee. I had an appointment to see Dr. Swartz on Wednesday, when I would have to tell him something. The dream journal on the bedside table still had mostly empty pages. It wasn't that I didn't dream. It was just that I had so little time in the morning before my daughter woke that I wanted to spend them in quiet, not re-living a harrowing dream. What would he say about this new development? That having Charlie coming around looking for money, made me feel like I was locked in a closet? Certainly my mind had come up with weirder things.

By nine-thirty that morning, I was sitting at my desk at work. Dr. MacIntosh, my boss and the head of the department, was in his office. For the past two weeks, there had been secret meetings in his office almost every week. The President of the college had come to visit, then the Academic Vice President. I tried to keep my ear tuned for rumors that the department was closing, but I heard nothing, which only made my anxiety worse. I kept reminding myself that I had a good relationship with Dr. MacIntosh, who was in his sixties, and looked like an anthropologist masquerading as Santa Claus. But when my intercom buzzed, and

Dr. MacIntosh asked me to come in, my heart raced.

I took up my steno pad and went in.

"Sit down, please," he said. But instead of 'take a letter' or 'I need these items Xeroxed,' he just sat for a moment looking at me. *Oh, oh. Not a good sign.* I ran through all the disaster scenarios I could imagine: they had decided to close the department, Dr. MacIntosh was retiring and the department would be merged with Archeology, or the worst one. I was being fired.

I almost made a fool of myself by blurting out how much I needed my job. The university had been generous with maternity leave, generous with sick time, not so generous with salary, but there was every chance I might move up. I couldn't afford to look for something else now.

"Don't look so worried, Mrs. Robertson. I hope this will be a pleasant conversation."

He stopped again. My heart was racing.

"How long have you been here? Three years?"

"Since before my daughter was born."

"How's she doing by the way?"

"She's fine." *She's getting used to regular meals, clothes that fit her, the day care center where she sees her friends. Her mom needs this job.*

"Let me get to the point. I've been offered an opportunity to move up. I don't know why they chose me, I'm a little old to be Vice President, but I've accepted the position."

"Congratulations," I said, wondering who I would be working for next, if they decided to keep me.

"I'll miss you Dr. MacIntosh," I said.

"Not so fast. I'd like you to come with me. Our new offices are in the administration building across campus. You'll have a larger space, a raise in pay, a longer vacation period, and a chance to take free classes here at the university. Your new title would be Administrative Assistant, which would mean you'd be supervising two secretaries and a file clerk."

"You want me to come with you?" *Why did I sound like such an idiot?*

"Of course. You're the best secretary I've had in years and I'm a man who hates change. Mrs. Robertson, would you consider coming to work with me as my new administrative assistant?"

I resisted the urge to get up on my toes and dance around the room as being too undignified for an administrative assistant, especially one supervising two secretaries and a file clerk.

"What do you say?"

"I'd love the job. Thanks for considering me."

"One more thing, and I'm sorry about this because I know you're a single mother. The president of the college has asked to meet with us this coming Saturday. She is traveling every day this week, and Saturday was the only day she could spare. The meeting should only last about an hour." He took a piece of paper and scribbled something on it. "This is the time and place. Can you be there?"

I nodded, thinking numbly about Mira. Saturday was our play day, my little girl's reward for a week when she hardly saw me. Only an hour, Dr. MacIntosh had said. I could do this.

I called my mother as soon as I got back to my desk and explained the situation.

"I'm so sorry, honey. I can't." she said. "Clint and I are going to New York City this weekend. We're going to see a play, eat at Tavern on the Green, stay in a posh hotel and you know..."

Yeah, s*crew like rabbits.* "Thanks anyway, Mom," I said.

"Any other time, I'd be happy to do it."

I called Hillary Collins, my go-to babysitter who regularly sat for me during the week. Every Saturday she traveled the two hours to visit her mother in a nursing home. Maybe, just this once, she could make an exception to the no-Saturday-or-Sunday rule. But Hillary was not bending. Since she worked every day, she only saw her mother on weekends, and yada, yada, yada. Damn.

I dialed Sara Goldsmith, a seventeen year old, who would babysit in a pinch. The fact that she emptied my refrigerator every time would be a small price to pay for having an hour on Saturday morning. But Tina was now on the track team and they had a meet on Saturday.

I tried Jennifer Hanks, who was fifteen, but she was going to Boston to a rock concert with her dad. Had I done any of those things when I was fifteen? I thumbed through my address book, desperately searching, but I was all out of babysitters. I could take Miranda with me and have her play on the floor, while the president and I talked. But Miranda would toddle over to some expensive knick-knack in the president's office and want to touch it, or she would cry because she was wet, hungry or bored, and all of it would be a distraction. I had no choice. It was time for Charlie to step up and do his daddy duty. Reluctantly I dialed his number but the phone rang and rang, which considering the fact that he rarely rose before noon and it was only ten, was a rarity. I left a message and went back to work.

He called me at three, breathless like he'd been running up a flight of stairs.

"You talked to your Mom?"

"No, not yet. She's got a new boyfriend and she's preoccupied at the moment."

"Bernie, I need that money. This is the chance of a lifetime for me, but if I don't jump at it soon, the offer will go away. You said you'd talk to her. Don't you want to support me?"

And how often have you supported me, either financially or any other way? I took a deep breath. "Charlie, I need someone to take care of Mira for an hour this coming Saturday. Can you do it?"

"I'm pretty busy getting this new job up and running. I'm not sure I can spare an hour in the middle of the morning."

At a time when you are usually sleeping?

"Charlie, she's your daughter. You complain that she doesn't know you. Here's your chance to spend some time with her. I'll pay you the usual rate. In fact, you can take Mira to the mall and I'll give you extra money for snacks."

"And you'll talk to your mother about lending me the money?"

"I'll talk to my mother." I was *not* going to talk to my mother about money and Charlie would realize that fact sooner or later. Hopefully, this would be the last time I would ever need him to babysit, and maybe, with luck, the last time we would see each other. With a raise in pay, and a larger pool of babysitters, I could care for Miranda without his help.

On Wednesday, I had my appointment with Dr. Swartz. I told him about the scene from *Jane Eyre* where I had burst out crying, and then my dream of saying good-bye to my mother. Maybe I should have told him about the notice in the paper that my mom had hidden from me, but I didn't.

"I can't give you the answer, Bernie. This is something your mind is trying to deal with. Have you dreamed again of being in the desert? "

I shook my head. "But the Chihuahuan desert is very close to Laredo, Texas where I was adopted."

"So it's possible you've been there."

" I'm pretty sure not."

"And the trigger for the dream you had last weekend was the movie you were watching?"

"That and a little dress my mother said I was wearing, when the cops found me wandering alone in Laredo."

He looked down at his pad and tapped the pencil gently against the paper, a gesture I was getting used to. "Have you thought any more about our doing hypnosis? I think it might help."

"Do you want to do it next week?"

"No, I think today would be best."

I could feel myself tense. I am not a brave person, and traveling to a place that had been the source of so many terrifying dreams filled me with dread.

"We won't do anything you are uncomfortable with, Bernie. If at any time, you feel anxious, or ill at ease, we'll stop. My goal is to gently pry open that door to your past. I want you to get comfortable in the chair, while I dim the lights. Are you ready?"

"Relax, Bernie," Dr. Swartz said. "This isn't going to be painful. And I am not going to make you do anything you don't want to do." His voice was soft and soothing. "I'm going to count back from one hundred. Just concentrate on the sound of my voice."

I woke to bright lights and the sound of Dr. Swartz' voice. I sat up and stretched. Usually, having a nap in the middle of the day leaves me groggy and punch drunk, but my head felt clear.

"How did I do?"

"You did fine. Fine." He seemed distracted, jumpy.

"Did I talk about being in the desert at night, in a snowstorm?"

"Yes, you did. I think your dreams reflect a memory of an actual event, but your conscious mind has still blocked it. It's a kind of amnesia."

"Amnesia?"

"The mind has the ability to erase things that are too terrifying to remember. Think about a child who is in an auto accident that kills his whole family, but he's too young to process those deaths. It's a wound that is still open and bleeding. I think the event that prompted your dreams happened when you were very young. It may also have been that there were other events that were deeply sad or scary, that followed on the first wound. Your mind just shut them away for a better day."

At that moment, Dr. Swartz' secretary poked her head into the office. "I'm sorry to interrupt the session, Doctor. There's a patient here. He says it's an emergency."

"Of course." He looked at me. "I'm sorry we can't talk longer today, but by next week, I'll have had a chance to go over my notes, then we can discuss them."

I nodded and went out the door.

On Saturday, I dressed with extra care, wearing a pale blue suit my parents had given me. I'd worn it for the first time more than two years ago, when Charlie and I had been invited by my parents to a Christmas event at the country club.

The party was a disaster for me: too much noise, too much wine, too many people wearing designer dresses and talking about vacations in Maui or condos in Antigua. I was pregnant and not feeling well. Charlie quickly got drunk and after asking one guest "How much do you make anyway?" we were escorted out.

I hadn't been sorry to leave. All the time we'd been standing there I'd been painfully aware that my 'jewels' were from Wal-Mart and the limo we'd arrived in was Charlie's old red pickup.

After that event, my father had gifted me with a single strand of real pearls, telling me that no matter what other people thought, I was still his jewel. Now I put them on along with the matching earrings, and brushed my hair until it gleamed.

"How do I look, sweetie?" I asked my daughter, who was sitting on the floor regarding me with a serious expression. "Will Mommy get the job?" I twirled and the baby clapped, thinking it was a new game.

"I'm happy for that vote of confidence, Miss Robertson," I said getting Mira into her coat and grabbing my purse. A car honked outside. It was Charlie.

Lugging the baby, and all her gear outside, I walked quickly to my own car.

"Hey," Charlie said. "I thought we were going in my truck. It's been cleaned for the occasion."

"You can't attach her car seat," I said, buckling the baby in and stowing her stuff in the trunk.

"I'm taking my truck," he said. "I might need it when we're done." He ran to his truck and roared off before I'd even said a word. I caught up with him at a red light, but then I had a hard time following him as he wove in and out of traffic. I didn't want to go over the speed limit, but sometimes it was all I could do to keep him in my sight. I finally pulled in beside him at the mall. As soon as he saw me, Charlie got out and began walking toward the stores.

"Wait, Charlie. I have to get the stroller out."

"Hurry up, then. I only got an hour." He looked at his watch just to make the point.

It's like this child isn't even his, I thought as I struggled to get the stroller out of my car. I stashed the bag containing sippy cup, spare diapers, change of clothes, snacks and toys in the bottom. Last I took Miranda from the car and strapped her into the stroller, covering her with a warm blanket and followed Charlie to the entrance.

He was standing just inside the door, tapping his foot with impatience. "Ready?" he asked. I followed him into the mall and handed him some money. "This is for babysitting, and here's some extra cash in case you need to buy snacks." I pointed to a Sears store. "I will meet you here in EXACTLY one hour. If I am early I will wait for you. If I am late, YOU will wait for me. You sure you can do this?"

"I'm not a child, Bernie. I think I can spend an hour with my own daughter." He looked down at Miranda, who glanced at him and then at me. Suddenly realizing that I was leaving and she would be left with this total stranger, the baby's face crumpled and she began to wail.

"She'll be OK, Charlie. Just walk her around, show her some stuff. I'll be back in an hour." Then I ran.

The interview went well, except for one awkward moment when I reached into my purse for a pen and dislodged a squeaky toy, and a container of dry cereal. It turned out that the college president, Angela Hartshorn was a grandmother of three and completely understood. As I walked out of the administration building with Dr. MacIntosh, I had the feeling that this new job was going to work.

"Thank you for coming, Bernie," Dr. MacIntosh said, as we got to my car. "I hope you'll take advantage of the educational opportunities this job offers. You'll get time off from your job to take classes. You're a smart young lady. You should set your sights higher. You might be a college teacher yourself some day."

On that note, I got back into the car and virtually floated to the mall. When I stepped inside, I glanced over toward Sears where I'd asked Charlie to wait. He wasn't there. I looked at my watch. It had been an hour and five minutes since I'd left him, no more than that. I walked inside the store and glanced around, but there was no Charlie. I trudged around a little bit, poking my nose into stores on either side of Sears. No Charlie. Panic rose in my chest; I started walking faster, looking into every store I passed. No Charlie.

"Lost something lady?" The security guy was short with an enormous belly that strained the buttons of his shirt.

"My husband. He has our daughter and was supposed to meet me near Sears, but he's not in that spot."

"You could try the office. You can have him paged there. If something has happened they'll know. "

I nodded and moved in the direction he'd pointed to. I could live with something happening to Charlie, but Mira was my life. What could possibly happen in a mall? It wasn't like they were surfing or sky-diving? I was running now, hyperventilating in my anxiety.

Inside the dingy office, a woman sat at a desk behind two telephones. She was probably in her late seventies with severely curled white hair, misshapen teeth, and the smell of an unrepentant smoker.

I gave her Charlie's name and asked that he be paged. The woman repeated it into the microphone.

"Is there anywhere in the mall where he might not be able to hear the page?"

"Toilets, and sometimes the bar 'cause it's so noisy?"

"There's a bar here in the mall?" I had been in this mall many times. Why hadn't I realized there was a bar here?

"There are two bars. The Brown Bear used to be a restaurant; now it's just a bar. Then there's The Last Call at the far end, near Best Buy."

"Page him again, will you." The woman paged. I waited. No Charlie.

"Lady, you ain't lost a baby, have you?" the woman asked.

"No, of course not. She's with my husband. I just don't know where he is."

"Someone left a baby in a stroller outside Best Buy. Poor little mite was just bawling her head off. If you ask me, some people are just too irresponsible to be parents."

My knees went weak. *Had Charlie abandoned Mira in the middle of a shopping mall?*

"Where did they take this baby? The one that was abandoned?"

"Police came and got her. Don't know where they took the youngster. 'Spect it was the station. I can't understand people just leavin' a kid like that? Probably one of them teen age mothers. They think it's cool to have a baby, but once it's here, they don't know what to do with it. Me? I had five kids. Five. And no man, neither. But I took care of all them kids and they turned out fine. Now my oldest Harry..."

"Page Charlie Robertson again," I said.

The woman paged again. A few minutes later the phone rang. The woman picked it up, listened for a minute and then handed it to me. "It's about your man," she said.

I picked up the phone.

"You the one looking for Charlie Robertson?"

"Yes."

"This is The Last Call. You want him, he's here."

"Does he have a baby in a stroller with him?"

"There's no baby here. But you need to come for him. He's getting to be a problem."

"I'll be there," I said, running from the mall office toward The Last Call. If Charlie Robertson had been standing there before me, I'd have pushed him down and sliced off his member with a pocket knife. Make that a *rusty* pocket knife. How could Charlie leave his own daughter in the middle of a shopping mall? I'd been such an idiot to trust him. I could only pray that Mira was safe.

I found him in the back of the bar, arguing loudly with two other men who had him pushed up against the wall. I moved toward them and grabbed Charlie by the arm.

"Hey," one of the men said. "We saw him first."

"You can have him when I'm finished," I said. "But there won't be much left by then."

"You saved me from near death, Bernie," Charlie gasped as we stood outside the bar.

I moved, so we were nose to nose. "Where is Mira?"

"Mira?" he asked. "She's around here somewhere. I left her stroller...."

"AROUND HERE SOME WHERE?" I was screaming. "You left our daughter AROUND HERE SOME WHERE? But you have no idea where she is, do you Charlie?"

He looked dazed, as though just realizing what he was supposed to be doing. "I owe those two guys money. They caught up with me and wanted to talk. I didn't want to take the baby into the bar so I...." his voice drifted lower.

"So you just left her? God, why did I marry you. I know that answer. Because I was pregnant. But why did I have another child with you, that's the question that I'm asking myself. You NEVER, NEVER leave a child alone. Someone could have kidnapped her..." My voice started breaking just thinking about it. I pulled myself together. "Come on, we're going to get our daughter." I dragged him by the arm down the length of the mall and when we got to the parking lot, I shoved him roughly into my car.

"My truck," Charlie said weakly.

I said nothing. I was so mad, I could have knifed him right there but then Mira would have had neither mother nor father. When we got to the police station, I stopped before we went in.

"I'm doing the talking," I said. "NOT ONE DAMN WORD FROM YOU."

"I'm sorry," Charlie said. He seemed to be sobering up.

We walked into the station and identified ourselves as the parents of a child found at the mall and were led back to a uniformed officer in a cubicle. The name on his desk said "Det. Arnold Landry."

"So tell me, Mr. and Mrs. Robertson," Landry said, " how did you happen to leave your little girl sitting alone in her stroller outside Best Buy." His voice was not friendly and he was looking at me as though I were the poster person for Bad Mothers.

"Bernie was going to watch her while I went into the store for a minute," Charlie said. "Then we were all going to get ice cream. My little girl just loves ice cream, doesn't she darling." He looked at me. *Why was he lying like this?* The cop gave me a murderous look.

"When I came out of the store, neither my wife or daughter were there. I had been there a little longer than I expected."

"That's not true," I protested. "I paid him to watch her while I went for...."

"You will have a chance to tell your side of the story, Mrs. Robertson. So what happened next, Mr. Robertson."

"This isn't what happened," I said. "He was the one who..."

"I'm talking to Mr. Robertson," the cop said. "You'll have your opportunity, Mrs. Robertson." He turned to Charlie. "What did you do then?"

"I walked around for a while, looking everywhere for my wife, and daughter. I went into every single store and finally I found my wife in Best Buy."

"She had simply abandoned the child outside the store?" Landry asked, looking at me.

I stood up. I'd had enough of this. "He is lying," I said, trying to keep my voice level. "He was the one who left her outside the store not me. I asked him to babysit for an hour, AN HOUR, and this is what happens."

"Mrs. Robertson, sit down and we'll get to the bottom of this."

"I will not sit down. You don't believe what I'm telling you, and I'm not staying here one minute longer. Where is my daughter?"

"Mrs. Robertson," Landry said, standing up. "I must warn you that child abandonment is a serious crime and you're in a police station."

"I've had enough of this crap," I said. "I want my child."

"I'm letting you off with a warning," Landry began, but I wasn't listening. I had left the office and had started down the hallway, where in the distance I could hear Miranda crying. I followed the sound of her voice, pushed open a door, and found her sitting on the lap of a policewoman, bawling her eyes out.

"Mommy's here, pumpkin" I said, taking her into my arms. She nestled into my neck and I could feel her sobs subside.

I walked back up the hallway, past Landry's office. He and Charlie were standing in the doorway and Charlie was shaking Landry's hand. "Don't take this situation lightly, Mr. Robertson," Landry said as I passed. "The next time could be much more serious."

I continued walking without even looking. Outside the station, I unlocked my car and put Mira in her car seat. Then I got into the driver's seat and started the engine. Charlie had followed me out to the parking lot and was knocking on the window of the passenger side, which was locked.

I rolled it down an inch. "What?"

"My truck is at the mall. Are you giving me a ride back?"

I shook my head. I could easily have run him over with my car, but I didn't want to risk the dents.

"How will I get back to the mall, Bernie?"

"Walk," I said and drove off.

Chapter Five

When I went into work on Monday morning, Dr. MacIntosh was in his office, cleaning out his bookcase, his face flushed with the effort. He had taken off his jacket and there were large sweat stains under his arms and on the front, making his shirt cling. Every once in a while, he would stop and mop his brow.

"Let me give you some advice, Bernie," he said as he lifted an armload of books and deposited them in a cardboard box. "Resist books. Books are an addiction worse than alcohol or cocaine." He held up a book. "Look at this one. I've had it since I was in college. The information in it is at least thirty years old, and for a scientific book that means it's useless. And yet I've lugged it around with me, through five jobs, moving it from bookcase to box and back again. It's not even worth giving to a library, and yet I can't part with it."

"And this one," he held up a small volume. *The Sonnets of John Donne.* "My wife loved his poetry and we spent every evening of our early married life reading his poems to each other. When she was failing---well." He tossed the book into the box. "I should give them all to a public school."

"Can I help you do this, Dr. MacIntosh?" I asked.

He looked up at me. "I don't want you to get that pretty suit all dirty, but sure, your help would be much appreciated. If we can get them boxed up, then the college will provide a truck and a worker to take them over to my new office."

We worked all morning, loading dusty books into boxes. I was sorry that I hadn't worn older clothes. Dry cleaning is expensive. And yet Dr. MacIntosh was more than a man I worked for, he was a friend. I sensed that under his somewhat gruff exterior, he was very softhearted. Once, because the daycare center had been closed, I'd brought Miranda to the office and he'd spent an hour entertaining her with paper airplanes. Later he told me that he'd never had so much fun. I knew he'd been married, but were there children, or grandchildren? The only picture on his desk was of a pale blonde that I assumed was his wife. He was such a genuinely nice man that I was tempted to bring Mira in again, just so he could get his baby fix.

At noon we stopped work, both of us sweat-stained and tired. Since it was a lovely fall day, Dr. MacIntosh suggested we send out for lunch and eat it out doors, near the Student Union where there were a few tables. When we got outside, a bunch of teachers and students were sitting there, also enjoying an alfresco lunch.

"Dr MacIntosh," a young man said. He came over to where we sat, and plunked himself down on a bench.

"Jeremy Sinclair. How are you doing?"

"I'm doing great. Actually, more than great. I've just been accepted into the Ph.D. program in cultural anthropology at Northwestern. "

"Congratulations." Dr. MacIntosh said, shaking his hand.

"You were the man who got me started in this field. I don't know how to thank you."

"You could buy me a beer sometime."

"How about this Friday? A bunch of us are going to Beefeaters to celebrate. Seven- thirty or thereabouts."

"What about it, Bernie?" he asked looking at me. "Shall we join them?" Turning to Jeremy, he said, "This is my new assistant, Bernice Robertson."

"You are welcome to come," Jeremy Sinclair said. He had blue eyes and dark blonde hair which kept falling forward over his eyes. I wanted to take my hand and ever so gently push it back.

"I'll have to find a babysitter," I said. "I have a daughter who's a year and a half, and I can't just leave her." *There, Mr. Jeremy Sinclair, that ought to put a damper on your interest. No man is eager to be saddled with someone else's kid.*

"I hope you can find someone," Jeremy said, rising. "It will be fun having you with us."

For the rest of the afternoon I thought about what I could wear to a casual gathering of friends at a local bar. Nothing too flashy. I didn't want to advertise that I was looking to meet someone. On the other hand, Jeremy seemed interesting and might even be interested. It would be nice to spend an evening with grownups for a change.

I called up Hillary Collins and she was willing to babysit for the evening.

"I'm glad to hear you're going on a date, Miss Bernice," she said. "You've been single too long."

I didn't have the heart to say that technically I wasn't single yet. "It's not a date, Hillary. Just a gathering of some of Dr. MacIntosh's students. I don't know why they asked me along."

"Because you're a pretty girl, that's why. Someone will see you and realize what a catch you are, mark my words."

At that moment I could have doubled her wages for babysitting. We agreed on seven o'clock for that coming Friday. On Wednesday morning, Dr.Swartz' secretary called to cancel our appointment for that afternoon. I was itching to find out what I had said during the hypnosis session, but that would have to wait another week.

That night I had no dreams at all. It was as though, given the chance to reveal themselves, those events decided to hide instead. In another week I would learn what was at the root of everything . If I had lived through some sad, scary events, it would be better that they be brought out in the daylight where I could face them head on.

On Thursday night, I had fed the baby and was just sitting down to eat, when there was a knock on the door. Miranda was still in her high chair, playing with some fruit, but she needed to be in bed soon. Reluctantly, I opened the door with the chain still on. Charlie was standing in the hallway. In one hand he held roses in a plastic wrapper, and under his arm was a doll.

"Can I come in?"

"Charlie, I'm eating supper and just about to put the baby to sleep. I don't want to see you again until our divorce. And even then, I want nothing to do with you."

He pushed the roses through the crack in the door and I thought, Look a gift horse in the mouth. Over the years I had learned that Charlie only gave things that were cheap, or that benefitted him in some way. The first year we were married, I'd received for Valentine's day a box of stale chocolates from the Dollar store. For the birth of our son, the gift was flowers from the grocery store, with the price ($6.99) still on the plastic wrapper.

"I brought you some money, Bernie," he said holding up a wad of bills. "But I'm not going to give it to you through a crack in the door."

I undid the chain lock and let him come in. "You have three minutes," I said, peeling the plastic wrapper from the roses. The flowers had been chilled, wrapped, stuffed into a truck and then carried to a supermarket where they had languished well beyond their sell date. When I put them in the vase, they slumped disconsolately forward, too apathetic to raise their heads.

"Look what I brought for you," Charlie said to Mira, putting the doll on the tray of the high chair. Miranda gave the doll one look, and pushed it onto the floor.

"She doesn't like me, does she," he said glumly. "You've done something to make her not like me."

"It's not that, Charlie. She's not into dolls right now."

I picked up the doll, which, now that I could see it closely, showed signs of wear. Lifting the baby from her high chair, I put her in his lap. "Why don't you hold her."

Mira looked at me and then at Charlie and I could see storm clouds forming. I grabbed my cell phone and gave it to Charlie. "Let her play with this." Charlie did what I asked, and the baby brightened, forgetting that she was sitting on the lap of a stranger, intent as she was on the phone. She put the phone in her mouth. He grabbed it and she began to scream again.

"Come on Mira." I said, "This is your daddy." I handed Mira her favorite toy, a stuffed bear with well-chewed ears. The baby settled.

"So, why are you here?" I asked.

He put the wad of bills on the table. "Money," he said, as if I couldn't see what it was. "To help out."

"And what is this money in exchange for?"

"Nothing. I got a little job, nothing much, but I wanted to share my paycheck with you."

I counted it out. A hundred dollars. I tucked it securely into the pocket of my jeans, just in case Charlie changed his mind.

" And oh.." he said, reaching into his jacket pocket. "I wanted to give you this." He pulled out a box and handed it to me.

Remember the Trojan horse. I looked at the box which was from an expensive jewelry store in the mall. I'd admired their stuff from afar, but had no way to actually buy anything.

I opened the box. Inside lay a silver bracelet set with garnets and turquoise. "How are you able to afford this, Charlie?"

"It's a gift, Bernie. You're not supposed to ask questions like that about a gift."

"This must have cost plenty. If you had that kind of cash, you'd be paying me child support."

"Bernie, when someone gives you a present, you're just supposed to say thank you."

I tried it on. It fit beautifully and it was very pretty, but that Trojan Horse was still looming beside me.

"Could I have something to drink?" Charlie asked. "I'm really thirsty."

"I guess I could get you some water. Thank you for the money, Charlie. It really helps." I looked at the droopy roses. "And the flowers, and the bracelet."

"You're welcome, Bernie. I'm sorry I never did right by you. You deserved better than me."

I didn't know how to respond. What he said was true, but he'd never said it before.

"Bernie do you still have that rum your parents brought back from Barbados two years ago?"

"Yeah. I think it's in a back closet somewhere."

"We could mix it with a little orange juice. Have a celebration."

"What are we celebrating, Charlie?"

"Our divorce, and my turning over a new leaf to be a better husband and father."

I got up to look for the rum, but the minute I did, Mira made the 'don't-leave-me' moan that she does. It was past her bedtime and she needed sleep.

"I'll put her to bed and get the rum," I said. "Give me a few minutes."

Ten minutes later, the baby was asleep, and I'd found the rum behind a bunch of Mira's outgrown clothing. In the living room, Charlie was standing by the door.

"I'm sorry, Bernie. I've got to go." He pulled the door open and then he was gone.

I glanced around the room. Everything seemed to be just as I'd left it, except that my purse, which had been on the couch was now on the table. I dived for it, and checked the wallet. My two credit cards, and all my cash, forty dollars and seventy three cents, were still there. And now I had some extra money to buy groceries.

In celebration, I made myself an ersatz Orange Blossom Special with Sunny Delight and excellent Barbados rum.

Chapter Six

Hillary Collins was standing at the door of my apartment offering me advice when I started out toward the bar on Friday night. I had decided to wear a bright blue sweater that showed just a touch of cleavage over jeans that I hoped didn't make my rear end look like two basketballs fighting under a blanket.

As an added touch, I wore heels that might make me seem a teensy bit taller, silver earrings and the new bracelet. In all, I felt ready to take on any man who might be interested.

Beefeaters was one of those wanna-be English pubs that dot the area around the college. Lots of dark wood, phony brass and signs advertising British beer. It even had a dartboard in the corner. When I stepped inside, I could see Dr. MacIntosh with a crowd of men and women at a large table near the back of the room and I moved toward them, hoping that I was giving people sufficient time to appreciate my assets over my liabilities. In truth, no one was looking at my entrance. They were laughing at some joke that probably had to do with anthropology.

"Bernie," Dr. MacIntosh shouted when I got within hailing range. "You made it. Come on over here." I squeezed in, so I was sitting between him and a woman who ignored me. Jeremy Sinclair was sitting right across from me, wearing a flattering red sweater over a checked shirt. He caught my eye and smiled. He actually remembered who I was.

"What would you like to drink?" Dr. MacIntosh asked.

Something sugary with lots of alcohol and a little umbrella on top. "Strawberry Daiquiri." I said. Everyone else at the table seemed to be British-beer or whiskey–and-soda kind of people and I'd probably already blown my chance to be cool, but when my drink arrived, Jeremy raised his glass to mine and smiled again. Then he swapped places with the woman sitting beside me and we were hip to hip.

"Tell me about your daughter," he said. "I think being a parent must be one of the most rewarding things a human being can undertake."

People who say things like that have no idea what being a parent is like, but I gave him the *Father Knows Best* version. I didn't talk about sleepless nights, projectile vomiting, a child who cries for two straight hours because she's overtired, or how sometimes I simply long to have a conversation that doesn't involve Rudy the Rabbit or Sammy the Sappy Squirrel. I did tell him about watching my child learn to walk, about hearing her say her first word, about watching her eat on her own. And the ultimate joy, watching my daughter's face light up when I come into the room and knowing that she is mine.

"Congratulations on getting into the Ph.D. program," I said.

"Originally, I wanted to teach college, but now I think I'll probably work with Native Americans. Give something back, you know?"

"I got an early high school acceptance to Cornell," I said. "I was going to be a lawyer."

"Great," he said, but he wasn't listening. He was scanning the room for someone. He turned toward me. "I didn't know you were a Cornell grad. That's a good school."

We seemed to have reached an impasse, conversation-wise. Even though I worked in the department, I knew nothing about the lives of undergraduate students and, of course, he knew nothing about being a single mom. Maybe he was just being polite? Maybe he was trying to get into my pants? At least he was paying some attention to me which most of the other people were not doing. Even Dr. MacIntosh seemed to be totally engrossed in a conversation about the religious practices of the ancient Inca. I decided I needed to pee.

I excused myself and squeezed out of the crowded corner. I thought I had seen a sign for a ladies room as I entered, but when I looked, it was nowhere around. It's a mystery to me that in a bar, where people imbibe a lot of liquid, you have to follow a maze through a deep wood to find the toilets. I had just spotted the washroom when I saw Dr. Swartz sitting by himself at a table. I went to the washroom and when I came out, he was still there. I walked over to say hi.

"You're here all alone?"

He smiled. "Bernie, how nice. No. I'm waiting for someone. Jim Walters called me, said he's read my book and wanted to talk. I suggested we could meet here, and now he's kept me waiting." He glanced at his watch. "I told my fiancee I'd meet her at the movies. If Jim doesn't show up soon, I'll have to leave."

"I didn't mean to bother you," I said. "I was here with some friends and I just wanted to say hello."

"Sit down, please. I'm sorry I had to cancel our session, but I wanted to talk with you. I've been looking over my notes and re-listening to the tapes." He sighed. "This is hard to say so I'll just say it. Most of the time during a hypnotic session I'm able to sort out the event that is blocked in the patient's past. Sometimes these events are very painful, but rarely are they something that could be called criminal. I'm beginning to think we might be uncovering a police matter."

"A police matter?"

"I think what you're trying to remember really happened, and from your description, it was horrifying."

"So I was dreaming about a crime? And it was connected to snow in the desert?"

"I'm not a detective, Bernie. I leave the solution of crimes to others. Something illegal happened in that place you are dreaming about, I'm sure of it. Maybe it was something you witnessed or were emotionally connected to. Something so terrible that you blocked it entirely."

And I had thought my life was boring. Dr Swartz had paused and was looking behind me.

"Here's Jim," he said. "We'll talk about this later." I followed his look to see a small, Asian man striding toward us. I thanked Dr. Swartz and moved back toward the table where the group was.

It was nine o'clock, and I needed to go home and get some sleep. As I walked toward the table, Jeremy saw me and his face broke into the biggest smile I'd seen that evening. Maybe the night wasn't a waste after all. He seemed like a nice man, good looking and... A man passed me moving toward Jeremy's table. Jeremy's eyes followed the person as he squeezed by the others to give Jeremy a hug. It wasn't just a hug, but a hug and a kiss. And then Jeremy stood up and the two men walked away from the table, waving good-bye to their friends.

It could have been worse, I thought. I could have thrown myself at him, finagled a ride home, begged to see his apartment and then after some awkward fumbling he would reveal the truth. It was better this way. Still, I watched the departing couple with envy.

Striding toward the bar, I asked for a check. I gave the bartender my credit card, but he returned a few moments later and put it on the bar.

"Sorry Miss. This one doesn't work?"

"Doesn't work? But I just used it last week, and I pay my bills on time."

He shrugged. I fumbled in my purse for the second card, the one I used for emergencies. He took that, and in very little time, he was back.

He put the card on the bar and I knew the answer without having to ask.

"It's over the limit," he said.

How could it be? My mind was reeling. I had forty dollars in my wallet. Barely enough for a cab ride home and payment to the babysitter. Then I remembered the hundred dollars Charlie had given me.

While the bartender waited patiently, I dumped my pocketbook on the bar and poked through every single pocket, trying to remember where I'd put the extra money and hoping that I had indeed put it in my purse. When I found it, I handed the bartender a twenty from the roll, praying that he would not come back and tell me it was a fake.

"Here you go," he said, handing me the change. I put most of it back in his hand. I normally don't tip a lot, but was grateful that I had enough to pay the babysitter and buy groceries for the week and wouldn't have to take money out of my savings account. The credit cards would be dealt with later. Then I went outside and hailed a cab.

When I got home, it was almost ten, but I called both credit card companies. I explained that someone had taken the numbers from my card, and I'd just discovered the problem. They told me that goods in the amount of five thousand for each card had been charged, and that they'd closed down the cards. Since I'd called as soon as I discovered the mistake, I wouldn't be charged but I would have to re-order the cards.

I had a pretty good idea who'd stolen my identity. I was careful with my cards, and the only opportunity Charlie had had was when I left him alone in the living room while I looked for the rum. Charlie and I wouldn't be legally divorced until the end of October. Could I be found liable for his illegal activity? Damn the man. Damn. Damn. Damn.

I poured myself a glass of wine and sat at the table thinking. Glancing down at the bracelet on my wrist, I realized that I should have paid more attention to my gut feeling about Charlie and gifts. If he'd come to visit in order to steal the numbers from my credit cards, why had he given me jewelry and money? Casually, I took off the bracelet. Maybe, if it were really worth something and not just made in China, I could sell the thing on e-Bay. I turned it over and started looking carefully at the inside. There was a mark that said sterling, a good sign. I kept turning. Then I saw the inscription. "To Alice, with all my love, J." Would a woman give a man a bracelet that another man had inscribed to her? And if it had not been a gift, how had Charlie acquired it? The answer was clear. Charlie had stolen it. Had he stolen the money I'd just used to pay the bar bill, hire a cab and pay the babysitter? Quickly I took the money from my purse and counted it. I had fifty three dollars left, so in addition to giving up a pretty bracelet to the police, I would have to give up the hundred Charlie had given me, making up the difference from my own funds. Damn him. By now it was almost midnight, much too late to call my mother. Hadn't she said that her new boyfriend was an ex-cop? Maybe he could give me some advice.

My stomach churned with anxiety and in a few hours Mira would wake up and want Mommy fully present and accounted for. I took the wine glass to the sink and rinsed it and went to the bedroom where I undressed and lay down. But it was a long time, before my mind stopped working over my problems, and I was able to get some sleep.

Chapter Seven

The next morning I called my mother long before she usually gets out of bed. She was very gracious about the whole thing, but I'm sure she could hear panic in my voice. When I asked her what I should do about the bracelet and the money she asked me to wait a minute. *So, the boyfriend was there,* I thought.

"Hi, Bernie. This is Clint Morrison. How are you?"

"I'm fine." It felt funny calling him Clint, but it also seemed strange to call him Mr. Morrison, or Detective Morrison, especially since he was obviously sleeping with my mother. Should I think of him as my step-father? That was way too weird.

"I suggest you go down to the police station and tell them the whole story. If you're honest, they won't charge you. When I was working as a detective, we were following the activities of a local gang, mostly teens and young adults who were responsible for a rash of robberies. But now I've heard that a Chinese Mafia from Montreal has come in. I hope Charlie hasn't become involved with them."

"Will Charlie be arrested?"

"Possibly. Especially if he's involved in the crime. Will that be a problem for you, Bernie?"

"He hasn't been much of a husband, Mr. Morrison."

"Call me Clint."

"But Charlie *is* still Miranda's father."

"Isn't she about a year old? She probably won't even know that he's in jail. Bernie, if you do go to the police, get a signed receipt for anything you give them."

"Can I talk to my mom, please?"

When my mother came back on the phone, I said. "He sounds nice Mom. Think he's a keeper?"

She laughed. "Do you want me to come to the station with you?"

"No, that's OK. Mira and I need the walk."

After a good breakfast, the two of us set out. It was Saturday so lots of people were out doing their usual weekend chores. Tyndale was a town that had grown up around a river that in the 1800's provided the only reliable transportation for voyageurs bringing goods by canoe from the St. Lawrence River, or loggers running cut trees from the Adirondack woods to the mills. Now, the river was used for recreation and as I walked by, a couple in a canoe were moving inexpertly across the water. First they would both paddle on one side, and then both on the other, pushing the canoe in a zig-zag pattern. A gaggle of geese was trying to stay as much out of their way as possible.

I rounded the corner of the Civic Center, waved to Janice Armstrong standing in front of the grocery store in her weekly Peace Vigil and went into the police station.

"I'd like to speak to someone about stolen property," I said.

"You've had property stolen, or you've recovered stolen property?"

"I've received what I think is stolen property," I said, putting the bracelet on the counter. The policeman picked it up, looked at it and then set it down. "Let me see if there are any detectives here," he said.

When he returned he said, "Follow me," and led me back to a cubicle. There, large as life and twice as beautiful was my old buddy Detective Arnold Landry.

"Well, Mrs. Robertson, lost any babies lately? Nope, I see she's here. " He looked down at Mira who regarded him sourly. "Hiya sweetheart."

"Detective Landry," I began. "my husband and I are separated. In fact, by the end of this month we will be divorced."

"Congratulations."

"A couple of nights ago he came to visit me and he gave me this." I pulled out the bracelet and put it on the desk between us. "I think it's stolen."

"Why do you think that?"

"Look inside. There's an inscription."

Landry picked up the bracelet and turned it around. "To Alice with all my love, J." he read.

"My name is Bernice, and my husband is Charlie."

"How do I know that *you* didn't steal this bracelet, Mrs. Robertson?"

I stared at him dumfounded. "Why would I bring a stolen bracelet to the police? That would be putting my head in a noose."

"Listen to me. A woman who would leave her child unattended in a shopping mall while she goes gallivanting off to Best Buy will do anything. Maybe you thought there would be a reward. News flash. There is none. Maybe you're mad at your husband and think it would be neat for him to spend a few nights in jail while the police race around trying to match the bracelet to a list of stolen property. While the police are doing this, the bracelet which you've owned for a dog's age, is sitting in a drawer. When you think your husband has been sufficiently punished you'll come back and say, 'Sorry, I made a mistake. It was really mine all along.'"

I stared at him unbelieving. Did this man really hate women in general, or was it just me?

"I want a receipt for the bracelet," I said. Landry pulled open a side drawer and extracted a pad. He scribbled something on it, and pushed the pad toward me. "You got to sign it," he said.

"Put the date on it," I said. "And I'd like you to say more than 'bracelet.' I want you to write 'silver bracelet set with garnets and turquoise, engraved 'To Alice with all my love, J.'"

"You seem pretty good at this. Why don't you write it."

I did. My hand was shaking with anger, but I finally managed to write what I thought was an accurate description of the bracelet. Then Landry signed it and I signed it. He tore off a yellow copy and handed it to me. "Are we done?" he asked.

"Not completely." I hated doing this. Why should this fool have cash that I could use myself? But my parents had raised me to be an honest person and dishonesty always has a way of catching up with you. I took the remainder of the cash Charlie had given me, augmented by funds from my meager savings account and put them on the table. "That's one hundred dollars. I want a receipt for it."

"You're ex give you this too?"

"He did."

"Why did he do that, do you suppose?"

Would it be worth my while to try and explain Charlie's twisted mind to this man? I gave him the short answer. "He hasn't paid child support for a while, and he was hoping I would be nice to him."

"So you think he stole the money?"

That was a good question. If Charlie had actually earned the money he gave to me, then I was being a fool to give it to this cop. On the other hand, if the money was stolen, and I kept it, I would be dishonest. Charlie would have told me I was being stupid. Keep the money, he would say, even if you think it's stolen.

"I don't know whether it was stolen or not. Is there some way the police can prove that? Don't the banks record bill numbers of money that has been taken?"

"If an item is engraved like the bracelet, it's fairly easy to prove that it was stolen." Landry said. "Cash is a different matter. Banks keep track of the bill numbers. But most people don't, even when they keep large amounts of money in a safe."

Landry took the cash and counted it. Then he tucked the money into his pocket.

"I want a receipt for that," I said. "I'm not leaving until I get one."

He pushed the pad toward me again and this time I filled it out completely with the date, the words 'cash' and my signature. I wasn't sure if I needed identifying numbers for the bills on the receipt. If I did, I had no idea where to look for them. He signed. I signed. I put the slips for the cash and the bracelet in my pocket and stood up.

"One more thing, Mrs. Robertson. Do you have an address and phone number for your soon to be ex?"

I did. I gave Landry Charlie's social security number, date of birth, the make, model and license number of his old red truck. I could have told Landry the last place Charlie worked, the location of his favorite bar, the names of three of his friends, what kind of underwear he wore and what he ate for breakfast. But Landry didn't ask for any of those details.

"Nice doing business with you Detective Landry."

"You, too. Mrs. Robertson. Stay out of Best Buy." He waved sweetly at Miranda. "You too, little girl."

I walked out of the station, mentally calling Landry a few names my mother would be embarrassed to hear me say. Outside the day was bright and clear. The sky was blue, the leaves shedding their gold onto the ground. I needed something sweet and high calorie to settle my soul.

We stopped at Katie's Koffee Kupboard where they had home-made blueberry muffins and a variety of coffee drinks. I bought a small bottle of milk for Mira and I had cocoa piled high with whipped cream and drizzled with chocolate. We split a muffin. It took me several sips of the sweet drink to settle myself down. There was nothing I could do about Detective Arnold Landry. He was the man that he was. I had no idea whether he was a good cop or a bad cop, a good detective or a bad detective. But I had the distinct feeling that I would not want to be a woman accused of a crime that came into his line of sight.

After the snack, Mira and I walked around for a while, watched the geese on the river, threw bread to a bunch of squirrels and chased after pigeons. In a few years, my daughter would be old enough to paddle with me on this river, which would be fun.

The image of Miranda and I on the river morphed into Jeremy Sinclair with his arm around his lover. Damn, that had been such a nice dream. Then, my cell phone rang. It was a woman from the credit card company. She wanted additional information if I had it.

"Do you have any idea who might have taken the cards, Mrs. Robertson?"

"I do," I said. "I think it was my husband." I gave her all the information I'd given Detective Landry, but this person seemed more interested. I hoped someone would investigate what Charlie was doing, but I had my doubts that it would be the detective I'd just met.

I called my mother and told her the whole story, starting with Detective Landry pocketing the hundred dollars Charlie had given me.

"You got a receipt though."

"Two. It was the best I could do."

"I'm proud of you honey. You returned the money even though you weren't sure it was stolen. Let's do something special tonight. Dinner. A movie. I think there's a new kid's flick at the Rialto."

"Sure, both of us will take a nap right now, so we'll be bright and cheery for the movie."

"Pick you up at five thirty."

After a long stressful day, at least I had something to look forward to.

Chapter Eight

My mother called me at ten o'clock on Monday morning when I was at work. Since Dr. MacIntosh and I had moved up to the Vice President's office, my job had become busier. It was Fall with lots of students back in school and lots of people coming in and out of the office. In addition, I was trying to get the hang of supervising two secretaries and a file clerk.

"Dr. Swartz is dead," my mother said.

"What did you say?" I had been thinking about my new job, and not listening.

"His obituary is in today's paper. Apparently he died of a heart attack."

"But I just saw him on Friday night. He seemed healthy enough then."

"Heart attacks can happen anytime. Remember your father. One minute he was playing golf, and next minute he was in the emergency room."

I felt my muscles go weak. I liked Dr. Swartz. He seemed to be a genuinely caring human being. And then I remembered the hypnosis session. "I wonder what happened to his notes on our session? Do you suppose I can get them?"

"If it were me," my mother said, "I'd go to his office right away and ask for them. You want to do it before they clear things out."

I asked if I could take an early lunch and went downstairs and out the door.

There was a newsstand just around the corner from the building, and I picked up a copy of the local paper *The Bugle*. Sure enough, there on

6B, the obituary page, was a photograph of a much younger Dr. Swartz.

"Easton Harrison Swartz, Jr. 53 passed away in his home as the result of an apparent heart attack.

"Born in New Hope, Pennsylvania, the son of Easton and Rachel Swartz, he attended New Hope High School, graduating with high honors, then Harvard College, graduating Magna Cum Laude in the pre-med program. In 1978 he received his MD degree from Johns Hopkins University, and did his psychiatric residency at Texas Tech University in Lubbock, Texas. In 1983, Dr. Swartz became a staff psychiatrist for the Boston University Medical Center. The same year he married Margaret Anne Weis. The marriage ended in divorce in 1990. There were no children. Dr. Swartz established a private practice in psychiatry in 1991, specializing in therapeutic hypnosis. He was the author of *Into the Past: The Challenge of Human Memory* (1997) and numerous scholarly articles. He leaves a wife, Margaret Anne Weis. Arrangements are with the Taylor Funeral Home. A private interment will be held in the spring."

Besides being surprised at all the things Dr. Swartz had done with his life, there was a deep sadness. He had been an ally in dealing with the demons that haunted my sleep. I suppose I could have gone out and found some other doctor, but in the brief time we had known each other, I'd come to like him and I didn't know if I had the energy for a new therapist. I walked to my car, got in and drove to Dr. Swartz's office.

I walked in through the front door of the building and up to his floor. I had been to this office twice now, and usually each visit was accompanied by some kind of anxiety. In the beginning it was, Will he believe me? Will he think I'm crazy? and the last time we met it had been Will this hypnosis work? What will we learn? Now, there was somber silence about the place. The waiting room was empty and nobody sat behind the glass partition ready to check me in. I could hear a noise from behind the door to Dr. Swartz' office. Gently I knocked.

I knocked again and waited.

The door was opened by Dr. Swartz's secretary, a woman I'd seen only twice before. The last time I'd seen her, her red hair had been smartly styled and she'd worn a pretty print dress. Today, her hair hung limply around her face and she was dressed in jeans and a shirt. I struggled to try and remember her name. Alice? Eleanor?

"The office is closed," she said. Her eyes were red and she kept dabbing at them with a tissue.

"I know. I read the obituary."

"If you had an appointment, it's been cancelled." She broke down and began to cry hard. "He's dead."

"I'm sorry Miss..."

She was sitting in a chair, weeping. I sat down near her and touched her hand.

"I worked for him for ten years. After his divorce, we...." She looked at me. "I shouldn't be telling you all this."

I put my arm around her shoulder. They'd obviously been more than employer and employee.

She stopped, overcome, and then pulled herself together. "We had plans to get married. It was going to be a small wedding, just our closest..... Oh God. I can't believe he's gone."

"I'm so sorry." I tried to remember the details of the obituary. " When did he die, Miss...?"

"Maynard, Ellen Maynard . We were going to movies at eight on Friday night, but then he called and said he was having a drink with someone, and could we go to the nine-thirty show instead. When he didn't show up at nine-thirty, I got concerned. He never missed a date, and he wasn't ever late. I called his house but there was no answer, so I drove over and.... he was there, sitting in his chair."

She burst into another round of weeping, and I sat with my hand on hers until it subsided.

"Did Dr. Swartz have any history of heart trouble?"

"No, no. He was very healthy. He played squash twice a week and ran in marathons. He watched what he ate. He knew that he was in a sedentary profession, and he tried to stay healthy." *Even apparently healthy people can have heart attacks,* I thought. *Look at my father.*

"Did the medical examiner do an autopsy?"

"I don't think so. When I found the body, I called the police and they came with the rescue squad. I followed them to the hospital, where they declared Easton dead. When I tried to find out what they were going to do with him, the hospital told me that he'd died of a heart attack and that they'd called his ex-wife, to make the arrangements. Even though she and Easton had been divorced for a long time, she was still the next of kin. Margaret insisted that she didn't want an autopsy. She would deal with the body herself. She took him to be cremated. I never had a chance to say goodbye."

"But they will have a funeral. The paper said it would be some time in the spring."

"His ex-wife wrote the obituary, and I think she just put that in because people expect there to be a service. There's nothing left of him now, just a bunch of ashes in a....." She stopped and tried to compose herself. "We were going to have such a nice life, maybe even adopt children. Easton always wanted chil..."

"Did he have any extra stress in his life? Someone who might have been angry at him because of a diagnosis, maybe a colleague whose toes he stepped on? Was he battling with his ex-wife over money?"

"I can't think of anything. But you can't delve into people's lives without making them feel uncomfortable. Psychiatrists deal with people who are sometimes really crazy and the therapeutic process sometimes makes their psychoses worse. There was a doctor in Maryland who was shot to death by a patient last year. After that happened, Easton and I had a long conversation. He tried to reassure me that it would never happen to him. He was careful in choosing his patients, and he always met them here in the office where he had some control."

We sat in silence for a moment, then I said. "I know this sounds crass, but I wonder if you could get his notes from our last session. He hypnotized me, but he wouldn't tell me what he'd learned."

"The doctor/patient relationship is confidential."

"But the doctor is gone. Can't I get access to my own information?"

She nodded numbly and then turned to me. "After your last session, did he give you any hint what you'd said?"

"Not much. I remember as soon as the session ended, he seemed unsettled. He said he thought my dreams weren't just anxiety, but reflected something that had actually happened to me. And then Friday night, I saw him at a bar."

"You saw him? Where?"

"Beefeaters, it's near the college."

"I don't think I've ever been there. Was he alone?"

"No, he was waiting for a man whose name was....let me think. Jack, no Jim. Dr. Swartz said that Jim had read his book and wanted to talk."

"Maybe this guy was the reason he changed the time for our date."

"Maybe."

Ellen stood up. "I've got to inform the other clients of Easton's death." She looked at me. "What's your name?"

I thought I had told her, but maybe she'd forgotten.

"Bernie Robertson. Your records would be under 'Bernice.'"

"Wait, let me write it down. Do you have a phone number?"

I gave it to her, then I reached over and hugged her, feeling how thin she was. Her body started to shake and we just held each other for a while.

"Bernie," she said. "Do you think we could get together sometime. I have nobody I can talk with about this. I'd really appreciate it." She took out a piece of paper and scribbled her phone number on it.

"Of course. I work full time and have a little girl, but I can make time."

"Meantime, I'll try and find out what happened to your records."

"He must have left something."

"I know where he keeps his notes. I can't promise anything, but I'll take a look."

"Thank you, and I'm so sorry for your loss."

The words seemed a weak response to something so life-changing. What do you say to someone who has fallen in love with a man and waited for years to be with him, only to have him die before you marry? Ellen had been convinced that Dr. Swartz' death wasn't an accident, but heart attacks happened to seemingly healthy people. It was possible that if someone had been with Dr. Swartz when he had his attack, he might have lived. But, even with friends around him, a quick trip to the ER, and the best care possible, my father had died, so even with an instant response, Dr. Swartz might not have survived either.

I hurried out the door to my car. I still had half an hour left of my lunch time. I should have gone back to work, eaten lunch at my desk and returned to the job for which I was being paid. Instead, I had an overwhelming urge to play hookey, so I went over to Lord and Taylor in the mall, and browsed. The dresses I loved, at one hundred twenty five dollars at pop, were way above my budget, and the dresses that I could afford looked frumpy and cheap. I did buy a bracelet for twelve dollars and some fake diamond earrings that were on sale. After a latte with extra whipped cream, I felt cheered enough to return to my job and finish out the day.

That evening I called my mother, but there was no answer. I was vaguely jealous that she should be out, having a wonderful time, while I was stuck at home. On the other hand, I knew that she'd been lonely without my father. She deserved to have some fun.

Chapter Nine

I'd been thinking a lot about Ellen Maynard. It is one thing to have a husband you've had a child with. It is another to love a person for years, and, as you are about to marry, have him die. Though I'd never had a partner die, I knew what heartbreak and loneliness felt like. A week after I'd seen Dr. Swartz' obituary in the paper, I dialed Ellen's number.

"I'm sorry," the answering machine said, "Dr. Swartz is no longer seeing patients. The office is closed."

"Ellen, it's me. Bernie Robertson. I came to see you about a week ago. Do you remember me?"

Her voice came on the line. "Bernie. Of course. I haven't found anything yet. I'm sorry."

"That's OK. I know it takes time. How are you doing?"

There was a long sigh. "I'm alive. Sometimes I wish I weren't."

"Want me to come over?"

"Sure. When?"

"I can get off for lunch tomorrow. Will you be there?"

"Yup. I'm just cleaning out the office. Easton's wife cancelled the lease, and so everything has to be out of here by next week."

"I'll be there at noon."

Ellen and I had some things in common. We both had had hopes for a relationship that didn't work out. In her case, death had put an end to her romantic hopes. It my case it was divorce. We were strangers, but in a lot of ways we were sisters.

When I got to Dr. Swartz' office the next day, Ellen was standing just inside the glass entry way, wearing an old shirt and blue jeans, her hair flying in random strands around her head. She looked prettier without her makeup and her business attire, but there were dark circles under her eyes, as though she hadn't been sleeping. On the floor were dozens of boxes which she was rapidly filling with books.

"Hi," she said.

I gave her a hug. "Come on," I said. "You need to have some lunch. I brought Mickey D's. We can sit and eat, and then I've got a half hour to help you pack books."

"You don't need to do this," she said.

"I know." I moved some papers off a desk and pulled up a chair. Then I laid out our lunch, two Big Macs, fries and two large sodas.

"Do you know, you're the first person who's asked me how I'm doing? His wife knew about us. They've been divorced for a long time, but she pretends that I'm only the secretary and I'll just move on to another job." She started to sob, and I put my arm around her while she pulled herself together.

"How can I go on with my life? What am I going to do? I need to support myself, but I can't bear to work for anyone else." She wiped her eyes, and took a sip of her soda. "I'm sorry to put this on you, but you're the only one who's been kind to me since it happened."

"He was a good man," I said. He'd only been my therapist for two sessions, so I hadn't known him very well, but that seemed to be the case.

"I know I'm not supposed to ask, but why were you seeing him?"

"I've had these dreams that started about a year ago. I was walking through the desert in the snow and someone was following me."

She nodded. "Lots of people have stress dreams. Once the cause of the stress is found, the dreams go away."

"That was what Dr. Swartz said. But for me, it was always the same dream, or some version of it. When the dreams first started, it was the snow that fascinated me. I felt like I'd never seen it before, light flakes falling softly on the ground in front of me. And then I realized that I was in a desert and there were cacti and scrub bushes all around. Later, after I'd had the dream a few times, there would be something following me, hiding behind rocks. I could see its red eyes and imagine its teeth sinking into my flesh. In later dreams, it was a man with a gun screaming at me to stop. I would start to run, and you know how it is with dreams, your feet keep slipping and as much as you try to move, you can't. I would always wake with this feeling of terror. Dr. Swartz said the dream could have been based on a real event."

She nodded. "It happens."

"Something about that hypnosis session spooked him. When I saw him in Beefeaters he said that we might be uncovering something that could be a police matter."

"He said that?"

I nodded.

"And he was with someone in the bar. What was his name again?"

"James Walters. Didn't I tell you that?"

Ellen was writing all this down. She looked up at me. "If Easton was with James Walters on Friday night, that man might have been the last person to see him alive. If we could get in touch with him, he could tell us what happened."

We were silent for a moment. "What will happen to all this?" I asked, indicating the boxes of books and files.

"All this stuff will be sorted out by his wife. I expect most of it will be shredded and go to the landfill."

"You've got my phone number," I said. "Call me."

"We could have a real lunch together," Ellen said. "I don't have anyone to talk to."

"Of course." I glanced at my watch. I had fifteen minutes to get back to my job. We hugged again and I dashed back to work.

Chapter Ten

It had been a while since Dr. MacIntosh and I had moved to our new place, and I was still trying to master the art of being a supervisor. I had heard nothing from Charlie, which was what I had expected, but the fact of his silence made me nervous. I was especially careful where my daughter was concerned, repeatedly warning the caregivers at Little Tots never to give her to anyone but me or my mother. Charlie would be very angry when he learned that I'd turned the bracelet into the police. I needed to protect myself from him.

On Saturday, I called the locksmith and had him put another lock on the front door and locks on the windows. After the locksmith had gone I walked around the apartment, testing his work. It would have to do. I had no other way to keep myself or my child safe. And even though I was secure inside, I had no protection if Charlie decided to ambush me as I left the apartment. Finally, I left the living room and walked back to the bedroom, but it was a long time before I fell asleep.

On Monday, Ellen Maynard called me.

"Did you find the notes?"

"Nope, but I found where your files should have been. Dr. Swartz filed all his patient's notes and the original tapes from the sessions in a locked drawer. That drawer had been jimmied open and things had been rearranged, as though someone pulled files out and then put them back out of order. I remember all those names. Your file was the only one missing."

"Bernie," she said. "I think someone is watching me. He wears a shapeless coat and a brimmed hat, and hangs out on the street outside the office. You mentioned the man who was with Easton on Friday night at the bar, Jim Walters. What did he look like?"

"Let me think, short, balding, Asian features. I don't remember much because I was more interested in talking to Dr. Swartz. Is this man the one you think is watching you?"

"It could be him, but he always disappears before I can get a good look."

"Ellen, be careful, please."

"Bernie, I have something I want to show you. Something I found, but I don't want to tell you over the phone. Can you meet me at Fancy Beans tomorrow at three o'clock? It's that little coffee shop just off Madison Street."

I knew where it was. Three o'clock was in the middle of my working day, but I could postpone my lunch hour and plead a doctor's appointment or something. The next day I walked to the coffee shop, arriving there just at three. I looked around. Ellen wasn't there.

Maybe she'd gone to the bathroom, or was somewhere outside looking for me. I went up to the Barista, a young woman with bright purple hair and ear plugs to match. When I asked about Ellen, she said no one matching that description had come in. Had I made a mistake on the time? She'd said today at three, hadn't she?

I ended up waiting for almost forty minutes and then going back to work. Just before the end of the day a call came in on my cell.

"Bernie, it's Ellen. I'm really sorry about leaving you at the coffee shop. Something came up, and I've decided I need to get away." Her voice seemed distant, as though she were already a long way from Tyndale. "I want to thank you for being my friend."

"We'll see each other again, Ellen," I said. "You'll be back in a week, won't you?"

"It might be longer," Ellen said. "You won't forget me will you?"

"Of course not." We were friends and it was only going to be a week. Why would I forget her?

A week later I walked over to Dr. Swartz' former office and discovered that everything had been cleared out: furniture, files, pictures on the wall, everything. Even his name "Easton Swartz " had been removed, as though he'd been a figment I'd dreamed up. I tried looking Ellen Maynard up in the phone book, but there was nothing, which didn't surprise me, because a lot of people have cell phones these days and so aren't listed. Still, I felt let down. I wanted to ask where she'd gone in such a hurry, and what she'd learned that had been so important she needed to tell me right away, and then decided against it. She had been one of the few friends my own age I had. And now she had vanished as though she'd never existed.

The next day was Saturday, a cool October day with the smell of winter in the air. I was crossing the street in the late afternoon, pushing the baby in her carriage as we headed for home. Suddenly a red truck sped toward me, its lights off, the windshield dark. I panicked, thinking *That truck is going to hit me*, but still I couldn't move. With all my strength, I pushed the baby carriage toward the sidewalk and fell. There was a rush of air behind me, as the truck sped by, only inches from my legs.

I managed to crawl to the sidewalk. The baby was crying but she was OK. My heart was racing and I was dizzy. I looked down at my pants which had been torn when I fell. Someone had deliberately tried to run us over. Was that person Charlie? I had not seen or heard from him in seven days, not since he'd stolen my credit card numbers. I thought of calling the police to tell them that my ex-husband had just tried to run me and my daughter over, but they would ask me for the make, model and license number of the truck. I would have recognized Charlie's truck, if it were parked on the street, but this truck had taken me by surprise, and I hadn't thought to get a glimpse of the driver. Shakily I got up and walked the few blocks to the apartment. I let myself in and leaving Miranda in the stroller, I locked the two security locks and then walked around, checking the locks on the windows. I was safe for now, but I couldn't stay in the apartment twenty-four seven. I had a job to go to. I put the baby on the floor to play and then dialed my mother. Her answering machine picked up.

"Hi, you've reached the house of Cyndi Sorengard. If I'm not answering the phone, it means I'm out playing. Call me later."

Playing at what? Probably at the indoor tennis court, or shopping, or having her hair done, or catching an evening movie and supper with Clint. I didn't want to bother my mother when she obviously was having such a wonderful time with her new boyfriend. At the same time, I just wanted a grownup to talk to. I poured myself a glass of wine and watched the baby playing on the floor.

"What will your story be, little one?" I asked out loud. She looked up at me. "If my story is 'How I Found You', what will yours be? Maybe it will be 'How my Mother Survived my S.O.B. Father, Long Enough for Me to Get Born'."

I walked over and picked her up. "Time for supper, sweetie. And then bed."

My daughter is a good sleeper. Almost as soon as you put her down, she goes out. Of course, if she's overtired and doesn't have her favorite toy, it can be a different story, but I am very lucky that I don't have a fussy girl.

I, on the other hand, took a long time to get to sleep that night. My mind was racing through the day's events, trying to find a reasonable explanation for someone running me down in the street. I thought about Dr. Swartz's death and Ellen's leaving. Maybe Dr. Swartz had written a will, leaving everything to Ellen, and his ex-wife had objected and, instead of going to court, she'd hired a hit man. Maybe Ellen had found out about this, and had simply run. She didn't want to tell me where she was because she was afraid of being followed, and she didn't want to draw attention to me. At three o'clock in the morning, still unable to sleep I got up and went into the kitchen for a cup of tea.

From my living room window, I could see out to the street below, and there standing on the sidewalk opposite my apartment building was a man. Was he waiting for someone, but if so, why here? There were no bars or restaurants near my apartment, and he looked like a man just standing there, not like a man waiting to be picked up and eager to be home in bed. Then he looked up at my apartment, and it seemed that he was looking right at me. Swiftly I drew back from the window. Was he actually watching the place where I lived? And, was this the same man that had been following Ellen?

I spent the rest of the night sitting in the chair in my living room, terrified that the unknown person would decide to break in. I must have fallen asleep at one point, because I woke to the sound of Mira talking to herself. It was Sunday morning, a day when we would be together and do whatever we liked. After I made breakfast for the both of us, I dialed my mother's number. "You're home."

"Well, why wouldn't I be."

"The last couple of times I called you were out."

"Oh that. Clint and I went to New Hampshire for a few days."

"How was it?"

"Well, you know I haven't been there in years. We did a little bit of hiking, ate at the most fabulous little restaurant, and the hotel had a hot tub..."

"Don't tell me any more, Mom. "

"Sorry, honey."

"So you really like this guy? Are you going to marry him?"

"I think it's a little soon, don't you?"

"But you're having fun."

"I am. How's the baby?"

"She talking up a storm. Last week, she pulled on the cord for the table lamp and knocked the whole thing off. Luckily I was right there. Mom, someone tried to run me over with a truck just as I was crossing the street. Do you think it could have been Charlie?"

"When did this happen?"

"Yesterday afternoon, about four."

"Bernie, Charlie got arrested last night."

"Arrested?"

"Apparently he was involved with a gang. The police raided a vacant house and found three men and a woman living there. Charlie was one of the men. The group had been selling drugs to make money and also stealing from homes in the area. The only reason we found out about this, was because one of Clint's friends called him."

"How come no one called me?"

"Charlie refused his one phone call. Said 'his family' would take care of him. He has no money for bail. He's still in the village lockup."

"You said he was arrested last night?" *Had Charlie been the one driving the truck that tried to run me over yesterday?* "Mom, do you know how long Charlie will be in jail?"

"Maybe until the rest of the month, maybe longer. That's what Clint said. At least you won't have to worry about him harassing you. Bernie. I need to talk with you. Can you come here this weekend? It will be just the two of us."

"What about Clint?"

"He's going to a tennis tournament. I like playing the game, but watching it is a total bore. It will be fun having you and the baby here. Come on Friday."

When I'd hung up the phone, I sat for a minute thinking. Charlie and I would be divorced soon, but I needed to know what the charges were against him, and how long he would be in jail. I couldn't go by second-hand information; I needed to talk to the source.

I put on our coats and set up the stroller. Then I pushed Miranda down to the police station, hoping that I would not run into Detective Landry.

I entered the building where a young police-woman sat at the desk . She looked up at me and smiled, a good sign.

"I'd like to talk to someone about Charlie Robertson; he was arrested last night."

"Are you a relative?"

"His wife. Well, soon to be ex-wife."

"Do you want to see him, Mrs. Robertson?"

"No, not really. I was just wondering why he was arrested."

She rose and returned several minutes later with a tall, slender, red-headed man I guessed to be in his early forties. "This is Detective Anders," she said.

Anders nodded hello, and then I followed him back to a tiny cubicle that was his office.

"You're asking about Charlie Robertson?"

"Why did he get arrested?"

"I wasn't the arresting officer, you understand, but I'll try to tell you what happened. We have been experiencing a higher-than-usual string of robberies in town. At first we thought it was a change of leadership in local gangs, most of whom are young people trying to fund a drug habit. When a new leader comes in, gangs sometime become more aggressive or daring. I suppose it's just a way for a new guy to prove that he's more macho than anyone else."

"Anyway, we identified a house where we thought this gang (they call themselves Slash and Burn) were living and on Saturday afternoon we raided the place. We found plenty of evidence of local theft, plus a good supply of cocaine and marijuana. Fortunately for Charlie, he was a minor player in all of this. He'd just come on board a few weeks ago, had never actually broken into a house, but had helped to fence stolen property. We found no evidence that he was one of the men selling drugs. I don't think they trusted him to that extent."

"Everyone we picked up at the house was put into the county jail, and will stay there until the hearing which is scheduled for next Thursday.

Bail will be set at the hearing, lawyers will be assigned and the judge will decide on the sentence."

"Will Charlie go to prison?"

"Criminal possession of a stolen object can get Charlie a jail sentence, a fine and parole. But it depends on the value of what he stole. I think you brought in a bracelet, that he gave you, didn't you?"

I nodded.

"The bracelet was from a recent robbery and in spite of the nice gemstones, it was only worth about two hundred fifty dollars, which makes it a Class A misdemeanor."

"What does that mean?"

"The judge can give him up to a year in jail."

"What about the hundred dollars in cash Charlie gave me?"

"What hundred dollars?"

"I turned it in to Detective Landry about twelve days ago."

"You have a receipt from Landry for this money?"

"I do."

"Let me look into that. But, that won't make much of a difference in Charlie's case. It still brings the value of the stolen items to about three hundred fifty dollars, less than the thousand it takes to move the crime to a Class E felony. Unfortunately for Charlie, he had a little dustup with the arresting officer which might get him slapped with an assault charge. The officer was bruised, but not seriously hurt, which could reduce the charge to a misdemeanor, instead of a felony D. That charge also means jail time, or three years probation."

"So Charlie will do time in jail?"

"It's hard to say. He has no prior arrests which might make the judge more lenient. And if he agrees to testify against the other members of the gang, that will help him. He might be lucky enough to come up against Judge Maloney, who could give him community service instead of prison time.

Damn, I thought a year in jail sounded like a good thing for Charlie.

"You sure you don't want to see him?"

"OK," I said.

Anders rose and led me down a corridor to a door. I followed with Miranda in the stroller. We crossed a parking lot and entered another building. A policewoman in a grey uniform sat at a desk, just inside the door. Behind her was a locked gate.

"We'd like to see Charles Robertson," Anders said. He gestured toward me. "This is his ex-wife." I held up my driver's license and the guard looked it over carefully. "You taking the baby in there?" she asked. I nodded. I had no choice. Miranda wasn't fond of her father, but it was the only way Charlie and I would be able to talk. The guard led me to a room with a table and two chairs and in a few minutes Charlie came shuffling in. He was wearing a bright orange jumpsuit and his hands were cuffed. A large bruise darkened the side of his face and his lip had been cut. The guard looked at me. "You two OK being alone with him."

I nodded. I looked at my ex-husband. "Did the cops do that to you, Charlie?"

He shook his head glumly.

"Do you have a lawyer Charlie?"

He shook his head. "I guess the court will appoint one."

"What about bail. Can your parents get you out of here?"

"They don't want anything to do with me. Said I needed to learn my lesson." He sat down in a chair and I sat opposite him. Miranda was starting to squirm in the stroller, so I took her on my lap and took out my phone, a 'toy' that would keep her occupied for a few minutes.

"I blame you for this, Bernie," Charlie said sourly. "All I needed was a little bit of money to start my own business. I begged you to get it from your mother, but you wouldn't do it, not even for me."

He stood up and started pacing around the small room, stopping to look at me again. "You forced me into this, you know. If you'd been willing to give me a chance, things might have been different. I wouldn't have gone in with these guys, or done what I did. I was only trying to do right by you and Mira. You always complained that I never did enough to support you, and when I tried to get something going, you turn me into the police."

None of this was true. Charlie had been the author of his own woes. He alone, had made the decision to join a gang.

"You don't know what I'm going through," he said angrily, crossing the space between us and pushing his face into mine. The baby began to wail. "Do you know what will happen when I get out? The men who loaned me money will be waiting for me, and if I don't have the dough, they will find a way for me to pay.'"

"Keep your voice down, you're scaring the baby."

"The hell with the baby." He sat, and looked at me. Then he said, very quietly. "I blame you for what has happened to me, Bernie. Don't forget that. And when I get out of here I will come after you. You can run or you can hide, but I will find you."

I stood up shakily and walked to the door where I called for the guard. Miranda was sobbing in my arms, her face pressed against my chest. In a few minutes the guard appeared.

"You done?"

"We're done," I said. I couldn't wait to get as far away from Charlie as I could.

I watched as the guards came and took Charlie away. As Charlie was leaving he turned toward me. "You're a cold bitch, you know that?"

"Did you try to run me over with your truck, yesterday?" I asked. "Maybe it was one of your pals, angry because I turned in the stolen stuff."

Charlie just shrugged and turned away, an irritant I would never be completely rid of.

On Wednesday I arrived home to find my divorce papers sitting in the mailbox. I should have had a celebration, but instead I felt drained.

I fed Miranda and put her to bed, and then made myself some supper. As I was eating, I glanced out on the street, wondering whether the man who'd been watching my apartment was back. He had disappeared, and instead, a small group of costumed children came running past. And then I realized that of course, it was Halloween. Miranda was too young to go trick-or-treating and I had no friends with children her own age to share the evening with. I watched as the children ran past. It would have been fun to see them up close, but I had no candy to give out. I left the window and went to the couch, where I flipped on the television, but there was nothing that appealed to me. Finally, tired but not really sleepy, I took a book from the shelf and went to bed and finally fell asleep.

On Friday evening, Mira and I traveled to my mother's house, where my mother was waiting at the door and the fragrant smell of Chicken Mirabella filled the house. There were two glasses of wine already poured on the counter.

I took off Miranda's coat, leaned over and gave my mother a kiss. Then I put Mira on the floor. Immediately she walked to the cupboards and started grabbing pans.

"Come on sweetheart, let's get you a toy," I said, pulling puzzles out of my bag and settling her on the floor.

I took a sip of wine and began telling my mother about my visit to Charlie.

Chapter Eleven

"He blames me for not asking you for the money to start this new business venture, Mom. I think, frankly, his business was selling things he and the gang were stealing." We were standing with our arms around each other and when Miranda saw us, she got up from the floor and came over, wrapping her arms around my legs. My mother bent to pick her up and Mira put her arms around her grandmother, hugging her tight.

"Do you think Charlie will come after me once he's released?" I asked. "Maybe I should have given him some money, just to keep him off my back."

"No," my mother said, balancing Miranda on her hip as she moved around the kitchen. "Once you get start giving him money, you'll never be free of him."

I looked at my daughter, mine and Charlie's. After the death of our son, when I'd made the decision to stick with Charlie, all I wanted was another baby. I hadn't thought that Miranda would have Charlie as a father and that I would be tied forever to a man I'd come to hate.

"You could move somewhere else." my mother said. "Start over again."

"Move? Where? I've got no money to move, Mom."

My mother paused and looked at me. Then she said, "I have something I want to tell you honey. Don't blame me for this. It was your father's idea and he wouldn't let me talk him out of it."

She handed me the baby and I put her on the floor. Miranda walked over to the refrigerator and began hitting the door with her stuffed toy.

"Sit down, Bernie," my mother said. When we were sitting across from each other she said. "Do you remember the trust fund your father set up for you when you were twelve?"

"He used the money he made from the book he wrote about his early days in the oil fields. I loved that he put us all on the back cover."

"You were supposed to get the money when you graduated from college."

"Instead I got married. What happened to that fund, mom?"

"What happened to that fund has to do with your wedding. I know you weren't feeling well, but you remember what that was like."

"Of course, Charlie's mother in that horrible pink dress that was two sizes too small, with her boobs hanging out."

"And your bridesmaid slugging Charlie's brother on the dance floor."

"And Charlie's father making that awful speech. It was like they were royalty and I was just some trashy thing they picked up on the street."

"I think if your father had been in a dark corner with Charlie's dad, he'd have strangled the man. I've never seen him so mad. When we got home from the wedding, he went into his office and stayed there for an hour. The next day he went to see the lawyer, and when he came home he told me he'd changed the terms of the trust. He never told me the particulars, but after he died, I learned that you would not receive any of the money while you were still married to Charlie."

"How could he do that? I was his daughter."

"I'm so sorry, honey. Since New York is a community property state, your father was determined that neither Charlie nor Charlie's family would get any of his money. I know what it meant for you, believe me. I felt so bad, seeing you living in that horrible little apartment, having to make do with worn clothes and hand me downs for Miranda. I could not change his mind, Bernie. I tried, but he wasn't going to budge. He hated Charlie and his family, with a determination I've never seen before. He thought you would divorce Charlie after your little boy died. I think he really expected it."

"I don't know if I ever thought about divorcing him then. I guess I didn't realize how unhappy I was, and the truth was, I wanted another baby so I was willing to stick it out for a while more."

My mother leaned forward and took my hands. "We should have done something sooner. We tried to help you out when we could, but I know it wasn't enough. When you are divorced from Charlie, all of the money in that fund reverts to you."

"I got my divorce papers on Tuesday," I said. "Charlie and I are now officially not married."

My mother nodded. "I'll transfer the money to your bank first thing on Monday." She named a sum that staggered me. All those years of shopping at second-hand stores and scrimping on groceries, and I'd had this money. I realized then how much Charlie had cheated me, not only of a better education, but of a better life.

I spent a sleepless night thinking about the money. If I stayed where I was, I could buy a modest house with a real back yard for Mira and me. On the other hand, if I stayed in Tyndale,

Charlie would know it, and probably try to come after me and the money. If I stayed where I was, my little girl would be able to remain with people she knew: day care workers, babysitters, her grandmother of whom she was particularly fond. Moving to a new place would be disruptive and I would have to say good-bye to Dr. MacIntosh who had been good to me, even giving me a promotion. I thought of Charlie who would never be my daughter's loving father, and of the stranger trying to run me over with the truck. Maybe it would be safer to go somewhere else.

By morning I had made no firm decision. It would be so much easier to stay where I was, to let things slide and deal with dangers as they came. I spent Saturday and Sunday with my mother, letting her feed and coddle both of us, and then on Sunday afternoon I went home.

Chapter Twelve

I had just got the baby out of the car seat when I glanced up at my apartment. The door was open. Had Charlie been released already and come back to get his revenge? Cautiously I crept up the outside stairway and moved toward the door.

"Just keep looking, it's got to be here somewhere." a male voice said.

I ducked against the wall and cautiously moved away from the door. Trying to make as little noise as possible, I walked toward the stairs to the third floor and crept up the stairway, finally hiding behind the railing directly over my place.

"No luck," said the first man. "Tell J.W. we couldn't find it."

"J.W. not *my* friend. *You* tell him this."

"I will. Come on, let's split." From the sound of their voices, I could tell they were standing in the doorway, or on the porch in front of the apartment. Miranda began to whimper. She was tired and hungry.

"What's that?" one man asked.

"Cat maybe. Upstairs."

"It's not a fucking cat. Are you deaf?"

"Not deaf, need to go."

Cautiously I moved my hand toward my purse, trying to find the container of dry cereal I use to soothe a hungry toddler. I located the container and, as noiselessly as I could, began to pry off the lid. The lid flipped open, the container fell over and cereal spilled out, the sweetened oat circles rolling through the open railing onto the porch below.

"What the hell?" one man said. "I'm going to see what's there."

Grabbing my purse and the baby, I sprinted from my hiding spot. On each floor was a trash room where residents deposit things too big for regular garbage. It was supposed to be locked, but in a place like this, the lock was often broken and I was praying that this was the case. I could hear the man's footsteps behind me as I raced around the corner of the balcony to the trash room. Grabbing the handle of the door, I yanked hard. It was locked. Not daring to look back, I moved down the row of apartments, looking for something, anything. A door was open, and without a second thought I ducked inside and slammed it shut.

"Leave it open, Gladys," a man said from inside the apartment. "I like the air." He was sitting in a recliner watching TV. The apartment smelled of mildew and old age. I watched as he turned and looked at me.

"You're not Gladys."

"Nope, I'm not." I could hear the men outside, yelling and pounding on doors. Miranda had started to sob.

"Don't answer that, please," I said.

"How do I know you ain't here to rob me? Mind you, I ain't got anythin' that's worth taking." He was rising with difficulty from the chair, reaching for a desk lamp that sat on the table beside him.

"Sir," I said, moving toward him. "My name is Bernie Robertson. I live downstairs with my baby and someone just broke into my apartment. I need to stay here until they go."

He peered at Miranda, who had hidden her face against my shirt.

"I seen you before," he said. "You and your husband lived downstairs. What happened to him?"

"We divorced," I said.

"Happens a lot." He put the lamp down, lowered himself gingerly to the chair and flipped off the TV. "So why are those guys in your apartment?"

"I don't know," I said. I looked at a couch which was opposite the old man and in the same sad shape. "Can I sit down?"

He nodded. "Want some coffee? A soft drink? A whiskey?"

Whiskey sounded good, though I don't normally drink that sort of stuff. But I needed to deal with the men in my apartment, and to figure out where the two of us were going to sleep that night.

"I need to call the police," I said.

"Yup." He pointed to a desk in the corner where an old fashioned phone sat. "Don't have a cell phone. Too expensive, and what if it's an emergency and my battry's dead? Just dial 911."

A woman who turned out to be a dispatcher answered on the second ring. She wanted the particulars about the break in. I give her my apartment number. "But I'm not there," I said. "I'm in apartment... " I looked at the old man.

"Herb Steiner. 3H." he said.

"3H, it's a floor up from mine. I have a baby and I don't want to go back there until I know it's safe."

"Good idea," the dispatcher said. "We'll send someone right over."

Next I called my mother and told her what had happened. It seemed as though I was spending more time with her these days than I was spending in my own home, but I was grateful for the availability of her secure abode. What would I do if she lived in a different state?

"Do you want me to come and get you?" she asked.

"No, Mom. I can take care of this. I have to wait for the police, and then when they leave, I'll come to your place."

"How did they get in? I thought you just had new locks installed."

"I did get new locks, but the door and the frame are so cheezy that someone could pry them open with a butter knife. Anyway, I'm upstairs with a man named Herb Steiner." I heard a siren and cautiously opened the door. A police car was in the parking lot. "I think the police are here, Mom. I'll talk to you later."

There was a knock and I opened the door to a slender police woman. Even with all the gear strapped around her waist, I probably outweighed her by fifty pounds. Was she really capable of dealing with two hardened criminals?

"You're thinking what they all think, aren't you," she said. "How's this little woman going to deal with some thugs. Come on, let me go first and clear the place, and then you follow and we can talk."

I trailed behind her down the stairs and around the corner to my apartment. At the open door I froze. Miranda was half asleep in my arms. "What if they're still there?"

The policewoman drew her gun. "Police," she called and went in. I could hear her walking around. Luckily it is a pretty small apartment with only a kitchen, living room, two bedrooms and a bath. Since we'd taken off the closet doors, there were no places where a person could hide.

She came out to the porch. "Looks clear, but I'll stay with you, just to make sure."

I walked into the apartment, seeing the mess the two men had created. Lamps had been dismembered, their parts on the floor. Drawers had been pulled open and their contents scattered. One of Mira's stuffed bears had been sliced open and dishes, cups, pots and pans lay all around.

"I wouldn't touch anything if I were you," the police officer said. Her name tag identified her as R. Gonzalez. "We're going to send someone over here to dust for fingerprints."

"I need to put the baby to sleep," I said. "Will you come with me just to make sure no one is hiding in the bedroom?"

Although she'd done a thorough check of the apartment just a few minutes earlier, Officer Gonzalez walked with me into the bedroom and stood in one corner as I got Miranda into her PJ's and into bed. As I was tucking the baby in, I could see the officer inside the closet, pushing aside clothing and moving stuff around. I looked down at my tired child, thinking I should really give her some supper, but she seemed close to sleep, and maybe that was the best thing. When she had closed her eyes, the police woman and I went out the door and closed it behind us.

We sat in the living room, across from each other. I desperately needed a drink, but didn't know if I had any unbroken cups left. "How about some coffee, Officer Gonzalez?" I asked. "I know you said not to touch anything, but I need something to drink."

"Call me Reena. And coffee would be fine." I found some grounds and put coffee on to brew, poured myself a glass of wine, and returned to my seat.

"So tell me what happened from the beginning."

I started with seeing my apartment door open. Reena pulled out a notebook and began to write.

"Did you actually see the men who were in your apartment?"

I tried to think. "Briefly. They stood outside the door while I was on the balcony above. One was short and looked like a Latino, and the other was tall. They were both wearing dark wool caps and leather jackets. When the Latino man heard me crouching on the floor above him, he took after me and I ran."

"You heard them talking. Did either man have an accent, speech impediment, something you might recognize later?"

"One guy sounded like English wasn't his native language. The other man was American."

"But you don't know which of the two men spoke with the accent."

"I was so panicked by the fact that they were in my apartment, that I didn't pay any attention."

The coffee signaled that it was ready. I poured Reena a cup. "Cream or sugar?" I asked. "I think I still have some around."

"Both," she said with a smile. "I'm trying to cut back, but I can't stand black coffee."

I handed her the cup, the sugar bowl and the carton of milk. She doctored her coffee.

"Did you get a glimpse of the car these guys were driving?"

"Nope, " I said. "I was hiding out in Herb Steiner's apartment. That's where I called you from."

She nodded. She took a sip of coffee. "You weren't here when they first broke into the apartment, were you?"

"No, I was at my mother's house. She lives about ten miles from here."

"I know you haven't spent much time here since the men broke in, but have you noticed anything missing?"

I looked around. A small flat-screen TV that probably cost me a hundred dollars at Wal-Mart was still there, and my computer was still in its place on the desk. I stood up and walked into the bedroom where my jewelry case was, knowing that there was nothing of value except the pearls my father had given me, but the jewel case was untouched.

When I came back into the living room, Reena said, "I have to tell you that most burglars would take things like the computer or jewels which are easy to fence. Why didn't they do that? Burglars aren't very smart, and they strike when the owner is away. At the first sign that he's back, they flee. Why would a burglar risk your being able to describe him by chasing you? It doesn't make sense. So you have no idea who might have done this?"

"My ex-husband Charlie Robertson was arrested a week ago. He was part of a gang that was stealing locally. He even brought me a stolen bracelet and some money. Detective Anders said he would be in jail until his hearing on Thursday."

"If he was in the lockup, he certainly wasn't here," Reena said. "Although..." As I watched, she put on a pair of thin rubber gloves and began walking around the apartment, picking up lamps, turning them upside down and peering into the base then doing the same with knick knacks.

"When your husband brought you the stolen bracelet and money, did he bring anything else?"

"Some flowers. They were practically dead, oh, and a doll." I got up and went into the bedroom and got the doll. Putting it on Reena's lap, I said, "My little girl didn't like it, and I don't even think it's new."

"So you don't care what happens to this?" Reena asked.

"Nope."

"Do you have a pair of scissors?"

I handed her the scissors and she proceeded to cut a wide swath up the back of the doll's cloth covered body. She pulled out stuffing, feeling around in the arms and legs. Then she snapped the head off and peered into the cavity. It was empty. "Was Charlie ever by himself in the apartment?"

"On the day he came to give me the jewelry and other things, I left him in the living room while I looked for a bottle of rum."

"Your husband could have hidden cash or drugs in the apartment. Something he was going to come and get later. Maybe the people who broke in here knew about his stash and were looking for it."

"Where would he have put it?"

"A canister in the cupboard, behind the frozen foods in the refrigerator." She held up the ruined doll. "In a toy."

"In the meantime?"

"I don't think the men who broke in found what they wanted, so they could return."

We sat in silence for a moment, considering the possibilities.

Reena got up and looked closely at the door locks. "If I were you, I'd find somewhere else to sleep tonight."

"I'm going to my mother's house," I said. "So, what happens next?"

"It depends. It's possible the police will send a tech team over here, but unless they have suspects, prints won't do us much good. Try not to touch anything though."

"I met Detective Anders when I went to see Charlie," I said. "He seemed very nice." *Please, don't send Detective Landry.*

Officer Gonzalez made no comment. She had taken my phone number and said that she would call me if the tech crews came to fingerprint the apartment. On her way out, she looked again at the ruined lock.

"I'm not staying here tonight," I said. "And I'll get the super to fix the door tomorrow."

After she'd left, I packed a suitcase and then bundled my sleepy daughter into her car seat. Walking down the stairs to the car, I half expected one of the men who'd ransacked my place to jump out at me from the darkness, but nothing happened. Tonight I would be with my mother, and tomorrow, I would deal with everything else.

Chapter Thirteen

Miranda and I spent Sunday night with my mother. It was lovely to feel safe, but it didn't help me deal with the mess that had been created at my place, so on Monday, before work, I went back to my ruined apartment and tried to put things in order. While I was gone, the landlord had replaced the door and put on a new lock. But even with that protection, I felt shaky and uncertain. A fundamental part of my life had been brutally violated and I was no longer safe. I could have lived here again, but it would never be mine.

I had to make the decision to do something else, be someone else, live differently. It would be a disruption, but maybe it would be a disruption for the better.

When I got to work, Dr. MacIntosh was already in his office, a place that looked like he'd always inhabited it.

"Good morning, Bernie. How was your weekend?"

"Not good," I said. I told him about the break-in to my apartment. I didn't tell him about the man waiting outside on the street or almost being run down by a truck. Even though I had lived through all those things, the stories seemed too unreal to be believed.

"I'm thinking of moving away from Tyndale," I said. "My husband has been put in jail because he was part of a drug gang, and I don't want to be here when he gets out. I hope this doesn't mean leaving my job, but I'm afraid it might."

Dr. MacIntosh sat back in his chair and stared at me for a moment. "I'm sorry that all this has happened to you. I had no idea. I understand if you need to go somewhere safer, but I'll really miss you. You've been my good right hand."

"I'm sorry." It was all I could say. He'd been a good boss and, if I moved away, I would miss him.

"You can stay for two more weeks, can't you? Give us time to find a replacement?"

I hadn't even thought where I was going to be, but as long as Charlie stayed in jail, I was OK.

"I'm not happy with your leaving, but I understand," Dr. MacIntosh said. "But it's better that you be safe."

That evening, at home in my ruined apartment, I started to consider where I would go. I needed to be far away from Charlie and his gang of thugs, even though moving would separate me from my mother and everything familiar. I flipped through the atlas. Florida had the advantage of being warm, but it might be too close. I could move further west, Michigan, Iowa, California even. What about Texas? I hadn't, until now, thought about Texas as a place to live, but the state had one thing going for it that no other state had.

I had been adopted in Laredo, Texas and the more I thought about it, the more I realized that if I went west, I might be able to find the mother who'd given me up. If I went to Texas, I might be able to solve the great mystery that lay at the center of my life. What had happened to my birth parents?

I got up and went to the dresser where I kept the little dress I'd worn when I'd been found in Laredo, and sat with it, feeling the softness of the worn cloth. I tried to imagine my Texas birth mother choosing this dress from a store and watching me proudly as I paraded before her. But this was all an illusion. For all I knew, the dress could have been provided by the orphanage. If I were seriously going to look for the woman who bore me, I needed to be prepared for disappointment. Nevertheless, Texas, and the chance to learn something about my early life, beckoned.

I went to the computer and found a national website for jobs. As much as I would have loved to be a salesman, I couldn't take a job that required travel, and being a teacher wasn't something I was qualified to do. I Googled administrative assistant and scrolled down through a list of jobs listed everywhere but Texas. And then, finally, there was a small advertisement.

"West Texas Fair Trade Coffee Company looking for applicant with secretarial skills who has the following attributes: a strong ability to multi-task, a collaborative personality, an interest in learning higher office functions, and the ability to work independently and to follow specific instructions." A salary, that was a lower than my current wage was mentioned. But then there were the magic words: "Housing provided in addition to salary."

I would have a salary, and a place to live. The job didn't seem that different from what I was doing now, and the company was in Rosalita, Texas, which when I looked at the map wasn't far from Laredo. All I really needed besides a job and a place to live, was a convenient day care center and a good used car.

Quickly I e-mailed a response to Mike West, the name given in the ad, giving a brief synopsis of my qualifications. Almost as soon as I'd hit the 'send' button there was a response. "When can you start?"

This company must be really desperate, but now that I'd made the decision to leap into the unknown, I needed to get my feet moving.

"Two weeks," I responded.

"Great. I'll pick you up at the airport in San Antonio. Send me your arrival time."

I'd given myself two weeks and in that time, Dr. MacIntosh needed to advertise for a new administrative assistant and I needed to clear out my apartment and terminate my lease. The thought of those two things was daunting, but I was also excited. I was like a bird, preparing to migrate for the first time, not certain what to expect, but ready for the journey. I didn't know what kind of job West Texas Fair Trade Coffee would provide, but if it didn't work out, I had enough money to find something else. I looked around my small, shabby apartment, the place where my daughter had lived all her life, but also the place where my dreams of a loving marriage had been crushed. I was ready to find a new life.

Though Dr. MacIntosh was generous about my need to leave, not everyone was as understanding. The landlord charged me an extra month's rent because I'd not given him two month's notice, and it would take him that long (he said) to find another tenant. I went through the apartment and made a list of everything I couldn't take with me, and then put ads in the paper for the goods, so the next week and a half was a flurry of people coming to look and buy. Three days before I was due to leave, I called a local charity and asked them to bring a truck to take what was left.

I had made my plane reservations from Syracuse to San Antonio two weeks before. I held back essential items we would need for travel: a stroller which could double as a bed in a pinch, bottles, toys, some clothes for me and Miranda. I also knew that everything I took with me, had to be carried by me. The apartment was empty, so the night before, I stayed with Mom. She would drive us to the airport and then store my car. I had rejected the idea of driving alone to Texas as being too difficult for a woman with a toddler. I'd made all the important decisions, and those decisions, like a great tide, were carrying me forward to the time I would leave.

I was in tears when my mother and I said good-bye and the baby, not understanding, kept patting my cheek, trying to cheer me up.

"Call me," my mother said.

I held up my new cell phone. "Every day," I said.

And then we were boarding. I looked around at the people streaming through the jetway onto the plane. How many of them were making a break with the place where they had grown up, gone to school, had their first kiss, and their first sex? How many were leaving behind people they had known all their lives, and buildings they had walked by every day? Would I ever see any of these folks again? I hadn't even left, and I missed them already.

I checked the stroller at the door to the plane, and managed to stuff most of the other things above me or under me. Miranda was cheerful until the plane began to move, and then she started to howl. She didn't calm down until exhaustion kicked in half an hour later. By then, most of the people around me were giving me looks of sympathy or those that could kill on contact. We had a plane change which necessitated gathering all my stuff plus baby and schlepping it across miles of airport and then waiting When we finally touched down in San Antonio , it was two in the afternoon, and I was exhausted.

Part Two

Texas

Chapter Fourteen

The first thing I noticed about Texas was the heat. Suddenly, the fur-lined boots and down jacket that had been so necessary in Syracuse, were just things that took up space under the stroller. The second thing I noticed was that everyone, including toddlers and little old grannies were wearing cowboy hats and boots. Some of the hats were lavishly decorated with feathers and silver studded medallions. The boots were equally outrageous, hand tooled with silver toe tips and fancy heels. These things were worn by people who looked like they'd never been twenty miles from a ranch. Any self respecting New York cow would roll on her back laughing at the sight of these 'cowboys.' Maybe Texas cows were more tolerant.

I got to the area where people were waiting for relatives and friends. Suddenly my phone rang. It was my mother.

"You had a good trip?" she asked.

"It was long. And it's hot here."

"Mr. West is supposed to meet your plane. Is he there yet?"

I looked around, expecting to see a grizzled old cowpoke, with stained teeth and scraggly hair, smelling like he'd just come in from the range.

"I don't see him, Mom. Wait. Oh my God."

"What is it?"

"Mom, how old do you think Mike West is?"

"I don't know. Sixty, seventy?"

"Try thirty five, tall, slender, dark hair and sunglasses, wearing a blinding white shirt that hugs his body, immaculate blue jeans, boots and a cowboy hat, holding up a sign with my name on it."

"Well, go for it, honey. I'll talk to you later."

I hesitated. While Mike West looked like he belonged in a "Hunks of the West " issue of *G.Q.* , I had the unmistakable odor of one who has been cramped into a tiny seat with a crying baby for hours. My clothing was sweaty and rumpled, and was decorated with a variety of stains (coffee, baby food, crackers, milk and spitup) and it felt like months since my body had seen water and soap.

I held up my hand and caught his eye. I didn't want to admit I was the one he was looking for, but it was that or hitchhike all the miles to Rosalita.

"Bernie Robertson?" he asked.

I nodded.

He seemed to be on the verge of saying something, then he turned toward the luggage area. "Let's get your luggage, Ma'am."

Ma'am? Oh my goodness. The word made me feel about eighty years old. We moved to the luggage carousel and with no trouble, he humped my two huge suitcases onto the cart, along with the baby car seat. "My truck's out here, Ma'am."

There it was again. When we were walking toward the door he asked, "How did you get the name 'Bernie.'"

"My name is really Bernice. I was named for my mother's favorite aunt."

"And your little girl?"

"Miranda Jane. We call her Mira."

He smiled.

"What's so funny."

"In Spanish, 'Mira' means 'look." People use it all the time."

"Are there many Latinos in Texas."

"Lots."

"And Mike is short for Michael?"

"Miguel. My Mom's a Latina, my Dad was an Anglo."

We got to Mike's truck which looked like it had seen a lot of Texas sun and Texas mud.

Mike lifted all my stuff and put it in the back. Then he looked at the baby. I pointed to the bottom of the car seat and together we secured it to the truck's seat belt system and buckled her in; I got into the front and we drove away.

"You hungry?"

"Starved." I had eaten very early that morning, and the small snacks offered by the airline seemed to be eons in the past.

"There's a taqueria not far from here. They've got wonderful Chili Rellanos."

"What's a taqueria?"

"Texas fast food. When the original cowboys worked the range, they would fry up a some meat and sauce, slap it on a tortilla, and eat it on the move. Most Mexican food around here is Tex-Mex. If you want to eat real Mexican, you got to eat my Mom's cooking."

I watched the scenery rush by. Palm trees near the city gave way to pasture that stretched to the horizon, dotted with scrub trees and pump jacks. There were ranches too. One was named "The Texas Twostep" and had a metal cutout of a couple dancing over the name. The Texas I was seeing, seemed to be mostly endless pasture, where cattle with long, deadly-looking horns grazed. With all this sameness around me, I felt myself drifting off to sleep.

"We're here." Mike said.

I jerked awake. "I'm so sorry. I must have fallen asleep."

"What time did you leave home this morning?"

"I had to catch a nine-thirty flight in Syracuse, so we left home around six. I didn't sleep much last night, worrying about whether I'd forgotten something or if the move to Texas would be a big mistake."

"Texas isn't for everyone," he said slowly. "But people are friendly, and if you spend enough time here, the scenery grows on you." He got out of the car and stood behind me as I undid Miranda's seat belt, and lifted my sleeping child into my arms.

"Can I help?" he asked.

I remembered Charlie and our trip to the mall. How could two men be so different. "Could you grab the diaper bag on the floor and my purse?"

He lifted both bags and followed me into the restaurant, which was full of people all talking at top volume. The smell of onions drifted toward me, reminding me how hungry I was.

I put Mira in the high chair and pulled some cereal out of my pocketbook. Sometimes the cereal is as much plaything as food. Mira looked at Mike, but didn't seem afraid of him. I desperately needed to change out of my sweaty clothes, but I couldn't do it in the bathroom with a toddler clinging to my legs.

"Can you watch her for a minute while I change?" I asked.

He nodded. "Want me to order for you?"

"Sure, whatever you think is good. I could eat a horse."

"I don't think those are on the menu, but I'll get you something."

Racing back to the truck I found my suitcase and pulled out shorts and a t-shirt. The perfume that I was hoping would make me smell more presentable was in the bottom of the bag and I couldn't spare the time to find it. Soap and water would have to do.

In ten minutes I was back, cooler, if not cleaner. Mike had put some salsa and chips on the tray, and Mira was pushing them around. Normally, at this point she would have been in tears, being left, as she was with a stranger, but she was smiling and laughing-- flirting really. You shameless hussy, I thought.

"I ordered you a quesadilla," Mike said. "A tortilla sandwich with chicken, sauce and melted cheese inside."

"Sounds great," I said. I took a sip of water and dipped a chip in the salsa. I took a bite-- whoow. The salsa was burning its way down my throat. I grabbed again for my water.

"Texans like things hot," Mike said. "But we'll make a Texas gal out of you yet."

When our food had arrived, Mike turned toward me, looking serious. "I'm afraid the house isn't much, Bernie. I use it as temporary housing for my workers, while they find a better place to live. If you're going to stay for long, you might want to put in some things, like central air and heating."

I thought about Rosalita, the town I was going to. I had expected a city, but the idea that Mike might have to offer his workers temporary housing made me think otherwise.

He looked toward me. "Changing your mind about the job?"

"No. No." I said. "It's just that this is all so different from what I'm used to."

"Which is?"

"A small town in northern New York. I went to grade school through high school there,   got married there, had my daughter there, and got my first job there. I've never lived anywhere else."

"So why did you leave?"

"I had some things I had to get away from," I said. The image of my wrecked apartment rose up and I pushed it away.

"Bad relationship?"

"Something like that."

"You're not running from the law, are you?" He said this with a half smile.

I shook my head.

He looked at Mira who was pushing refried beans and chicken around on the tray.

"What about you, little lady. Got the FBI tailing you?"

Mira smiled and raised a hand covered with mashed beans and patted him on the arm, leaving a nice brown stain on his pure white shirt.

"I'm sorry about that. Let me get you a wet cloth," I said.

"No problem. Soap and water will get it out." He stood up. "Let me work on it now."

"Thank you Mike, for coming to get us, and being so nice about it."

He nodded his head and I expect if he'd had on his cowboy hat, he'd have doffed it. Oh dear, I thought, Oh dear, oh dear. This man was courteous and kind, and easy to look at. I wasn't even divorced for two weeks and it was way too soon to think of a relationship, but I was being tempted.

When he returned, he had a wet splotch where Mira had branded him with the beans. Through the thin fabric of his wet shirt I could see the dark hair on his arm and it didn't take much imagination to picture that hair over his chest, belly and further down---oh dear, oh dear.

To change my thoughts, I asked "How far is it to Rosalita?"

"Another forty minutes," He looked at his watch. "We should get on the road."

Against my protest that I could pay my share, Mike took care of the bill.

"At least let me help with the cost for gas," I said. "You've driven all this way from Rosalita and then back, to pick up two people who are strangers."

"Well, we're not strangers now," he said.

We returned to the car and pulled away from the restaurant. A soft sunset was resting on the horizon, filling the sky with yellow and rose.

"Miranda's a pretty name," Mike said. "From Shakespeare, right? *The Tempest?*"

"You read Shakespeare?"

"You think all a Texan does is sit around a campfire, singing 'Home on the Range' to his cattle?"

"No, of course not," I stammered.

"I have an M.B.A. from U.N.T. Dallas."

Too many initials, but I felt silly asking. Charlie didn't even have a high school diploma, and here I was with a man with an M.B.A. Was he really too good to be true? I thought of Jeremy Sinclair and his delight over seeing his male lover. He'd also been too good to be true.

"You're not gay are you?"

Mike looked like I'd slapped him. "No," he said slowly. He looked at me. "Any other intimate personal questions you'd like to ask?"

I could feel my color rising, and if we hadn't been going seventy mph on the highway, I would have opened the door and jumped out, preferring to walk the rest of the way to Rosalita.

"Let me see," he said. " I am thirty-five, single, not currently in a relationship. I wear boxers, and drink my coffee black. My father was Otis West. Actually, it was Westenmeyer when his family emigrated from Germany, but that was too much for most folks to spell. Anything else?"

"You said your mother was Hispanic."

"Guadalupe Maria Garcia. Her family was here when Texas was still part of Mexico. *Una Familia mui orgulloso*. Very proud of themselves and their heritage. It was definitely a step down for my mother when she married my father. And what about you?"

"My father's family came from Norway, my mother's family from Sweden, but of course they were both born in the U.S."

"You don't look either Swedish or Norwegian. Aren't those folks usually blonde?"

"My parents adopted me when I was little."

In the next forty minutes we talked. Mike told me about growing up on a Texas ranch and I talked about Tyndale, New York and its strange characters.

I leaned back in the seat, feeling myself relax in the warmth. "It will be nice not to wear that heavy winter jacket again."

"Don't get rid of those jackets yet. You'll need them."

"But it's so warm."

"It gets cold at night."

And sure enough, as we drove into the yard of the ranch at six, it was starting to cool off. We went up a rutted road and came to a small weathered house with a sagging porch and a cord hanging between two trees that would be my clothes dryer. Mike came over and opened the passenger side door for me. This, I thought, was something I could get used to. A man who opened doors. Then he retrieved Mira's seat from the back. We walked up the steps and entered the house.

I hadn't known what to expect, but the reality of the place was still depressing. There was a living room, with a couch, and two straight chairs facing a fireplace. The floors were wood, buckled with age. We walked through to the kitchen, which had a white cast iron sink, a 30's era stove, and a refrigerator of the same vintage. A tiny microwave sat on the counter. There were two bedrooms. One held a double bed, with a single bedside table, a dresser and a straight chair. The second bedroom was empty. I resisted the urge to turn around and do the whole of my long day's journey in reverse. No, I couldn't. This was my new home; I needed to get used to it.

"Mike, would you be willing to take me shopping?"

"Of course," he said. "What do you need?"

"A crib, clothes, diapers, food. I can rent a car for now, but later I'll need to buy one, so I can shop for myself."

"Tomorrow is Saturday. We can go to San Antonio, then on Monday I'll introduce you to Tina, your office mate. You do have office experience, don't you?"

"I was the administrative assistant to the Vice President at Tyndale College," *Hadn't I e-mailed him this information?*

'This was before they caught you cooking the books?"

Was he serious? I looked over and saw the sly smile at the corner of his mouth. A sense of humor was something I wasn't used to.

"Yeah. I got away just before they caught me."

I could feel the chill in the house, but when I looked around for a thermostat, I couldn't see one. "How does the heat work?"

Mike pointed to the fireplace. "That's the heat source," he said. "Let me start it for you."

"No, no." I said, but he had already started crumpling some newspaper and piling the logs on top. He had the butane lighter in his hand. "I'll be OK," I said. "Just leave it."

"It's the only heat you're going to have in this place, Bernie.

"We can be OK." *How cold could it get? This was Texas for heaven sake. Wasn't the West supposed to be hot?*

"Look, why don't you stay at my house tonight. I've got plenty of room and it's a lot warmer and cleaner. No one has lived in this house for at least three years. I feel bad that I didn't do anything to spruce it up."

"We'll be fine," I said. "You've done an awful lot for us Mike. I don't want to put you out any more."

"You haven't put me out, Bernie. I want you to be comfortable. At least let me give you some supper."

What I wanted at that moment was to sit down and accustom myself to my new surroundings, but Mike seemed determined.

"Come on," he said. "We're going up to the house. At least I can give you a cup of coffee, and you can stay the night if you need to."

"We'll sleep here, Mike," I said. "You can give me coffee, but I'm going to stay here in this house."

"OK," he said, finally. He was probably thinking he'd never met such a crazy woman in his life. That, or I was running away from something truly awful.

We got back into the car and drove up to the house, which was a large structure made of reddish adobe. We stepped into a huge hallway with an ancient credenza against one wall and above it a painting of cactus. Clearly a lot more money had been spent on Mike's house than on the little shack where I was staying. We stepped through into a living room where two comfortable leather couches faced a fireplace with a fire burning. Above me stretched a high ceiling with rough wood supports. The opposite wall seemed to be all glass, looking out toward a pasture where cattle grazed. The walls were a bright mustard color and had paintings of horses, cowboys, old barns and cactus in bloom. Best of all, the house was warm.

Mike walked toward the back of the house, calling "Maria." In a minute a woman came into the room. She was middle aged with dark hair worn in a long braid and was wearing a white blouse and dark skirt. "Mister Mike," she said. "I thought you would be late coming home."

He said something to her in Spanish and she nodded, then disappeared.

"Maria will make us coffee," he said. "And anything else you like. Soup? Tortillas?"

I wasn't hungry, but then I remembered the cupboards in the house where I was staying, empty except for mouse droppings. I had nothing in my bag except some pretzels leftover from the flight and two jars of baby food. "Maybe a little soup," I said. "Something to tide me over until morning."

Mike motioned to one of the sofas. "Sit down. I'll bring the coffee in here."

I sat with Mira on my lap. In one corner of the room was a recliner facing a flat-screen TV, and on a table beside it was a sculpture of an eagle in flight. Mike was obviously a man who liked art. Mira started to squirm, so I bounced her up and down. This house wasn't toddler proof, so I wasn't ready to let her wander around. In a few minutes Mike came back with two steaming cups of coffee.

"Do you want milk and sugar?" he asked.

Mira looked at Mike. "Soooga?"

"She talks," Mike said.

"Once she gets to know you, she won't stop talking. It's just that this is all so strange, and she's adjusting." I reached into the diaper bag and pulled out one of her sippy cups. Mike was still standing there, watching us as he drank his coffee. I held up Mira's cup. "Could we have some milk?"

"Sure," he said. "Follow me."

I followed him to a large kitchen with a granite countertop running along one side. On one wall was a gas range, refrigerator and a deep, stainless steel sink. Maria was standing at the stove, stirring something in a pot. I held up the sippy cup.

"Leche, por favor, Maria." Mike said.

Maria turned and saw the baby and her face brightened. she rinsed the cup in the sink and then filled it with milk. She leaned in toward Miranda and smiled warmly as she handed my daughter the cup.

I set Mira on the counter while she drank her milk.

"This is a beautiful kitchen," I said. The tiles on the walls were reds and blues and greens. I ran my fingers over one.

"Made in Mexico," he said. "When I moved in here, I had the place completely re-done."

On the wall hung a carving of a man's head wearing a hat with a fish coming out of the top. "You like to collect art," I said.

"I do. It's my only weakness. While Maria is getting our supper, I'll show you the house."

I hoisted Miranda up on my hip and we started walking away from the kitchen, down the hallway that had doors on either side.

"When I bought this place, it was a wreck, " Mike said. "Captain Siphers was a cattle rancher here, but because he had no family when he died, the place sat empty for years. I wanted somewhere to start my business and the land and the house were cheap."

I was looking at the paintings and prints that lined the corridor. Longhorn cattle stood among fields of bluebonnets, bright pink flowers bloomed against Adobe walls. In one photo, a cowboy rode a bucking bronco, his hat waving in the air.

"My first job as the new owner was to gut the place and shore up the collapsing roof. I was redoing the house and trying to grow the business at the same time, so it took me a while before I finally made it livable." He opened the door to a screened in porch. In the growing darkness, I could just see buildings that were probably the roasting sheds. A smell of coffee hung in the air.

Another door opened to a small office, with a single desk on which sat a computer, and a leather arm chair. One whole wall was lined with books.

"Did you live here while you were working on the house?"

"No, I lived in the place where you're staying. I was so busy that all I did was sleep there. Lunch was usually eaten out in the field where I was building the roasting sheds, or here in the house, where the workmen were remodeling."

We peeked into a bathroom whose bright blue tiles glowed. On the wall was a striking picture of a young woman, her face partially hidden by a shawl. Blue and green towels echoed the color of the walls. We walked on and he showed me the master bedroom with a large double bed, and side tables and wardrobe made of some dark wood. The beige carpeting on the floor was accented by a woven rug in shades of red and pink.

"Mr. Mike," it was Maria's voice calling us.

"Supper is ready. Let's eat in the living room."

We sat on the sofa. I put the baby on the floor with her sippy cup and ate my soup and part of my tortilla. I broke off some of the cheese and gave it to Miranda.

"My mother runs a day care center," Mike said. "She'll be happy to take care of Miranda while we go shopping tomorrow."

"Your mother runs a day care center?" This place was more and more surprising.

He nodded. "When I moved here, she came with me. She'd been living in a tiny house in Amarillo and I think she was lonely. My mother should have had ten children, she loves them so, but she only has me. When she got here, I suggested opening a day care center. It's hard work, but she has a couple of women who work with her. If you think Mira would be OK with someone she'd never met before, my mother would be happy to have her."

I looked at my daughter who was yawning. It was eight-thirty, past Mira's bed-time, and I wouldn't mind putting in an early night myself, especially if we had a long day tomorrow.

I finished the tortillas and put my dishes on a nearby table. "Thanks for the meal, Mike," I said. "I think we'll go back to the house now."

He nodded.

It had turned chilly. I slipped into my jacket and got Miranda into hers, grateful for their warmth and mindful of Mike's earlier comment that we would need them. We drove to the house, and Mike plugged in a little space heater that he'd brought with him. It wasn't much, but it would have to do.

"Thank you for everything you've done for us," I said. I reached for his hand and held it. "You have made us feel very welcome."

The color changed slightly on his face. He nodded, turned and was gone.

When the door had closed I looked back at the room. The house was still dirty, and though the space heater was working hard to warm us, the house had less than half the heat of Mike's house. I walked around again. In a cupboard I found several wool blankets that hadn't been chewed by mice and I threw them over the bed. It was only quarter to nine, but I was exhausted. I put Mira onto the double bed, fully dressed with her winter jacket on, and within minutes she was asleep. Then, still in my jacket, I lay down, pulled the blankets over both of us, and slept.

I woke the next morning to biting cold. In the living room, the space heater was working valiantly, but there was ice in a water glass. It was too cold to undress and take a shower, too cold even to remove my down jacket. The baby woke crying and I rummaged around in the bag and found a jar of strained pears and a spoon. Sitting on the edge of the bed, I fed her the pears. When I touched her hands they were ice cold, so I wrapped her in the blanket. I was glad I had not given in to what I thought was 24/7 Texas heat. Clearly this was a land of extremes.

There was a knock on the door and when I answered it, Mike was there wearing his usual dark jeans but with a leather jacket and gloves.

"Jesus, it's cold in here," he said. "Why don't you let me start a fire?"

I watched him carefully as he went to the fireplace, crumpled paper and then laid some logs on top. The flames caught, filling the house immediately with smoke.

"Some bird has built a nest in the chimney," Mike said, opening the door. Outside the sun was shining and it actually seemed warmer. I picked up Mira and we stepped outdoors.

Mike came out after us. "Well," he said. "It looks like we need to do more to this little house than I thought."

Tear it down and put something else in its place, I thought.

"I'm sorry, Bernie. I didn't realize it was such a wreck. I haven't been inside here in years. When my employees stayed here, I just let them fix it up to suit themselves. I should never have let you stay here."

"It's not your fault. I agreed to stay here, sight unseen and I'm going to make the best of it."

"You're a good sport. Most of the women I know would have made a beeline for the nearest motel."

I wondered how many women he knew, and what those women were like. I thought Texas women, like the men, could tough out anything. Maybe not. I, however, had made my decision and though the bed was lumpy and not very warm, I was going to lie in it.

"Let me take the three of us out to breakfast," Mike said. "And then we'll go see my mother at the daycare center."

"Sounds good."

The daycare center run by Guadalupe Maria Garcia-West, called Texas Babies was at the end of a short tree-lined street. The front yard and the area around the front door was a riot of flowers, some of which I recognized. Hibiscus grew on small bushes, purple coneflower and small red poppies crowding around it.

Mike knocked on the door and then opened it.

"Mama," he called.

"Miguel," came a call from the rear of the house, and then a small plump woman came toward us. She had dark hair streaked with grey, which she had pulled back severely, and she wore a print dress with an apron over it. But it was her face that caught my attention. It was unlined, in spite of her age, which I guessed to be mid fifties, and her eyes sparkled.

She looked at me briefly, but her attention was drawn to Miranda. They were like two magnets, the older woman and the baby. Miranda had reached that age when anyone who wasn't her mother was a stranger to be shied away from. But Mike's mother held out her arms and Miranda, with no fussing, went straight into them.

"Come on, you two," Guadalupe said, as she walked away from us toward the back of the house, carrying Miranda. "I'll show you the place."

The house, narrow at the front, widened out in the back to a large playroom with a kitchenette, and windows that looked out onto a yard filled with flowers. Clearly, one of the things Guadalupe loved, besides babies, was gardening.

Sitting on the floor of the room, surrounded by toys, were four babies. Another three toddlers were busily pushing and pulling and jumping and tussling over toys as the sunlight poured in through the windows. Two women were fully occupied, one feeding a baby in a rocking chair, the other reading with a toddler on the floor.

"What is your baby's name?"

"Miranda. We call her Mira."

Guadalupe smiled at that. "I shall call her Miranda."

"This is Bernie," Mike said.

"Short for Bernice."

"And this is my mother, Lupe."

"Short for Guadalupe."

I pulled off Mira's coat and set her on the floor. Several other children began to crowd around studying the new arrival. Mira gave me a look of concern and I wondered if I was right to leave her. We'd been traveling with strangers yesterday, had slept in a strange house last night, and now were in a daycare center with people she didn't know.

Lupe saw my concern. "She'll be all right. Just you wait, when you get back later, it will be as though she's been here for years."

I nodded, hoping it was true.

Chapter Fifteen

We drove from Rosalita toward San Antonio, reversing the trip we'd made the day before. On the way, Mike and I talked about where I could get the cheapest goods. By noon, I had purchased a flat screen TV, washer and dryer, a computer and a grate that would keep the baby away from the fire, plus a bunch of other stuff. The TV, computer and fire grate we had in the car. The washer and dryer would be installed later. Mike knew a guy named Ewald Jackson who he thought could help me. By noon, we decided to break for a meal. San Antonio has a lovely river walk, so after we'd parked the car we walked along it, looking for a place to eat.

Above us stretched old buildings, mostly high rises, and before us was the winding, coffee-colored river, with riverboats taking tourists up and down. Strolling beside the river with Mike beside me, I thought I'd never been so happy. We chose a small restaurant just off the Riverwalk, and after our Margaritas and chips had come, we sat, waiting for our meal.

"Have you ever been to the Alamo?" Mike asked. "It's not far away."

"I've heard of it," I said. "Davey Crockett and Jim Bowie were killed there, weren't they?"

He nodded and went on to give me the shortened version of the story, which was that Texas had once been under Mexican control, and when General Antonio Lopez de Santa Anna decided to reign in the troublesome Texians, a band of men, including Davey Crockett, Jim Bowie and William Travis. took over an old mission, named "El Alamo" which was being occupied by Mexican forces.

He started relating the history, but I found my mind wandering as I watched the people strolling the tiled walkway in front of me. Had my parents come here before I was born, walking this same path, or eating a meal at this same table? Maybe they had taken me, an infant, to this very spot.

"The battle raged from February 23 until March 6, 1863, and almost everyone, except a few women and children, who'd gone to the Alamo with their men, were killed. " Mike turned to me. " You aren't listening, Bernie."

"Sorry," I said. "Did I tell you that my birth parents were Texans? At least that's what I think. It's one of the reasons I came here."

"That makes sense," he said. "Actually it makes more sense than the story you told me yesterday which was that you needed a change of scene."

"I didn't say that," I said.

"No, I guess you didn't. I don't mean to pry, Bernie. and you don't have to tell me why you decided to move all the way across the country to work here in Texas. My only concern is that you will stay, and not decide that you hate the country and leave in a week."

"Have your other employees done that?"

He looked uncomfortable. "I own a small company and I'm trying to make it profitable. It's hard training people who come here on a whim and then decide that the heat, the cactus, the isolation, or even the Texans are things they hate. I've done that a few times. I don't want to do it again. That's the only reason I keep asking why you came."

"Fair enough," I said. "I promise I'll give you six months."

"Even if you hate the job?"

I was making a huge commitment, but what other choice did I have? I could go back to an ex-husband in New York who might decide to murder me, or stay here where I had a job and a place to live and the friendship of a gentleman.

"Even if I hate the job. Though if I hate it, I hope I can tell you why."

He leaned back in his chair and took a sip of his drink. "The Alamo's not far away," he said. "We have time to see it if you want."

"Why not."

The Alamo was smaller than I had expected and full of noisy people. It was hard to imagine that it had been a mission before becoming a fortress and the site of a famous battle. Mike showed me the places where defenders had scratched their names into the soft limestone walls.

We walked through the adjoining gardens, and though they were interesting, I was getting tired and wondering how Miranda was doing without me.

"Time to go home?"

I nodded.

I had put my head back on the seat rest and was half asleep when Mike asked.

"Where is Miranda's father?"

"What?"

He gestured toward my wedding ring. "Your husband. If you don't mind my asking, where's he?"

I was half asleep and caught off guard. "He died. In a car accident. A year ago." *Why had I said that? Because I didn't want to be seen as a woman married to a criminal, even though I was guiltless. If I were a widow, I could be the object of someone's pity, instead of a manipulating, self-centered divorcee. But now I was with a good looking man who'd been nothing but a gentleman and I was lying to him. Not a good start to a relationship, if there were going to be a relationship.*

"I'm sorry," he said.

"His car flipped over on an icy road. He was driving to the drug store to get medicine for the baby."

I looked over at Mike. Was he buying any of this? Me, the sweet, grieving widow, and Charlie the selfless father and husband? I didn't believe any of it myself, how could I ask him to believe it? There are many problems with a lie, but one of them is remembering the details of the story. Did Charlie die six months ago, or a year ago? Was he going to the store for baby diapers or medicine? What kind of illness did the baby have that required medicine? What kind of car was he driving? What was his name?

"Charlie," I said aloud. "His name was Charlie." At least I wouldn't have to make that up.

"When my dad died, my mom never came out of the house for six months. All of her friends came by with food, with invitations to the movies or to Bingo, which she loves. I think it took all that time to adjust to the fact that he was gone. She says she'll never love anyone else like she loved my father."

How nice for her, I thought. But I was envious. When I first married Charlie, I was awed by him, and proud that I had married the man every girl wanted. But I was only seventeen. I'd never had a real boyfriend, and the only man I'd ever slept with was Charlie. It wasn't until much later that I realized the truth of the situation. While I was being swept up into the newness of being the perfect little housewife, Charlie was feeling trapped.

"What did your husband do?"

"He taught Anthropology at Tyndale College. We met when we were both undergraduates." I had chosen anthropology because Professor MacIntosh was an anthropologist, and I knew something about his work. But the thought of Charlie teaching college was ludicrous. The most he ever thought about anything was when he was working out the odds at the horse track. I put my head back on the seat and closed my eyes, hoping that this pretense of sleep would stop further questions.

Chapter Sixteen

The next day was Sunday and with Lupe agreeing to take Mira for a while, I set out to put the house in order. First, I scrubbed every room from top to bottom, especially the cupboards in the kitchen, the stove and the refrigerator. Then I began painting. Half way through the first room, there was a knock on the door. I went to answer it and standing there was Mike.

He looked me up and down, taking in my paint spattered jeans and shirt, the dirt on my face, and the old bandana that smushed my hair down.

"How about some help?" he asked.

I nodded, too overcome by his generosity to say more. I showed him the can of paint, the paint roller and paint tray, the plastic gloves. I put on the radio and for the next three hours we painted. By the time we'd finished, the bedrooms, kitchen and living room had at least one coat of new paint. Things weren't newer, but at least they were cleaner.

Mike looked over at the boxes of stuff piled in the corner, a crib for Miranda, new curtains and bedspreads for the bedroom, cups and dishes and silverware still in their packaging.

"Want help with any of this?"

I shook my head. He'd been so generous, I felt I was using him. Once the paint had dried, I could put the rest of the house together. "I'll call your friend Mr. Jackson. Once the washer/dryer comes, he can help me install them."

"I don't mind staying for a while," Mike said.

"Mike," I said, walking over to where he was standing by the door. "You've done so much. I can't ask you to do any more."

He reached forward and gently brushed his hand over my head. "You've got cobwebs in your hair," he said. Then he touched my cheek, "And dirt on your face."

I brushed my hand over my hair, unable to control the trembling. He was so close I could have reached up and kissed him. We were both sweaty and dirty, but it wouldn't have mattered, none of it would.

"I need to get Miranda from the day care center," I said. He nodded, the moment between us gone, but as we drove to Lupe's I couldn't help imagining what it would be like to be in his arms.

On Monday morning Mike showed up at my house early. We had just finished our breakfast and I was rushing around to get dishes in the sink (ah for a dishwasher), and getting clothes and snacks ready for Mira's day. We went to the day care center where we dropped off the baby. Today I would begin my new job working as a secretary in Mike's business.

We drove back toward the ranch, to a series of low buildings. I smelled roasting coffee, and I could see trucks parked by a loading dock and men carrying boxes in and out. Mike drove up to one of the buildings and stopped the car. "Before I take you to the office, let me show you the plant."

He led me to a large room that had two machines, one at each end. The room was warm, but two industrial sized fans stood blowing air away from the machines. A man wearing a white coat and a billed cap stood beside one machine.

"This is Jose Merida, my roastmaster," Mike said. Jose smiled. Clearly they had a lot of respect for each other. "Jose's nose is the heart of my business."

"No, no. Mr. Miguel. It is my heart that is the heart of your business."

"That too," Mike said, laughing.

As Mike walked away, Jose pointed to the roaster, and started explaining how coffee was roasted, but my attention was on Mike as he moved away, waving to one of the workmen as he left.

"You see the golden yellow color coming up to a mustard. We are nearing the first crack, when the moisture in the beans pushes out. Wait, you will hear it," Jose was saying.

"Miss?"

I hadn't been paying attention.

"You don't just look at the color, you smell," Jose said, lifting his nose to the air. "Between now and the second crack, the smell changes, becomes sweeter, more rounded, but you must watch carefully, not to burn the bean." He pulled at a handle sticking out of the machine and drew out a small sample of the beans and put his nose to them. "*Esta bueno*," he said. "The less roasting time a bean has, the more caffeine the coffee has. People think the darker the coffee, the more jolt, but it's just the opposite." He held up a bean. "French roast is basically just burned coffee."

Jose was still talking about coffee roasting as Mike disappeared from view. I might see him later. It was a small business, but he was also a busy man.

"Carmelita," Jose called.

A woman wearing a white smock came forward. "Can you show Miss Bernice where the packaging room is?"

I was led to the packaging room where two women were running a machine which bagged the coffee beans and labeled them. Then Carmelita took me to a door and pointed to a building where I could see the word "office." Outside the sun beat down fiercely, and I was sorry I'd not worn a hat and sunglasses. One more thing to shop for.

I went into the second building, passed the employee break room, where two men were sitting drinking coffee, and arrived at the office. Sitting behind a desk with papers spread out before her, was a young woman. She looked up as I went in.

"You're Bernie," she said. "Mike said you were coming this morning. I'm Tina Grasmere." She held out her hand to shake mine. "I'm terrible at filing? Have you done this before?"

I nodded and in the next hour, Tina and I worked out a filing system to replace the papers that had been pushed haphazardly into the cabinet. Once in a while the phone rang and Tina would scribble down something on a piece of paper.

"What are those?" I asked, pointing to the slips.

"Orders," she said. "When someone calls, I scribble the order on a piece of paper, which eventually goes to packaging."

I reached over and picked up a slip. It was hard to decipher the writing.

"What happens if the people in shipping can't read your writing?"

Tina blushed. "They call me." She pulled out a large ledger from under the desk. "When I have time, everything goes into the book."

I suppose the book was a good back-up plan, but it seemed fatally prone to errors. Ledgers were the stuff of Victorian novels---men working in dusty, unheated rooms, scribbling numbers into dusty tomes by candlelight. "This is a crazy system," I said. "Whoever designed it was nuts."

Tina's face fell. "It wasn't me," she said.

"I designed the system," Mike said, stepping into the room. "My dad was the foreman on the Rocking J ranch and this was the way he did things. It worked for him. Why do you think it won't work here?"

I had no business telling the boss how to run his show, especially since it was my first day on the job. I should have been considering my other employment options before I opened my big fat mouth. I didn't have a car, and if Mike fired me, I'd have a hard time begging him to drive me to a job interview.

Mike settled himself into a chair. "This is a system we've used successfully since the business began. Tell me why you think it needs to be changed, and if I'm convinced, I'll consider other options."

I took a deep breath, reminding myself, that as a new employee I needed to keep my opinions to myself, but he had asked and so I told him. I talked about having redundancy in a system so that orders, the lifeblood of his company, didn't get lost. As I talked, he nodded, and I relaxed. He knew I was right and he was willing to let me research a system.

"OK," he said. "Run your ideas by me before we order anything."

"Bernie needs a computer, too Mike," Tina said. I expected him to respond with something sharp. I've seen other bosses take criticism poorly, but he just nodded and left. Fifteen minutes later a computer arrived. It wasn't new and the operating system was at least five years old, but with it, I could research programs to manage product in a company like Mike's. I found an ad for a scanner that would transfer Tina's slips into the computer. More insurance against getting things lost. I had just finished writing all the particulars down, so I could show them to the boss, when he poked his head in the door.

"Lunch, ladies," he said. "We're having fajitas with refried beans." Tina and I followed him back to the break room, which was now filled with eight people, all chowing down. On one counter was laid out a large pan of meat and vegetables, another of meat, a lidded dish with warm tortillas and paper plates and plastic ware.

"Guys," Tina said. "This is Bernie Robertson. She just started work today, and she's found a program that will do away with my handwritten slips. From now on you can get typed slips."

"Typed slips?" one woman said. "What a great idea. No offense, Tina, but being able to read a slip without knowing Chinese will be a treat."

Tina colored. I don't think she'd actually realized how much extra work the "system" had created.

"We organized the filing system," Tina said, between bites of food. "And Bernie ordered a small scanner that will save things into the computer."

There was a scattering of applause and some smiles. I looked at Tina, but she didn't seem unhappy about these changes. I vowed that I would be very kind to her in the future.

Mike came into the room and began helping himself to food. There seemed to be an easy friendliness between him and his workers. He turned and faced the room.

"So you've met Bernie," he said.

There were nods.

"She's only been here a day, and already she has some good ideas."

More nods. I flushed with pride. This was going to be a good job, I thought. Whatever reservations I'd had about leaving New York were starting to melt away.

People had finished eating and leaving. I turned to Tina. "Do you eat like this all the time?"

"Only once a week. It's a way for people to get together, to feel like we're more than just a business."

That evening, at home, I moved the new crib, the rocking chair, and the toy box into the baby's room. With curtains, matching throw pillows and a rug, the room was now bright and cheerful. In my bedroom, I had a new down comforter, bedside table, lamps and a small desk with a chair for my computer.

I had covered the old sofa in the living room with a new throw and purchased a recliner. On my new table, I laid out candles, place mats, china and silverware, imagining a lovely dinner, though whether this dinner was going to be a romantic meal for Mike and me, I didn't know.

The kitchen, with its newly painted walls and cupboards was marginally better than it had been. The aging cast iron stove was still there, as well as the white enamel sink, and the avocado green refrigerator, but the cupboards were clean enough to put food and dishes into. I ran water into my new teakettle and put it on the burner. Then, taking a cup from the cupboard, I put in instant coffee and sugar. I took my coffee into the living room and sat in the recliner, tucking Miranda and her sippy cup in beside me. I was home.

I had acquired a pretty-good Nissan Sentra, which had only been driven by an elderly couple going to church, or maybe rock concerts, but I still needed lots of stuff, especially a baby gate if I wanted the door open. I'd only been in Texas for a few days, but I'd begun to think of this place as a permanent abode.

That night I called my mother whom I hadn't spoken to since we'd talked at the airport.

"Bernie," she said. "How are you, honey?"

She sounded like she was at the bottom of a rain barrel. "Where are you, Mom?"

"Clint and I are in Belize. It's beautiful here, soft sand..."

"Don't tell me. You're eating seafood, drinking rum colas and having sex on the beach."

"Bernie."

"OK, I won't talk about the obvious. Have you heard anything about Charlie?"

"He's still in jail as far as we know, though we've only been away for a week, so Clint doesn't get the latest news. How's your new job? And my little Miranda? I miss that baby terribly."

"The house has no central air or heating system. No dishwasher, washing machine, or clothes dryer. But I'm coping. Yesterday we painted three rooms, and today I moved new furniture in. "

" *We* painted? "

"Mike West, was here."

"The cowboy that met you at the airport. That Mike West?"

"Mom, I know what you're thinking, and the answer is I only just got divorced from Charlie."

"But Charlie may be in jail for a while. If you've got a good-looking man out there, take advantage of it."

"Thanks Mom," I said. "Stay well, and while you and Clint are romping around naked on the beach, try to keep sand out of your you-know-what."

"Is that any way to speak to your mother," she said, but I heard laughter in her voice.

That night, lying in bed, I awoke with a start to a strange noise. Someone was in the room, or maybe in the house. Please, not in the house. Cautiously, I threw back the cover, grabbed my robe, stuffed my feet into slippers and stepped into the living room, which was eerily quiet. Long streaks of moonlight were spread across the floor, but there were deep pits of darkness in the corners.

"Who's there?"

No answer. In truth, it was highly unlikely that a burglar would say "Just me, Ma'am, robbing your house."

"I'm giving you one more chance to get out of here and then I'm calling the cops," I said turning on a lamp that threw a weak glow into the room. I was sure I'd heard something, but there was nothing there.

I crossed to the front door and threw it open. The wind was blowing, moving branches back and forth against the clapboards of the house. No doubt this was what I'd heard. Something rustled in the bushes nearby. Charlie? Charlie with a gun? The rustling continued and then a fat raccoon waddled out onto the grass.

"Git," I cried. The raccoon looked at me as though I'd lost my mind and waddled away unconcerned. If I couldn't scare a raccoon, I was certainly not going to scare Charlie

Chapter Seventeen

On Wednesday Mike came into the office. "Can I talk to you Bernie?" he asked. He gestured toward the empty break room. "In here?"

I got up from my desk, wondering what was wrong. Nothing is wrong, Bernie. I said to myself. He likes you.

"Are you happy with what we've done with the system?" I asked even before we'd sat down.

"I am. I'm always embarrassed when we make mistakes. The women in packaging are asking why we didn't do this before. But that's not why I asked you here."

I waited. If it wasn't about the work, what was it?

"Want to come to a dance with me on Friday night? I think it would be fun."

The last time I'd danced was at my wedding and then I'd been pregnant and running off every ten minutes to throw up in the john. Charlie had been plastered, so he wasn't doing much dancing either. I'd had dance lessons as a kid, but now I couldn't even remember the basic steps to a waltz. Was it too late to fly Fred Astaire in for a few pointers? If Mike wanted to waltz me around the floor, he'd have to deal with my two cement shoes.

"How about it? Friday night at seven. Mom will sit with Mira, if you want. Most folks wear jeans so don't worry about getting dressed up."

He was serious about this. "Sure," I said.

On Friday night, we drove to a dance hall named The Starlight Cafe. The outside walls of the building had painted images of stars and planets

146

glowing with fluorescent paint and near the driveway was a neon sign advertising Kurt and Kountry Kowboys. We walked into a huge room with a bar at one end, and walls covered with branding irons, cowboy hats and what looked to be ranching tools. A raised platform held a collection of microphones and amplifiers, with no musicians in sight, but already most of the tables were filled with people laughing and talking.

We ordered a beer for Mike and a rum and coke for me. Then the band members came in, warmed up, and in no time had launched into a favorite song, "The Yellow Rose of Texas." Soon the dance floor was filled with people doing the jitterbug, the waltz, the polka and a few folks in the corner doing some complicated dance step in unison.

"What's that they're doing?"

"Line dancing." He stood up and grabbed my hand and I followed his lead toward the floor. He pulled me to him. As I said, I'm not a dancer, but Mike is, and so we were off, moving around the floor smoothly with no hitches. If I stepped on his toes, he never said a word. He seemed to know exactly where he wanted to go, and I would have followed him anywhere.

If you watch people dancing you can tell something about their relationship. Are they awkward and stand-offish? Does one partner have wonderful rhythm while the other partner is clueless? Does the woman lead and the man follow, gritting his teeth until it is over? As I danced with Mike, I began to sense what being partners with him would be like. I rested my head on his chest, and he put his chin on my head and we danced more slowly, getting used to our physical closeness.

The music ended and we waited for the next song, which turned out to be "Crazy," a song that must be the Texas national anthem because every single man and woman and a few kids got up and began dancing. It was so crowded we kept bumping rear ends and elbows, but no one seemed to mind. Then it was "The Boot Scooting Boogie" and the whole room got up to line dance. Then "May I Have This Dance For The Rest Of My Life" and "Waltz Across Texas With You."

When the song had finished, the leader stepped up to the mike. "We're taking a little break folks. We'll turn on the juke if you want to keep on dancing."

There was a buzz behind me, and the whole place grew quiet. I looked around. Coming through the door and heading toward us was a tall, blonde woman wearing skin-tight jeans that had rhinestones running down the side seams, a t-shirt with a rhinestone cross emblazoned on the front, a red cowboy hat with a sparkly band and red cowboy boots.

Every male in the place had turned to watch her pass, and someone in the rear let out a "Yee-hah." She stopped at our table.

"Hiya Mike," she said.

"Caylee."

"Who's this?" she asked looking at me.

"This here is Bernie Robertson. She's staying in the cabin on my land." He gestured toward the cowgirl. "Caylee Harder."

I'm sure we had the attention of everyone in the place. Most people were probably wondering why Mike was with the little Yankee gal when he could have had this cowgirl goddess.

Caylee sat down and glared at me. If looks could incinerate, I would have been a pile of ashes on the floor.

"You staying in Texas awhile?" she asked.

"I don't know," I said. Wrong answer. It should have been "Show me the door, and I'm outta here."

Mike reached for my hand. "Come on Bernie. Let's dance."

"She's very pretty," I said when we'd reached the dance floor.

"Yup."

"Obviously knows you."

"Yup."

Since this conversation was yielding nothing, I started watching dancers. First are the theatrical ones who take up all the space on the floor because they are twirling or dipping, or one partner is trying to flip the other. Then there are the hopelessly inept but trying, couples who have no sense of rhythm and keep bumping into other people and have to stop every once in a while and begin the waltz count again. These are the people I love. They know they'll never be Fred and Ginger, but they are game. The guy has a grim look on his face. He's determined to do this, and maybe if he's lucky he'll be rewarded with some sex tonight.

And then there were Mike and me waltzing across a field of bluebonnets under a bright Texas sky.

Someone tapped me on the shoulder. It was Caylee. "I'm cuttin in," she said.

Mike looked annoyed.

She was standing beside him, tapping one bright, red, cowboy-booted foot in annoyance. "We need to talk," she said. Mike shrugged. "One dance," he said. They started off and I returned to the table to watch. They were in animated conversation, but I don't think the subject was a happy one. About half way through the dance they stopped and just stood. They might have been talking or they might have been shouting; it was hard to tell because the music was so loud. Then Caylee turned abruptly and left.

Mike returned to the table looking weary. "Let's sit the next one out," he said.

"It's not too late, Mike. You can go after her."

"Why would I do that?"

"Because she's pretty and..."

"You're the one I want to be with tonight, Bernie. Not her."

As much as the words warmed me, I didn't feel comforted. It's not a good policy to come between a woman and the object of her affection, even if the man doesn't return her feelings. I had made an enemy tonight. I had few enough women friends here in Texas; I didn't need enemies.

At ten the music stopped, the dance floor was cleared and two huge tables of food were brought out. Not just crackers and cheese, but chicken wings, plates of sliced ham, fruit platters and whole chocolate cakes.

"They do this once a month," Mike said. "Everyone pitches in."

"I didn't."

"You can next month when we come again."

After the band members had eaten, everyone else had a chance. Then the music started up again and we danced some more. By eleven I was fading. Miranda Jane would be up at six and I would have no chance to sleep in.

Mike drove me back to the house, where he would pick up his mother. He got out of the truck and opened my door but when I got outside, he said "Wait," and then leaned forward and kissed me.

I put my arms around his neck and kissed him back, not even caring if his mother was watching from the window. I loved the taste of him, the feel of his arms around me, his slightly sweet aftershave. I wanted to bottle him up so I could take him inside and savor him privately.

After a while we pulled apart. "I had a good time," he said. "Can we do this again?"

Do it again? Was he kidding? I would do it every night for the rest of my life if he asked.

He kissed me again right there in front of his mother who was standing outside the front door watching. I went into the house feeling like Cinderella. I'd met my prince, danced with him, held him and kissed him. If Mike wanted to be with me, I would listen to that inner voice and obey that.

Chapter Eighteen

Mike

Mike started the car and waited for his mother to fasten her seat belt.

"You like that girl," his mother said. It wasn't a question.

"Yeah," he said, pulling away from the house.

"She's got a *niña*. You want to be a daddy to some other man's child. Most likely that child already got a daddy."

"Bernie's husband is dead. He died in a car wreck."

"You know this?"

"She told me, Mama. I believe her. I don't think she's a person who sleeps around."

"She's younger than you, *mi hijo*. Lots younger."

"You were nineteen when you married Dad. He was twenty four. I know, she's younger, she hasn't much experience and she's got a kid, but for the first time in a long time, I've met someone I want to be with."

They had reached his mother's house and he stopped the car and got out to open the door for her.

"Mama," he said when they reached her door. "Don't you want me to be happy?"

"Of course, *querido*. I just don't want you to be hurt."

Her words hung with him as he drove back to his own place, where he switched on the lights and threw his jacket across the back of the chair.

Walking toward the bedroom, he remembered the elation he'd felt when the house had finally been his. But now that euphoria was gone. He had a beautiful house, but it had no inner beauty. It was just a big lonely space.

He undressed, remembering the feel of Bernie's body as they danced across the floor. God he wanted her. He'd had a lot of women in his life. Sometimes the relationships had lasted more than a year, and other times they were one night stands. In the end, there was always something that turned him away. Why was that? Had he been waiting all his life for someone he could give his whole heart to? And had he found that woman now?

He got up and went to the kitchen and found the whiskey. Maybe with a few drinks, he would sleep without wanting Bernie in his bed.

Chapter Nineteen

Bernie

The next day was Thanksgiving. Lupe had invited me and Mira to her house for a four o'clock feast. When I got to the house, I saw that Mike was already there, sitting in Lupe's garden, drinking beer. He had the barbeque fired up and I could smell ribs cooking.

"*Hola* my little enchilada," Lupe said to Miranda.

"Oola," Miranda said.

"You're teaching her Spanish?"

"Just a few words." Lupe pointed to her head.

"Cabasha," Mira said.

"*Cabeza*," Lupe said, emphasizing the z sound. She kissed Mira on the cheek and Mira laughed.

I put Mira down and she walked over and grabbed a book from the shelf, one that she seemed very familiar with. "Mama," she said. "My book."

She brought me the book and I flipped it open, seeing that it was in Spanish. Is this what Lupe had been using to teach my child?

"*Cerveza or vino?*" Lupe asked.

"Vino, please. Blanco."

"Good, good. I teach you Spanish too." She put a plate of warm tartlets on the table. "*Sopas*," she said. "Con chiles. But don't fill up on these. We're having big Mexican feast tonight."

"First, *Crema de Elote*, corn chowder with chiles for you gringos, *Frijoles Negros Refritos*, refried black beans, Tamales, Mexican Green Rice, and for dessert *Aroz con Leche.*"

"Lashay" Miranda said.

"Yes sweetheart. Milk."

"I won't be able to get through the door after eating all that food." I said.

"And Mike's doing his ribs."

I took Miranda up on my lap and took a bite of a sopa which was warm and spicy. When I gave a bit to Mira, she made a face. She was slapping her hands on the table, obviously bored, while I, with the food and wine was already feeling well fed.

"Here," Lupe said, putting a small dish of rice pudding in front of the baby. "She'll like this."

I fed Miranda the pudding, which seemed to settle her and then I put her on the floor with a toy. I watched as she walked around, pulling things off the shelves. She seemed so comfortable here, so much at home. Was I leaving her with Lupe too often?

Lupe put food on the table and we started to eat. "Do you think Kyle will get the job? The President is interested in him, no?"

Mike was silent, concentrating on his food.

"You should be proud of him, Mike. Director of Homeland Security is an important job," Lupe said. "You used to be his best friend. I never figured out what happened between you two."

"We grew apart that's all," Mike said.

"Remember the pranks you got into? Climbing the convent wall to watch the nuns, driving that old jeep out in the field when you were drunk, smoking in the boy's bathroom at school. I think you were eleven at the time. Your father and I sure heard about that one, didn't we?"

They seemed to be speaking in a secret tongue, deliberately excluding me.

"Who's Kyle?" I asked.

"Kyle Harder, big man in Texas politics. Kyle's daddy, J.W. Harder owns the Rocking J where my husband was foreman," Lupe said.

"You met his sister Caylee at the dance," Mike said. "She boards her horses here and comes around sometimes to ride."

"The three of them grew up together." Lupe said. "Like the three mouskateers, they were."

"Can we talk about something else." Mike said. "It's Thanksgiving. What do folks in New York do on Thanksgiving day, Bernie?"

"Eat themselves silly with turkey, mashed potatoes, squash, stuffing, cranberry sauce and six kinds of pies. Then the women go into the kitchen and do the dishes and the men veg out with the football game."

"Sounds good to me." Mike said.

I looked at Miranda, who had taken a quilt and dragged it to the center of the room. She must be ready for bed. I found another quilt and put it over her and watched as her eyes began to close.

"My dessert's better than any pie," Lupe said. She got up and went to the stove. "Coffee anyone?"

"Real coffee, Mama," Mike said. "Not that instant stuff."

"For you, *mi hijo*, real coffee."

She bustled around clearing the table and setting down rice pudding spiced with cinnamon. I looked at Mike. Some casual brightness had gone out of the evening, replaced in Mike's face by a hard tension.

He took a bite of the pudding. "Is good Mama. No one cooks like you."

Lupe smiled, but she seemed to have picked up on Mike's unhappiness, and her expression was forced. We ate the dessert in quiet, each of us working on our own thoughts. I offered to help with the dishes but Lupe refused. It was nine o'clock. Time to get home. I went and picked up my sleeping baby.

"Thanks for a wonderful meal," I said kissing Lupe on the cheek and then we left.

On Friday evening, the day after Thanksgiving. I was going to get groceries, and driving past the horse barn, I saw Mike and Caylee standing in the doorway. I was tempted to slow down, to try to hear what they were saying, but they were too far away. He's just letting her use the barn, I said to myself. It's nothing but friendship. But the two people standing in deep conversation looked like they were more than friends. Even though Mike had asked me to the dance and kissed me like he meant it, he had a longer history with Caylee than he had with me. I needed to get a grip on my emotions. Otherwise, I'd make the same mistake I'd made before, and find myself heartbroken again.

Two days later my new washer and dryer were delivered and I called Ewald Jackson, the man Mike had recommended, to install them. I'd already unpacked my new computer, but the television that I'd muscled into the house sat in its large box in the corner. I had no idea how to install it, so that, too, would have to wait for Mr. Jackson. With all I was spending, I'd decided to wait on a dishwasher.

At six thirty two evenings later, there was a knock on the door. I walked to it, followed by Miranda. When I opened it, a short, round man with a fringe of white hair was standing there.

"Mr. Jackson?"

"Folks call me 'Scrappy,'" he said, stepping into the house. "Hope I ain't coming here too late. " He looked down at Miranda. "Hello, little one. What do they call you?"

Miranda hid her face behind my leg. "Miranda goes to bed at seven, so we've got time to talk," I said, ushering him into the living room and showing him the boxes containing the washer and dryer. I picked up Miranda and we walked to the kitchen and then the bathroom.

"Wail," he said, when we were standing in the bathroom. "This would be best. That way it'll be handy to the dirties."

"Can you do the plumbing?" I asked.

"A course. I done a bunch of plumbing jobs."

"I have confidence in you, Mr. Jackson." Miranda, reached out and patted his arm as if adding her confidence to mine.

"Scrappy, Ma'am. Got the name 'cause I fought a lot as a kid."

"Scrappy, if you can help me hook up the washer and dryer I'll be very happy."

"That all?"

I led him back to the living room where the flat screen sat in its box. "Can you mount this on the wall and get it to work?"

He nodded. "Want me to get this up now?"

"That would be nice."

"Anythin' else?"

"Mr. Scrappy..."

"Just Scrappy, Ma'am."

"How hard would it be to have central heating in this place?"

"Wail. I ain't done none of that neither, but I got a cousin does. Want me to call em?"

"I'd be obliged."

"Gonna cost ya, Missy."

I nodded. *Thanks Dad. I forgive you for waiting all these years to give me the money.*

Scrappy measured the walls and found studs. Then he mounted the TV on the wall and plugged it in.

He flipped on the television, but there was almost nothing to be seen. "You won't get much TV here lessen you get cable, an antenna or somethin'," he said fiddling with the dial. "Get one of them DVD players. You can see plenty of movies that way."

He was putting his tools in the bag, when I asked, "Have you done much work for Mr. West, Scrappy?"

"Who?"

"Mike West, the man who recommended you to me."

"Miguel? Yeah I done some. 'Couple years ago he brung me to Mexico. Had me working on a school there."

"A school?"

"Cement block it was. We stayed a month and Mr. Miguel paid my whole way, room and food. Every day we worked on the building, and when the outside was done, we made tables and benches and cubbies for books. We put up a teacher's desk and chair and a blackboard. Like a regular U.S. school it was. Had a big fiesta when it was done, then we come back home to Texas."

"Why were you building a school in Mexico?"

"Don't know and didn't ask neither. If a man's willing to pay me to work, I ain't gonna ask why."

He closed up the tool bag and said, "I'll call when I'm ready to do the plumbing," he said. "Then we can put in your washer and dryer. I'll talk to my cousin about the heating. Get a DVD player if you wanna watch movies."

After he'd closed the door I moved toward the bedroom to put my sleepy child to sleep, but as I was watching her eyes close, I was thinking about Mike. Why would he build a school for children in Mexico? The next time we were together, I would make sure that I asked him.

Chapter Twenty

Saturday morning was the day Miranda and I had to ourselves. I was beginning to feel that Miranda was growing closer to Lupe than she was to me. She only saw me briefly in the morning and evening, and those times were generally rushed. We hurried to eat breakfast, get dressed and get ourselves out the door, and at night, I rushed to get supper and give her a brief playtime and story before bed. So on weekends, I tried to make our time together special. This morning I was making French toast when Miranda wandered in.

"Mama," she said. "Come see."

"Not right now honey. Let's wait. It's almost time for breakfast." I took her sippy cup, filled it with milk and handed it to her. She pushed it away.

"Mama, come now," she said, stamping her foot. Then she grabbed my hand and pulled me toward the living room. She pointed.

There in the center of the room was a snake, ringed with black, yellow and red.

My mind froze. I didn't know which snakes were poisonous and which were not, but a snake in the middle of a living room was not a good sign. I looked at Miranda who was moving forward to touch the snake.

"No, Mira," I said, grabbing her. "Don't touch."

She burst into tears and I took her into my arms. "Snakes are dangerous," I said.

"Danjarush."

We watched as the snake started uncoiling itself and began moving lazily toward me. I

161

screamed. Miranda wailed. I rushed her into the bedroom and slammed the door. She was sobbing loudly, but I needed to deal with this intruder first.

I am not a woman who is easily cowed. Keeping an eye on the snake, I went into the kitchen and got a broom, thinking perhaps I could just sweep the snake out the door. I lunged with the broom. The snake raised its head and hissed. I feinted with the broom, the snake tried to get around me. In spite of my best efforts, this was not working. I was running the risk of being bitten and then where would I be? On Monday morning, they would miss me at work and come to the house where I would be lying dead from snake-bite on the living room floor, my daughter dead from hunger or dehydration in the bedroom.

I needed a different plan. Again, keeping one eye on the snake, I tried to think where my cell phone was. In the kitchen, the living room, the bedroom? The bedroom. I opened the bedroom door. Miranda was sitting in the center of the room, bawling. Slamming the door, I picked up my baby and dialed Mike's number.

He answered on the second ring. I could hear a TV in the background, but no other voices. I hoped I wasn't interrupting anything important, but I needed him. "Mike," I said. "There's a snake in my house. He's red and yellow and black. I tried to get rid of him with the broom, but he just hisses at me. Can you come over and get rid of him?"

I hung up the phone, feeling a small measure of relief. Mike wouldn't let me die on his property, it would be too embarrassing. In five minutes there was a knock on the door. Cautiously, I opened the bedroom door, leaving Miranda behind me. The snake was still there, curled up in the middle of the floor.

I inched around it and opened the door.

"Are you OK?" Mike asked, concern written across his face.

I pointed to the snake. "It was there this morning. I was in the kitchen cooking and Mira was walking around." I burst into tears. "What if it had bitten her?"

He put his arms around me. I could smell soap and aftershave. He kissed me on the top of the head and if we hadn't had a snake right there in the middle of the room, I would have kissed him back.

"I think it's a milk snake," he said. "They aren't poisonous. Snakes are cold-blooded. That means when it's chilly, like it is this morning, they are slow moving and sleepy. This one is probably just looking for a warm place to den up."

"He'll have to find somewhere else. I'm not sharing," I said.

Mike took the broom and slowly moved the snake from the center of the living room to the door and gently swept it outside. "There, the problem's solved."

"What if it comes back?" I asked.

"Just do what I did. Sweep him carefully out the door."

"Mike, I'm not always in the living room. Sometimes I'm cooking or cleaning. Miranda is walking. I'm not worried for myself, I'm worried for my daughter."

"We can try to find someone who will come out to the property and snake-proof the place, but it might be a couple of weeks until they can do the work."

I didn't think I could survive worrying about snakes for a couple of weeks.

I could hear Miranda sobbing in the bedroom. Jumping up, I went to grab her and walked back into the living room with her on my hip. There seemed to be no easy solution.

"I could help you," Mike said slowly.

"Help me?"

"When I redid my house I watched the builders snake-proof the place. I think I know how it's done."

"Would you?"

"Sure," he said finally.

"Come have some coffee," I said. "I was just making French toast, would you like some?"

He nodded and followed me into the kitchen where I put Miranda into her high chair.

He sat down at the table and I poured coffee. "How's Caylee?" I asked.

He looked surprised. "She's fine, I guess."

"You two were together the other night talking outside the barn."

"She's making some improvements on her house and wanted advice."

"I know you two are close." *Are you still in love with her?*

He looked at me hard. "Let's talk about how we're going to critter-proof this house, Bernie. You have to think not only about snakes, but scorpions and spiders. Fire ants will stay outside, but if you step into a nest, those things can really sting."

"Welcome to Texas," I said.

He smiled for the first time since he'd come into the house. It looked nice on him, reminding me again of how attractive he was. *Keep your mind on the job at hand. That's what he's here for.*

"We need to make a list of supplies," he said. I handed him a pad and we started thinking together. He would go shopping the next day, and that coming weekend, we could start critter-proofing the house.

On Saturday, I asked Lupe to babysit Miranda, so I could work without worrying about her. Side by side, Mike and I cleared the brush from around the house. Side by side, we patched up cracks with foam and put up wire mesh where the house met the land. We sprayed fire ant mounds with poison and covered up holes in the ground. It was hot, dusty work and by the end of the day we were filthy and tired. We ended the day, sitting on the porch, drinking beer, looking out over what we'd done.

"Thank you for helping me do this," I said.

Mike reached over and took my hand, filthy as it was. He seemed to be struggling to say something, but then, finally he just smiled and nodded. "We make a good team."

I watched as he stared out at the surroundings we had just de-crittered, his thoughts unreadable. Then, he put his beer down and stood up. "Got to go, Bernie." He said. "I'll see you tomorrow."

Of course, he probably had a date. He needed to get home to shower and change. The only thing I had to do was pick up my daughter and then spend a lonely evening at home. I could have packed the baby into the back seat and driven into town, but there wasn't much to do there. In the end, Miranda and I decided to stay at home, and watch the few channels my new antenna could provide on the TV.

On Monday I decided that I would thank Mike for his help by inviting him to supper. With all he'd done, I certainly owed him that. The next afternoon I walked around the plant looking for

Mike and finally found him in animated conversation with one of the workers. I watched as Mike and the man inspected coffee beans, and then unloaded the bags. When he started walking back to the office, I trotted up. "Mike, I wanted to say thank you for all your help. Would you come to supper?"

"You don't need to do that, Bernie," he said still walking toward the office.

"Please."

He stopped.

"As a friend, nothing more. "

He nodded.

"Six- thirty," I said. "Wednesday night."

When I got back to the office Tina was sitting at her desk, puzzling over a piece of paper. "Where do I file this?" she asked, handing it to me.

It was a bill for twenty five computers to be delivered to the *Escuela de los Ninos* in Tapachula, Chiapas, Mexico. It was marked 'paid.'

Chiapas was the state where Mike bought his coffee beans. I had I seen that name on the license plates of the trucks delivering coffee. This was, no doubt, the school that Scrappy had spent time building.

"File it under 'charity'." I said.

During the rest of the day my mind kept wandering back to the school in Mexico. Mike bought coffee beans from all over the place, but he'd chosen to support a school in Mexico. Would Charlie have given his own money to support a school so poor children could have a better life? Not likely.

On Tuesday, after Mira was asleep, I made the dessert for Wednesday's supper and tucked it into the refrigerator, along with the batter for the corn bread. On Wednesday morning I would put the pot roast into the crock pot and when I got home, would put the bread in the oven, so it would be hot when we ate.

When I got home on Wednesday afternoon I put the baby in the living room with some toys, and went into the kitchen to put the bread into the oven and check on the food. Mira was walking, and I was hopeful that she couldn't get into much trouble while I was out of the room.

There was a knock on the door. When I opened it, Mike was standing there. He wore a bright white shirt and jeans. His hair had been slicked back and he smelled of aftershave and soap. It was all I could do not to throw my arms around him and kiss him.

"Maaak," the baby crowed. She toddled toward him. When she got to Mike, she clutched him tightly around the knees. "Maaak ," she said.

He bent down and lifted her high up in the air, so she squealed in delight. Then holding her under her tummy, he pretended to fly her around the room while she laughed and laughed. I watched, my heart full. Why hadn't Charlie ever done any of those things with Miranda? Why hadn't he loved this little girl who was so easy to please and who brought so much happiness?

When they were done with the airplane ride, Mike sat with Mira in the upholstered chair. Mira nuzzled his neck.

"She likes you," I said.

He nodded. "Sometimes I go over to the daycare center to see my mom. If the kids are still there, I sit and read to them."

I had an image of Mike sitting in a chair, like one of those Navajo storyteller statues, surrounded by little ones hanging on his sleeve, or crowded onto his lap. He would make a wonderful father, I thought.

"Come on Mira, it's time for bed," I said. I turned toward Mike. "Would you like to read her a story, while I get a bottle? All her books are on the bottom shelf of that bookcase."

I went into the kitchen all the while telling myself, *We are just friends. He has a girlfriend, her name is Caylee.* I repeated the mantra, but my poor heart didn't believe it.

When I got back to Mira's bedroom, Mike was sitting in the rocker reading to Miranda. I handed him her bottle and watched as he popped it in her mouth. Slowly she drank the milk and her eyes closed. When she was fully asleep, I put her in the crib and we tiptoed out.

"She's a great kid," Mike said when we'd reached the kitchen.

"She is. Would you like a beer?" I walked to the refrigerator and when I turned back, Mike was there, right in front of me. I went to move past him, but he put his hands on my shoulders and drew me closer. Then we were kissing, and he was running his hands down the side of my neck, over my breasts, his hands under my shirt, unhooking my bra. I didn't stop him. I didn't want to stop him, except that...

"Mike," I said.

He moved away. "It's OK, Bernie, if you think it's too soon. I can wait."

"No, I need to turn off the oven." I ran to the oven, then came back. "Now where were we."

"I'm so sorry, I have been distant. Things have been cra..."

I put my hand over his mouth and kissed him again, and then led him to the bedroom. We undressed each other, touching, kissing, running

168

our hands over the other's body, breasts, buttocks, legs, arms. Sex had never been something I craved, at least not with Charlie, but with Mike I was transformed to a world where nothing existed but ourselves. When he entered me, I was ready, eager for him. When we were finished, we lay back sated.

I must have dozed in his arms. By the time I awoke, the alarm clock beside the bed read two a.m. and Mike was awake beside me.

"How about something to eat. I have a wonderful dish in the crock pot. At least it was wonderful last night, and I can finish cooking the bread." He sat up and began kissing me on the neck, the breasts. "This is all I'm hungry for."

We made love again and then slept. When I woke again, it was four. Mira would be up in by five thirty, and if we were going to eat in peace, it would have to be now. Quietly I got out of bed so as not to wake a sleeping Mike, put on my robe and tiptoed to the kitchen where I put the coffee on to perk and lit the oven. The table was still set, so I lit the candles and checked the crock-pot. I started humming a love song.

"You're up," Mike said. He was standing in the doorway. barefoot, wearing jeans but no shirt.

"I thought you might be hungry. The coffee's almost ready, and the corn bread might still be good."

He came toward me and wrapped his arms around me, nuzzling my hair.

"I've never been this happy in my whole life."

"You deserve to be happy, Bernie."

"So do you, Mike. Look at all the good things you do---that school in Mexico that you support for instance."

His body tensed. "Who told you about the school?"

"Scrappy Jackson, the man you recommended. He helped me put up the new TV and he's going to install the new washer/dryer in the bathroom."

"Scrappy talks too much."

He seemed unhappy. Was he ashamed of having supported that school?

"You're doing a good thing, Mike. You're helping to provide an education for children who otherwise might have nothing."

He nodded.

"Is that why you buy your beans from Mexico?"

"I buy my beans from all over, but I get them from Mexico because I know the growers, and they sell me a good product."

There was a cry from Mira's room.

"Do you want me to get her?" Mike asked as though he couldn't wait to hold my daughter.

"Give her a minute. She might put herself back to sleep."

I took the cornbread out of the oven, and sliced it up. The pot roast was warm, and after being in the crock pot, all day and most of the night, it fell off the fork.

"What should we call supper eaten at breakfast time?"

"Supfest, brupper." There was another cry from Mira's room. This was determined and a little angry. Our meal for two was now going to be breakfast for three.

I went to the bedroom and picked up my half-awake child. When she saw Mike sitting at the kitchen table her face lit up. He held out his arms and she went into them, and he bounced her on his knee.

"Bernie," he said. "I need to tell you something."

I turned from the stove, where I had been slicing bread.

"It's hard for me to say this. You might think I'm a great man because I support a school in Mexico, but I'm not. I've done some terrible things in my life."

"Well, that's good news. No one can live with a saint, and I'm certainly not one." *Was Mike's secret worse than my own? If he were going to confess something to me, was I willing to tell him the truth about Charlie?* I waited.

He took a sip of coffee. "Well, it's just that. I've been around a while, and I'm not perfect."

I walked over to where he sat and kissed him.

"I don't want a perfect man," I said. "So you will have to do."

"Don't do that," he said.

"Why?" I kissed him again. "I like kissing you."

"You make it hard for me to say what I need to say? Bernie, I want to tell you something."

I waited. He seemed to be wrestling with what to say. He took a sip of coffee, but said nothing. Finally, he glanced at his watch and put the baby in her highchair. "Look at the time. Eight-thirty. I've got to get home and change."

I needed to get to work too. Would anyone, looking at the wide smile on my face, guess that I had just slept with the boss?

Chapter Twenty One

A week later it was Christmas. Though I'd seen Mike at work, we'd not spent any time together. I knew he was busy, but I kept waiting for a sign that our one night together hadn't been just a fluke. Now, on Christmas day, I was in his house which was lavishly decorated for the season. Starting with the front hallway, the house had been transformed into a fairy land with pierced paper decorations hung from the walls and an enormous tree dominating one corner. Folks were milling around and conversation in both Spanish and English filled the room. I put my presents under the tree and moved into the dining room where a long table stood spread with food. There was barbecue, tamales, chiles rellenos, enchiladas, tortillas, fruit salad, pies, and several kinds of beans. People were already helping themselves, and looking around, I spotted Lupe eating at a corner table.

"Bernie," she cried. I put the baby down and she ran to Lupe, who scooped her up and hugged her fiercely. "*mi linda bebe*," she crowed. I watched the two of them. It had been six months since Mira had seen my mother and in many ways, Lupe had become her grandmother. I expect that Lupe would have loved grand-children of her own and Mira was a substitute for those unfulfilled dreams.

I filled a plate with food that Miranda and I would share. Lupe told me that the barbecue was Mike's specialty, and the reason we didn't see him was that he was outside cooking.

Half an hour later, he appeared wearing a long denim apron and carrying a plate of ribs. Behind him was Caylee, her hair pulled into a ponytail. With her jeans, denim shirt and long apron, they could have been twins. I felt a sudden twist of jealousy. Had I been just a temporary fling?

"This is the last of the ribs," Mike said. A few people stepped up to the table and grabbed some, but my attention was fixed on Caylee who was touching Mike's arm in a proprietary way. I had made love to him with no reservations. Had I made a mistake?

After we'd eaten, the presents were distributed, with many going to the babies and toddlers. Then it was the turn of the adults. Mike had been very careful to see that everyone got something.

"OK," Caylee announced. "My turn." She reached behind her and picked up a box which she placed in Mike's lap.

"Open it."

He hesitated, embarrassed.

"Open it now, Mike." It was an order, not to be ignored.

He tore off the paper and opened the box, then held up the gift, a hand- tooled leather belt, with a silver buckle the size of a dinner plate. With something that size he could easily disembowel himself just bending over.

"You shouldn't have done this, Caylee. It's too much," he said.

She bent over him, showing him the tooling on the belt, which apparently featured scenes of the area.

"The buckle has your initials in silver," she announced. "I had it made in San Antonio."

"Thanks," he said, but there was no joy in his words.

She reached forward and kissed him on the mouth. He reddened. Then she sat back, pleased as a cat with a new-caught mouse.

Mike stood up picked up two gifts from under the tree. He handed one to me and the other to Caylee.

Caylee opened hers first. It was a jeweled cross on a long chain.

I opened mine. It was an identical jeweled cross. Mike was grinning like a man who'd just won the lottery. Poor fellow, he had no idea.

Caylee's face darkened. Grabbing the box she stood up and marched out of the room, slamming the front door behind her. I thought about following her to apologize, but in Texas anything could happen. Shootout in the parking lot?

For the rest of the afternoon, the group talked and ate, beginning to drift away as it grew late. I needed to take my sleepy girl home and put her to bed. As I was packing up our things, Mike said.

"Can we talk, Bernie?"

I nodded and we went outside where the scent of cooked meat hung in the air. Buckling Miranda into the car seat, I returned to stand beside Mike.

"I bought those crosses a long time ago," he said, "before..."

We slept together?

"It wasn't really what I would have given you." He fished around in his pocket and drew out a square box. "Here."

I opened the box. Inside was a bracelet made of clear stones that sparkled in the sun. I couldn't turn this one over and see if there were an engraving inside, and I wanted to believe that this was a gift from a man who really cared about me.

"You like it?"

"I love it. Thank you." I reached up and kissed him and we were in that position when people began coming out of the house. I drew away. Even though I was proud of loving Mike, I wanted some privacy in our relationship.

"Dancing on Friday?" Mike asked. "I'll pick you up at seven."

"Sure."

When I reached for my purse which sat on the ground, I looked up to see Caylee glaring at us. Somehow I needed to make peace with that woman.

Chapter Twenty Two

I drove back to the house and put my toddler to bed. She'd had a long, exciting day and I was pretty bushed myself. I tried my mother's cell phone but it went to voice mail. No doubt they were in some elaborate Christmas bash in some fancy hotel on the beach.

I got into my PJ's and tucked myself into a comfortable chair. When I flipped on the TV there was a program about a woman who had just found her birth mother and how happy they both were.

I had a birth mother too. One that I had not thought about for a long time. I'd come to Texas partly to find her, and yet I'd done nothing in the months I was here. I got up from my chair and went to get the dress my mother had given me.

Taking the dress in my hands, I felt the softness of the old fabric washed so many times that the colors were barely visible. It had puffed sleeves, a collar with lace trim, a tiny row of buttons up the back and a half-sash. I closed my eyes imagining my mother buttoning me into the dress, tying the bow, kissing me on the top of the head and telling me to be a good girl. Was all of this simply a fantasy? I *had* a mother. She was romping around in Belize with her new boyfriend. But I suddenly wanted my other mother, a woman I'd never met, but whose genes I shared. Would we even look like each other? Would we have things in common like our taste in food or hobbies we enjoyed? Had she ever loved me? If so, why had she given me up and why had she only started looking for me after I was adopted? If I were separated from Miranda, it would be unbearable. How had my birth mother been able to give me up?

I picked up the little medallion, the one my mother had called a *milagro*. Would a woman who didn't love her child, pin a lucky charm to her dress as protection? But maybe the medallion had come from the orphanage? I looked closely at the image, but it was worn and hard to see. On the front was a picture of the Virgin Mary and on the back the letters S.H.C.H., Lar, TX. This was the orphanage in Laredo where my mother had found me. What had she said the name was? Sacred Heart Children's Home I didn't know if the Sacred Heart Children's Home was even in business, and if they were, whether they would remember me and more importantly, my birth mother. Today was Christmas Day and tomorrow was Saturday. Would Mike come with me to Laredo on the day after Christmas?

"Laredo," Mike said when I asked him. "Why do you want to go to Laredo? It's nothing but a border town. People come over from Mexico to shop or to work. They buy cheap clothing and then they go home. Believe me, there's nothing in Laredo."

"I thought it would be nice to see something different," I said. "I've never seen the border."

"It's a bridge with gates on either side and fences running along the river. You're not going to like it."

"If you don't want to come, I'll drive there myself," I said.

"No, don't do that. I'll drive you, but honestly I don't know what the appeal is. Until a few years ago, Nuevo Laredo, the town on the Mexican side, was dangerous. Are you really sure you want to go?"

"Yes. Can we leave Miranda with your mother?"

"Sure."

On Saturday we drove to Laredo, and parked the car in front of the La Posada Hotel in the San Augustin Historic District. On one side of us was a park with a bandstand in the center and a large statue facing the hotel.

"We can have lunch here," Mike said, pointing to the hotel.

"Do you mind if we walk around?"

He shrugged. This wasn't his trip, it was mine. In spite of his reluctance to be here, he was willing to go along. We walked through the park, looking at the bandstand, the statue of General Zaragosa given by the Mexicans, and the smaller statue of St. Augustine. I kept expecting something to jump out at me with sudden familiarity, but it didn't. Across the street from the park was a large yellow-brick, two-story building that seemed to be unoccupied. Men were lounging by the metal fence in front, and every once in a while a car would pull up and a few men would get in.

"Day laborers," Mike said.

"That building was a school," I said. "Part of the convent."

"How do you know that?"

I didn't know how I knew, but as I looked at the building more closely, I realized that I had been there. I remembered the dream where I'd been saying good-bye to my mother. Had that event happened in this building?

Behind the yellow building was a large church, the St. Augustine Cathedral, but as I moved toward it, Mike balked.

"Bernie," he said. "I'm going to the hotel for a beer. You aren't going to be long, are you?"

"No," I said. Some residual memory, long buried but now rising up was drawing me toward the church and I had to follow. I didn't blame Mike for being bored. Laredo wasn't his thing, and I had resisted telling him the real reason we were here.

I walked around the corner toward the front of the church, past a parking lot. This was where we played, I thought. Near the school.

The door to the church was open and I stepped inside. It was a vast cathedral, with vaulted ceilings and tall stained-glass windows. I had a fleeing memory of walking down the main aisle with other children, kneeling, crossing myself, watching the priest say mass at the altar. I am not a Roman Catholic. In fact, I've never been a churchgoer at all, but the cathedral, the incense, the stained-glass windows, the altar with its images of Jesus and the Virgin Mary seemed to be imbedded in me, something I'd once known and lost.

I went to a painted image of the Virgin standing on one side of the altar. It showed the Virgin Mary in a red dress, and a blue cloak that covered her head. Imprinted on the cloak were gold stars, and around her head and body were incised rays of gold and red. This was the same image of the Virgin that was on the *milagro* my mother had given me, the one that had been attached to my dress. "Beautiful, isn't she?"

I looked over at the priest who stood beside me.

"She is the Virgin of Guadalupe. Do you know the story?"

I shook my head.

"On December 9, 1591 a peasant, Juan Diego had a vision. It was the Virgin asking him to build a shrine to her on the spot, Tepeyac Hill, near Mexico City. When Juan Diego went to the Bishop with the request, the Bishop refused, saying he needed proof that Juan's vision was real. On December 12, the Virgin reappeared telling Juan Diego to gather roses into his *tilmatli,* a cloak, and take them to the Bishop. When Diego opened his cloak before the Bishop, hundreds of roses fell out and there on the *tilmatli* was the imprinted image of the Virgin."

"I have a *milagro* with her image."

"She is very important. Whoever gave you the *milagro* wanted to protect you."

I looked at my watch. It was twelve thirty. Mike had gone to the Posada Hotel more than half an hour ago. He was probably fuming as he waited for me to join him. I rushed toward the door, out onto the street and into the hotel.

"Is there a dining room here?" I asked at the desk.

"You're looking for your young man?" the clerk asked.

I nodded.

"He's in the courtyard." She pointed to a door.

I made my way to an area where two swimming pools sat under the sky, surrounded by potted trees. In one corner of this courtyard, Mike sat at a table, two empty beer bottles and a basket of chips in front of him.

"I thought you'd decided to walk home," he said.

"I'm sorry. I went into the Cathedral and got distracted."

"You didn't tell me you were Catholic."

"I'm not." *How could I explain?* "It's just a beautiful building and I wanted to see it."

"I guess there isn't much else to see here," he said. "Did you see the bridge? The fences?"

I shook my head.

"After lunch, we can walk around."

We were in a corner of the open area, separated from the swimming pools by a colorful tiled wall, hung with potted plants. I ordered a Margarita and looked at the menu. The sky above us was blue and it was warm.

"It feels like Mexico," I said.

"You've been there?"

"Never. But this place feels exotic, decadent, like I should be lying naked on a secluded beach somewhere."

"There's no beach here, Bernie. Just a swimming pool."

"No one wants to see me naked in that swimming pool."

"I wouldn't mind," he said. He gestured toward the balcony directly above the tiled area around the pools. "The rooms are right up there. I'm sure they would rent us one."

"Mike," I said. "It's one o'clock in the afternoon."

"Bernie, we're grownups. No one is going to report us for having a little fun. Come on." He stood up and drew me up from my chair, then he put his arms around me. "Imagine you and I are alone on a secluded beach. The waves are lapping on the shore, the birds are singing, the sun is hot overhead, and no one is around."

Love in the afternoon? It was so unlike the life I'd lived before. Having drinks in an outdoor courtyard with a handsome man who was inviting me to join him for an afternoon romp. Who was this woman I'd become?

"Sure," I said.

After our meal, we got a room and made lazy love for an hour.

"I feel like a character from one of those movies, where people spend the afternoon in bed, au natural, smoking, drinking and making love."

Mike moved toward me and kissed a nipple. "I love your au natural," he said, kissing his way down from my breast to my crotch and then he did other things that brought us back to what we'd been doing for the last hour.

When we finally surfaced, it was late. I'd only had a little taste of Laredo and I wanted to see more.

We got dressed and left the hotel. Almost immediately behind the building was the river, the fence and a bridge being crossed by people and cars in one continuous stream.

"Is this what you wanted to see?" Mike asked. "The bridge to Mexico?"

I looked at the bridge. It seemed ordinary, routine, nothing special. The streams of humanity crossing back and forth probably did this trip every day. We crossed the street and strolled around the park, past stores selling cheap clothing. I'd already seen the cathedral, and the yellow building seemed to be empty. As we walked back toward the hotel, I saw a sign for the Rio Grande Museum. It seemed an imposing name for something so small and, when I poked my head in, didn't seem to have much to offer.

"I'm going back to the hotel," Mike said. "Take your time."

I stepped inside, saying hello to a young woman who was standing beside a counter. The museum had basically two rooms. One room was devoted to photographs of early Laredo and the second room to furniture and other objects. I walked by the photographs, which seemed to date from the early twentieth century to the nineteen-nineties. I had been in the orphanage in the nineteen-nineties. Could I be in any of these pictures? One photo featured a nun, standing behind a group of children, all of them ranging in age from six to eight. I took out my cell phone and snapped a photo.

"Are you interested in the school?" asked the young woman working there.

"Actually, the orphanage, the Sacred Heart Children's Home. Do you know where it was located?"

The young woman shook her head. "But I have other books about Laredo. You're welcome to browse through them."

I thought of Mike cooling his heels at the hotel. Maybe I shouldn't take any more time with this, but I was here, this was my chance. I nodded and the woman went behind her desk and began rummaging through a stack of books, pulling one out and putting it on the glass case between us.

"This probably has some of the information you want. We are grateful for these old photos, because we can see what the town used to look like, before the border fences were put up."

She flipped through the pages and came to a picture similar to the one I'd photographed. The same nun was sitting on a wall, surrounded by four children, three girls and a boy. She was young, maybe in her thirties, wearing a black habit and black veil over a white wimple. But it wasn't the nun I was studying. It was a child about three sitting to her left, wearing a dress imprinted with roses. She had dark hair and eyes, and was gazing unsmiling into the camera. I had seen pictures of this same child in my parent's family albums. I was that child.

"When was this picture taken?"

"I don't know. Wait, yes I do know, because the original was in the *Laredo Morning Times*. She moved to her desk, picked up a photograph album and found a newspaper article dated May 21, 1994. I'd been adopted in September, so I had been in the orphanage in May. I looked at the picture carefully. There were no names given for the children, but the nun was identified as Sister Beatrice.

"Do you think Sister Beatrice is still alive?"

The woman shrugged. "I have no idea. You would have to call the diocese in San Antonio."

"If she was in her thirties in that picture, she would be much older now, wouldn't she?"

The woman shrugged. This was beyond her level of expertise.

"Do you know where the convent was?"

"Convents. I think there were several." She took out a map of the square and put an X in several locations. "Some of these are gone. One was right beside the river, I think. Is there anything else I can tell you?"

"No, thank you. Can I take a picture of the newspaper article?"

She nodded and I snapped a photo with my phone.

Just then the door opened and Mike appeared. "We need to get going, Bernie. It will take us an hour to get back to Rosalita and my mother will be wondering where we are." I wanted to stay longer in the museum, but my time had run out. Reluctantly I headed for home.

Chapter Twenty Three

That night after Mira was in bed, I sat down at my computer and Googled Sacred Heart Children's Home. The home was now a school, staffed by nuns called Servants of the Sacred Heart of Jesus whose convent was located at the same address. I copied the e-mail address of the contact person, a Father Leary, and wrote a note.

"Dear Father Leary.

"I am looking for a nun named Sister Beatrice who is pictured in a newspaper article in the May 21, 1994 issue of the *Laredo Morning Times*. I would like to talk with her about a personal matter. Do you know where I can reach her?

Bernice Robertson"

He could just dismiss me out of hand and I wouldn't blame him. Sister Beatrice might still be working somewhere in the school, or perhaps she'd retired. What I was looking for was definitely a long shot.

I had almost closed down my computer for the evening when I heard a ping telling me I'd received an e-mail.

"Dear Bernice Robertson,

One of the beauties of computer technology is that one can correspond at any time day or night. I am a poor sleeper, so I was up already and intrigued by your request.

Sister Beatrice is still alive, though no longer a nun, and I have no idea whether or not she is willing to talk to you. What I will do is send her an e-mail with your request, and if she is willing to talk, she will contact you herself.

Yours in Christ Jesus

Father John Leary"

That was as good as I was going to get. I downloaded the picture of Sister Beatrice from my cell phone and looked at the picture. The young nun sitting with the children had a bright cheerful smile and the children sitting with her, with the exception of myself, were all smiling too. Didn't this bode for good? I hoped so.

Four days later I got an e-mail.

"Dear Bernice Robertson,

I received a message from Father John Leary about your request to see me on a personal matter. I have searched my brain for your name but nothing comes up. Were you one of my students? If so, I would love to see you. If the matter has to do with something else, you might want to refresh this aging brain of mine.

Cordially,

Beatrice Delgado

Professor, Women's Studies, Sul Ross University"

I looked up Beatrice Delgado at Sul Ross University in Alpine Texas and found her on the faculty page. She no longer wore a habit, but her smile was still warm and welcoming. Would she talk to me if I told her the truth? That seemed to be the only way.

"Dear Ms. Delgado,

Thank you for responding to Father Leary's request. On May 21, 1994 an article appeared in the *Laredo Morning Times* with your picture in it. With you were several children. I believe that I was one of those children. I have been trying to locate my birth mother, whose name I do not know, and wonder if you might meet with me and possibly answer some questions.

Bernice Robertson"

"Dear Bernice,
Shall I call you Miss or Mrs.? As you may not know, I left the convent of the Sisters of the Sacred Heart of Jesus, shortly after that picture was taken. This was done for personal reasons which I will not disclose. However, those children in the picture were all well known to me and I would be happy to talk about any of them. Would you like to come to my office at Sul Ross next Tuesday afternoon. I will give you directions.
Cordially,
Beatrice Delgado"

I would need five hours, to drive from Rosalita to Alpine and the same amount of time to get back. I think Mike would give me the time off, though I wasn't sure yet that I was ready to tell him the whole story. What could I say to him or to Lupe, who would be caring for Miranda. How about telling them I'd just discovered an old chum? That wouldn't work since I'd ostensibly come to Texas knowing no one. The chum would have to be a friend of my parents. One my mother had recently asked me to visit. My fabrication wasn't leak-proof, but it would have to do.

On Tuesday, I made my way to Alpine, Texas, and to the University, and then to the Department of Women's Studies, all of these things severely testing my fragile sense of direction. When I knocked on Beatrice Delgado's door, it opened to reveal a short, stout woman with iron-grey hair and horn-rimmed glasses wearing a blue sweater over a blazing pink shirt. Maybe one thing about not being a nun was that you never had to wear black again. She held out her hand to me and her smile was wide and genuine.

I shook her hand, not sure what I should call her. As if reading my mind she said,

"Call me Bea. It took me some time to not answer to Sister Beatrice. And you are Bernice?"

"Bernie." I reached into my pocket, pulled out the copy of the newspaper article and pushed it toward her.

"Ah yes," she said, studying the picture. "It was a beautiful day; we were out in the garden and ..." she began pointing at the children. "Tomas Garcia became a lawyer in Austin. Maria Perez, and Angelina Gutierrez were re-united with their parents. The mother of Graciela" she pointed to my picture "picked her up from the orphanage before I left. I heard that Graciela was later adopted and went somewhere East." She looked at me. "You think that you are one of these children?"

I pointed. "This one."

"Graciela Morales," she said. "Oh my dear. Push up your sleeve and let me see."

I pushed up my sleeve revealing the heart shaped birthmark.

"I never thought I'd see you again. Where did you go?"

"Ralph and Cyndi Sorengard adopted me in 1994," I said. " I ended up in New York state. Do you know what happened to my mother?"

She shook her head. "I'm sure they must have looked for her, when they found you wandering alone. Someone told me you had been adopted, but by then I had left the order."

She pulled out a pack of cigarettes, tapped one out and lit it. "A bad habit. One I picked up after I stopped wearing the habit. I wish I could break it, but that's how it is." She took a drag and blew out a cloud of smoke. "I'll tell you what I remember about your mother, but we need to start at the beginning."

"It was early in the morning of Christmas day, 1993. I remember the day because we'd had a snowstorm that night, and it was quite an event in this part of Texas. Your mother had been walking in the snow, and she'd crossed the river because her dress and shoes were soaked. Both of you were soaked through. We offered her shelter, at least until her clothes were dry but she refused. She seemed to be very anxious about something. She begged us to take you until she could find a place to live, and we said we would. You were heartbroken to leave her, but she was adamant that we take you. "

"Did she ever come back?"

"Every weekend from January through March."

"And then what happened?"

"At the end of March, she came and got you. She said she'd found a job and an apartment where you could both live. A few weeks later they found you wandering beside the highway in Laredo. No one knew what had happened to your mother. In May, I left the convent for good, and later my friends told me you'd been adopted."

All this time, I'd imagined that Beatrice would connect me with my birth mother, and that I would introduce her to her grand-daughter, Miranda. How could a woman who had come to visit her child every weekend from January through March, simply vanish? It was possible that she'd been offered a better job, and was planning to come back and get me later, but wouldn't she have told someone this? Why simply leave me to wander by myself in a strange city?

"A week after I last saw her, she sent me something," Beatrice said. She rose, and going to a file cabinet behind her, began rummaging through the files. "I should have left this at the convent, but then I thought if your mother came for it, she would try and find me, rather than going to the other sisters. Ah, here it is." She pulled out a manila envelope with something bulky inside and handed it to me.

"You never opened it?" I asked.

She shook her head.

"You weren't curious?"

"I was, but see what it says. 'For Graciela.' She intended it for you."

I tore open the envelope and lifted out a small leather-bound book. When I opened it up, I saw that it was a journal, the entries written in Spanish in a tiny, neat hand. When I flipped through the book, two pieces of paper fell out, one of them a black and white photo. Three people stood against a rude adobe house, two adults and a baby. The man had a wide brimmed hat, almost completely shading his eyes. The woman was hatless and smiling. The baby was smiling too.

"My birth parents?" I asked handing the picture to Bea.

"I expect so."

With the photo was a piece of paper folded into the same size. I unfolded it to reveal an official certificate written in Spanish. I put the certificate on the desk between us.

"This is a birth certificate for a baby named Graciela Estrella Morales Hernandez," Bea said. She pointed to the paper. "Born October 7, 1990 in Tapachula, Chiapus, Mexico. Your mother was Lilliana Carolina Hernandez. Your father was Mauricio Raul Morales."

I looked at the certificate. Was I really this woman with the Hispanic name? One thing was sure from the picture and the certificate. I had been a baby who was wanted, and from Beatrice Delgado's words, a child who was loved. Whatever had happened to my mother, she had not willingly abandoned me.

Beatrice reached across the desk and folded her hand over mine. "I'm glad to have met you again Graciela Morales."

As I was walking toward the door, Beatrice said "Graciela."

It took me a minute to realize that she was talking to me.

"I just remembered something. Many years ago a man came to me asking about the children who were staying in the convent around Christmas of 1993. He seemed to know your mother's name but he didn't know yours. I didn't tell him anything because, frankly, I didn't trust him. Have you had any relatives who might be looking for you?"

"Was he a Latino?"

"No, Anglo. I wondered why he was asking those questions. Have you been in Texas for a while? "

"I only got here recently. Nobody but my mother and my ex-employer know I'm here."

"Well, obviously he didn't find you. Stay safe, Graciela."

It was late in the day when I got back to the day care center and the parking lot was empty of cars. Lupe answered the door at my knock. She had Mira in her arms. I took my baby and we followed Lupe into the kitchen.

.   "A cup of tea, or maybe some wine?"

"Wine would be lovely," I said, setting Mira on my lap. Miranda started squirming and I reached into my purse and gave her a cracker from my stash. Lupe handed me the wine which was sweet and heavy.

"Could I ask you a favor, Lupe?" I asked, taking the journal from my purse and pushing it toward her across the table. "This was written by my birth mother and given to me. But it's in Spanish and I can't read it."

"Why don't she read it to you herself."

"She's sick," I lied. I didn't want to tell her about my mother's disappearance "But she wanted me to read it. It's about her life, I think."

Lupe opened the book. "It says 'To my daughter, Graciela.' Your name is Graciela?"

"Graciela Morales. I was born in Mexico."

Lupe brightened. "You will come here in the evening, and we will eat together, you and little Miranda. Then we will read."

"You don't have to cook for me, Lupe."

"If you don't want to eat my cooking, I don't want to read for you."

"I didn't mean that. It's just that I didn't want to impose on you. You're doing enough for me."

"But I like to cook, and I have no one to cook for, no one to eat with. We will feed little Miranda, and I will feed you, and we will talk about the book."

I stood up and walked over to her, kissing her on the cheek. "Thank you so much."

"Tomorrow night. We will begin tomorrow."

Chapter Twenty Four

El Diario de Lilliana Morales

"Tapachula, Mexico. *Para mi hija*, Graciela. I suppose, looking back on it all, I should have stayed in Mexico, in the lovely green mountains of my home. But at the time I had no choice. My husband had been bitten by a snake in the coffee fields and by the time they got him into the truck and driven him the sixty miles to the hospital, he was dead. Injury and death among the coffee workers is common. You often see boys as young as twelve or fourteen with machete scars on their hands and legs. I knew other women who were widows, saw how they had nothing but stale tortillas and sugar water to feed their children. I didn't want that for you.

"One evening, I was eating with my husband's family at dinner. Though they had little themselves, they were generous to me. My brother-in-law Enrique said he was going to America to work. There were good jobs in America. His cousin in Miami had a business trimming gardens and cleaning swimming pools. If Enrique could make it there, he could get work.

"I glanced over at Enrique's pregnant wife, Maria, and at his two children, Pedro, seven and Sofia, five. Maria touched her swollen belly, and looked at her husband. 'He may not be back before the baby comes, but he will come later,' she said, smiling at Enrique, the look tender and hopeful. I had a momentary pang of jealousy, remembering my bond with Mauricio when we were expecting you.

" 'The price of coffee has gone down,' Enrique said, 'We work the same but get less. I want to send my children to school so they won't work so hard.'

"As he was talking, I thought of you, mi hija, sitting in my lap. I was working six days a week cleaning houses for wealthy people in the city, but the job took me away for long hours. On the day that I worked, I would rise at four-thirty to get us our breakfast, and then take you from your warm bed, still in your night clothes, and give you to Maria to care for. Then I would ride for an hour on the bus to my job. At six a.m. I would cook and feed the family, including a child just a little bit older than you were. This child had everything: a clean room, lots of toys, and someone to cook and clean for her, while you, mi niña, lived at the mercy of a busy aunt. As I worked, I couldn't help think about the difference between this spoiled little girl and my own child.

"How can anyone name the moment when you make the decision that will change your life? I had a choice, though not a good one. I was twenty-seven years old, and had been married to a man I loved. I had you, mi querida niña. I could have stayed where I was, only seeing you in the evenings when you were asleep, but when you started calling Maria "Mama", I realized that we both needed a better life.

"I had the option to remarry. Javier Cruz Ramirez, who was foreman on the plantation and a widower with six children, and who had already begun walking me home from church on Sunday. He was bald with a big belly hanging out over his belt, and I'd once seen his wife with a blackened eye. I didn't love him, but if I married him, I would have the security of a husband.

A Casualty of Hope

"And so, that evening when I heard Enrique talking about going to America, I made my decision. You and I would go with him. My mother-in-law tried to talk me out of going. She wasn't fond of me, but she loved you and wanted you near. Since my parents and father-in-law were dead, she was your only grandparent. She begged and pleaded. We talked for a long time, but in the end, she could not find me a better job closer to home and I decided to leave.

"When I told my employer the next day, she cried, begging me to stay. But once I set my foot upon a path, I travel it. I sold my little house and the few things I could not carry. I would miss all that I'd had here, but I needed money for food and travel, and I knew that I would probably never return.

"My brother in law convinced his best friend Diego Guzman to come along, so instead of three of us there were six: Enrique, myself, you, Diego, his wife Adriana and their twelve year old son Jorge. With greater numbers we might be safer.

"We left Tapachula at the end of September. It is a beautiful time of year in this region, with soft breezes cooling the heat of the day. I tried to keep the picture of my homeland firmly in my mind as I hugged my sister-in-law, my niece and nephew and my mother-in-law. Then we stepped onto the road and with hopeful hearts began walking."

Chapter Twenty Five

"We will stop here," Lupe said, closing the book. "Is time to eat."

"Lupe, you don't have to feed us."

She rose and without a word began putting plates on the table, followed by glasses and silverware. Miranda, who had been playing on the floor, looked up. "Nana," she said, which had originally meant a banana, but now meant any food. I put her on my lap, pushed us up to the table, and with both hands Miranda dug in.

"Wait a minute," I said, grabbing a dish towel and wrapping it around Miranda's neck. At least one of us might stay clean.

Lupe put rice and beans and chili onto my plate, then drew out a pan of bread from the oven and put it between us.

"Thank you for doing this, Lupe."

"In the Latino culture, it is rude to refuse hospitality. I cook for you because I like your company, and of course the company of little Miranda." She smiled at the baby who waved a grubby hand in her direction. "We are very simpatico, aren't we *querida*."

"I am sad for your mother," Lupe said. "She had such a hard choice."

I nodded, thinking about the woman I hardly knew who was becoming less of a stranger.

"When I married my Otis, I made the same hard choice," Lupe said. "My family was very angry. They wanted me to marry a Latino with a proud heritage like my own."

"Your family has been here for a long time?"

"My great, great grand-parents came from Spain, and settled here as cattle ranchers when Texas was still part of Mexico. At one time they owned thousands of acres, but the land was gradually sold off. Otis's father worked as a ranch hand for my father, and so, growing up, we saw each other a lot. When I was eighteen, I was sent to Spain to study. My parents hoped that I would come back with a Spanish nobleman, but Otis started writing to me. He wrote me a letter every single day, sometimes he'd include poetry with his letters. They were poems about the beauty of the ranch, and once in a while love poems. How could I resist a man like that?

"When I got back from my year in Spain, I told Otis I would marry him. My parents tried to keep us from seeing each other, but when you are young and in love, that only makes the other person more desired. The year I turned nineteen, we got married. My mother cried; my father stamped around the house, growling like a bear. But they came around. I was their only child, and Miguel was their only grand-child, so in the end they allowed us back into the family."

She stopped and looked down at her plate. "My goodness, I have talked so much, that I forgot to eat."

I had finished my meal, and Miranda had moved to the floor where she'd found a toy. I put a blanket on the floor and she snuggled under it. When Lupe had finished eating, I offered to help with the dishes, but she waved me off. "I like having you here, Bernie. I never had a little girl to dress in pretty clothes, or to talk to, mother to daughter, as she was growing up." She put her arm around me and we stood companionably together.

It was getting close to eight o'clock and I needed to get home and put my sleepy child to bed. I lifted Mira from the floor and picked up my purse.

Lupe handed me the journal. "It belongs to you," she said. "We'll read again in two days."

After Mira was asleep, that night, I sat in my comfortable chair with the journal wondering how I would feel, heading off to an unknown life, knowing I might never see my relatives again. I began flipping through the pages, seeing again my birth mother's small, cramped handwriting. Did she write like that naturally, or was she just trying to save paper? I stopped. On the top of one of the pages was a tiny pen and ink drawing of rough adobe houses in front of hills. A shiver ran through me. Drawing, especially doodles of people and animals was something I'd done since I was in grade school, often as a response to stress. I'd even gotten in trouble for my cartoons of teachers that decorated test papers. My birth mother's drawings were more detailed and finely done, but our drawings were similar. We are each of us born with a whole set of skills, some of them acquired as we grow, and some just there. I'd never had a drawing class in my life and neither of my adopted parents could draw, but I loved the act of putting what I saw on a piece of paper. That skill, handed down to me, could only have come from one person.

I flipped through the diary and felt my breath catch in my throat. There on the page was an exact likeness of Miranda, from her soft curly hair to her sparkling eyes and funny little smile. It took me a minute to realize that of course it wasn't Miranda. My mother had never met Miranda. I was looking at a portrait of myself. Under the picture was a notation, *Graciela Estrella Morales el amor de mi vida.*

I could feel the tears starting. Why had I ever thought that my birth mother didn't love me? She had loved me enough to begin a long, dangerous journey to a different country so that I could have a better life. I studied the photograph of my birth parents, searching my mind for any memory of them. Had my father not died from snakebite, I might be laboring on a coffee plantation or working beside my mother in some gringa's kitchen. Had my mother given me up, so I could have the life of ease given by my adoptive parents? And if she had done this, how could she simply have walked away?

Getting up from the chair, I went to the bedroom where my child lay sleeping, her thumb in her mouth. More than anything, I wanted my birth mother to see Miranda, and to know that her sacrifice had given me stability and love. If my birth mother had walked away to give me a better life, I was ready to forgive her.

Chapter Twenty Six

El Diario de Lilliana Morales

"In the state of Chiapas people are very generous. They will give you food and sometimes allow you to sleep in the stables, or on a pile of straw near the house. Nevertheless, we are always on the lookout for the La Joda, the local policia. To keep our spirits up, Enrique tells us of life in America, about the big houses and television sets. Everyone has a television set, he says. Everyone can go to school if they want. Everyone has plenty to eat. He has heard stories about the mercados where fruits and vegetables are piled as high as a man. Twelve year old Jorge dreams of being an engineer, or maybe an architect, and his parents beam on him proudly. His father will get a job working in a fabrica, making cars, and his mother will sew clothes at home.

"Such dreams would never be possible in our home town. There a man is a coffee-field worker, or sometimes if he's lucky and has a little skill, a carpenter, a mechanic or a builder. Once in a while, someone becomes a teacher, but those with more skill, leave.

"We traveled north and our money, which we have carefully horded, becomes less. It is slow going, and traveling every day is hard on the children, especially you, *mi querida*.

"About a mile out of town we were picked up by a farmer going to market, who allowed us to ride in his truck. We tried to conserve our meager funds by eating small meals, or finding food in the dumpsters behind restaurants. I would never have done a thing like that before, but when you are hungry, or when your child is hungry, you will eat anywhere.

"Once, when we were eating from a dumpster, a man came and invited us to his church for a meal. There were many migrants there, some had come all the way from Guatemala and had stories of abuses by officials. At this point, we were only about thirty miles from home, still close enough to turn around, but when we discussed it, none of us wanted to turn back. We stayed for three days in the town, eating food provided by the church and sleeping against the back of the church where we were protected.

"On the outskirts of Mexico City we ran out of money and had to find work. Though I tried to stay clean, rinsing out my underclothes in the public toilets and hanging them on the bushes to dry, I was still wearing the same clothes day after day.

"I began dressing as a man. It was easier, especially for Enrique and Diego who had two women and two children to protect. Sometimes, the local police tried to trick us into showing that we weren't locals by asking us to pronounce local words. I learned to listen very hard, not just for words, but for gossip or news. If the local people wore a certain garment, a hat or boots, we tried our best to imitate that look. Wherever we went, we had to be on the alert for someone who wanted to turn us in.

"The other issue was work. Diego, who was a skilled carpenter, could only find a job lifting sacks of cement for a hardware store. Each day the men would gather at the hiring place, and the foreman would pick those workmen who looked strongest, or those who would slip him a little *mordida*.

Enrique only got three days work before the foreman stopped choosing him.

"Adriana and I went to work in the dump, while we left you with Jorge who could earn a few pesos selling slightly bruised oranges. The work at the dump was terrible. Even in October, when the days were cool, the smell could overpower you, so we learned to wear scarves around our noses. When the trucks rumbled in, I learned to push my way in, ready to snatch at anything that could fetch money: clothing, a ceramic dish, an old radio, a lamp. These we would shove into a large bag, later to be cleaned and re-sold for a few pennies. The hospitals used the dump too, so we had to be careful of sharp needles and once I saw a human fetus, perfectly formed, just lying in the trash.

"During that time I was always hungry, but though I saw a child eating bread from the dump, blackened with grime, I would not stoop to that. After two weeks near Mexico City we were ready to move on. But things had changed. In the beginning, we were able to beg for rides, in the back of a truck, tucked between vegetables going to market, but after Mexico City, people were less generous.

"One day Diego came and said he'd found a man who would drive us one hundred fifty miles for only eighty dollars. To be able to ride in a car seemed an unimaginable luxury. On the agreed-on day we met the man in the town square. The car he had offered to transport us in was a large American vehicle that was rusted both top and bottom. When we piled in, we could smell old food, sweat, and fear. The driver offered to put our things into the trunk, and some of the men agreed. I hung onto my meager bundle. It had two photographs that were very precious: one of the three of us, and one of my parents. Besides some clothing, I had little else. All the other money I possessed had gone for this ride in the car.

"The man demanded our money and Enrique handed it over. The driver counted it carefully and then got into the car. He turned the key in the ignition, but the car refused to start. We waited, my heart sinking. We had just given everything to a stranger, who could decide that we wouldn't travel today. And what choice did we have?

"But when the driver turned the key again, the car reluctantly growled to a start and we drove away, out of town on the highway toward El Norte.

"We had driven for about an hour when the driver pulled over by the side of the road, and got out of the car. I assumed that he needed to pee. I waited for him to turn his back on us, do his business and then get back in the car. Instead he said. 'Get out.'

"On either side were farm fields, but no one was working them. I could see no houses and the traffic was very light. Why were we getting out?

" 'Get out,' the driver said again. He pulled out a gun and aimed it at the back seat where Adriana was sitting closest to the window. She would be the first one to die.

"Slowly we got out of the car. 'We have paid you to drive us a hundred fifty miles,' Enrique said 'We have only gone about seventy.'

" 'We are stopping here,' the man said. He still had the gun. He moved closer to Adriana, and with his free hand began running his fingers over her breasts.

" 'Leave her alone,' Enrique said. He moved closer to the man, who pointed the gun at his chest.

" 'I could shoot you right here,' the man said. 'I could shoot you all, except....' He looked at Adriana. 'I might have to shoot this pretty little chicken.'

"Twelve year old Jorge, was standing behind the man. He leaned toward me, pinched me and pointed to the ground, where there was a piece of lumber with a nail embedded in it. 'Distract him,' he whispered. I'd been holding you in my arms, and I put you carefully on the ground, warning you to stay put.

" 'It's too dangerous. He has a gun.'

"But Jorge had already started toward the lumber. He picked it up and with very slow motions he moved closer to the driver, whose attention was still focused on Adriana. I bent down.

" 'Oh,' I said, 'I have terrible cramps. I need to take a *mierda*.'

"Without looking toward me, the man gestured toward the bushes. 'Oh,' I cried again. I squatted and pretended to do my business on the ground.

" 'Not here, you idiot,' the driver screamed. 'In the bushes.' He moved toward me, away from Adriana. Diego grabbed her and stepped away.

" 'Oh,' I cried again crouching. The man with the gun moved closer. I could see Jorge behind him.

"I bent forward and said to Jorge 'Now.'

"With all his strength, Jorge drew back with the board and hit the man in the head. The gun went off, the man fell forward.

" 'Run,' I cried, grabbing you in my arms and heading toward the scrub at the side of the road. I could see Jorge, hitting the man again and again with the board.

" 'Jorge. Come.'

"And then he was with us.

"We spent that night in an irrigation ditch, listening to the coyotes calling to each other. Once in a while a car would speed by, but we were too frightened to try and go to the road and beg for a ride."

Lupe stopped reading. "Let's stop here for a while. Would you like tea or coffee?" she asked.

"I can get it, " I said. I'd now spent several evenings with her, listening to the story and her kitchen was becoming as familiar as my own. I put water in the kettle and fetched down the jar of instant coffee. I have always been a real coffee drinker. If you are going to ingest the stuff, you might as well pile up the caffeine points. But Lupe likes decaf, doctors it up with sugar and 'coffee whitener', and in deference to her, I have started drinking the brew. I'm not giving up real coffee, but I've learned to tolerate the other stuff.

Lupe turned the page of the journal. "The next date is early November. It must have been hard for her to write every day, or maybe she wrote this diary later and couldn't remember everything that happened."

I nodded, stirring the coffee and setting a cup in front of her. On the floor, Mira twitched in her sleep.

Lupe began reading.

"Somehow we made it to San Luis Potosi. In early November, Enrique went to a center for migrants to make a phone call home. When he returned to us, his face was white and he was weeping.

" 'Maria is dead,' he said. 'She died giving birth. The baby, a little girl, is alive but the children are now living with my mother.' He put his head in his hands and began to cry hard. 'I thought I was helping my family, but now my children have no parents. My mother pleaded with me to come home. She says, my children have forgotten what I look like, and the new baby Angel will never know me as her father.' He looked at the other five of us. 'What should I do?'

"Diego put a hand on Enrique's shoulder. 'What would be the best way to honor Maria's memory? It is your decision, but we have already completed almost half the journey. If we continue, you will have a chance to make a better life for your children. You can give them money for good food, warm clothing. You could send them to school so they will have a better future. Think about this before you throw everything away.'

" 'I miss them,' Enrique said. 'I wish I'd been there to tell Maria I loved her, and to hold her one last time.'

"We nodded. Each of us had someone living or dead that we wanted to say those words to. Each of us had someone at home that we wanted to see again, or hold again. The cost of this journey had already been more than any of us expected.

"We ate in a small taquaria, a rare treat, and talked until late. Without Enrique, I would lose the protection I had learned to count on. Diego was a good man, but he had no blood ties to me and he felt no responsibility for my safety. Enrique was my husband's brother, someone of his family. I spent the night awake, worrying about the decision Enrique would make and whether I could make the rest of the journey alone. In the morning, Enrique declared that he would continue. His goal was to find a good job, to send money back to his parents and his children. Sometime in the future, he would bring them north so they could live together."

"In late November we were sitting behind a church having our lunch. We had learned to take food not only from restaurant dumpsters, but to steal food from the fruit trees and farmer's fields as we passed. I am ashamed to tell you that we stole food, but we had no other resource and food is life.

"As we were sitting eating, we were joined by a young man and a girl. He was Antonio Hernandez, his girlfriend Paloma Rivera. Antonio "Flaco" looked as though he'd never eaten a full meal in his life. His bones stuck out through his thin flesh, and even his face was skeletal. Paloma, on the other hand, was plump, with a corona of fine dark hair and dark flashing eyes. When she smiled at Enrique and Diego, I thought 'This child is trouble.'

"They were both sixteen, traveling, like us to Los Estados Unidos. Paloma told us she was going to be a movie star like Salma Hayak or Eva Longoria. Or maybe a singer like Selena Gomez. How can you say to a Latina who speaks no English that the chances of becoming a movie star are equal to pigs taking flight. We talked for an hour while we ate, and when we were done, Flaco asked if he and Paloma could travel with us.

"I looked at Enrique, by common consent our leader. He must have felt sorry for Flaco, or perhaps he was lonely and Paloma attracted him. Finally, he nodded his head.

"We might have changed so many things. We might have stayed in Mexico, or told Flaco and Paloma that they couldn't join us. But we did not know the future and all things are in the hands of God. He alone decides."

Lupe stopped reading, and looked at her watch. "It is almost nine o'clock. Perhaps we can do the rest tomorrow night."

"Of course," I said. I walked over and gave her a kiss. "You've been wonderful to read this to me."

She held the journal toward me. "Do you want to keep it for awhile?"

I hesitated, remembering my feeling of wanting to touch something over which my mother had labored. But Lupe would keep it safe. "You keep it for now, I'll take it back later."

Chapter Twenty Seven

Driving back to the house, I passed the barn and seeing lights, I stopped. Miranda was asleep in the car, so I gently opened the door and stepped out. It was a lovely cool night. I could hear a distant owl, and from inside the barn a horse whinnied. I walked inside to where Mike was whistling softly to himself as he brushed down a large reddish colored horse. We hadn't spent any time alone together since our trip to Laredo two weeks ago, and I wondered why he'd been so distant. He looked up and smiled.

"Bernie," he said. "You're out here late?"

"I found a journal that my birth mother wrote in Spanish. Lupe's been reading it to me."

He said nothing, just continued to rub down the horse. I moved closer and patted the horse's nose. "What's her name?"

"Red Beauty," Mike said. "We've just come in from a ride. The stars are glorious."

I walked to the door of the barn and looked out. As Mike had said, the stars above were jewels in the black velvet sky. It would be lovely to ride out with him, enjoying the soft evening air. Two weeks ago we'd been lovers, but something had changed between us that I didn't know how to fix.

I walked back to where he was still brushing down the horse. "I should learn to ride," I said.

"Uh huh." *He had nothing else to say? Didn't he want us to go riding together?*

"You could teach me, couldn't you?"

"I suppose I could, but right now I'm really busy. Ask Caylee, I'm sure she'll be willing."

I wanted to stamp my foot and yell, *You're the one I want to ride with, not her.* Instead I turned to go.

"Bernie, wait." I stopped and looked back at Mike striding toward me. "There's a dance at The Starlight Café next Friday. They'll be fireworks afterwards. Want to go?"

"Sure," I said. We were only going to dance, nothing more. I'd let my heart lead for too long in this relationship. It was time to give common sense a chance.

On Saturday morning, just by chance, I saw Caylee in the barn grooming a big gray stallion. I hesitated a moment before approaching her. She obviously didn't like me and I was asking a big favor. But, you can never get ahead if you don't try.

"That's a beautiful horse," I said.

Caylee nodded. "His name is Casper, like the ghost. Sweetest gent you'll ever meet."

"Have you had him long?"

"Six years."

"Caylee, would you teach me to ride?"

She looked up astonished. I'm sure it wasn't the question she'd expected.

"Well," she said thinking about it. "How about this afternoon. We could go out at about four, it's a little cooler then."

"Sure. What will I need?"

"A jacket, some water and snacks. We should only be out for about an hour." She looked at my shoes. "I might have an extra pair of riding boots that will fit you."

I could leave Miranda with Lupe for an hour. "Thanks," I said.

At three-thirty, I packed the things I would need for a horseback ride (think picnic/campout with snakes and spikey plants) and presented myself at the barn. Caylee was already there, saddling the horses. The sun had begun its descent down the sky, but this was just a short ride, we'd be sure to return before dark.

"You've met Casper already," she said, She rubbed the horse's nose and I swear he winked at her.

"And this is Rosie," she said, pointing to another horse in a stall nearby. "She's a little skittish, but I can handle her." She looked at what I was wearing: a pair of jeans, a long sleeved shirt and a sweater.

"You'll need a helmet," she said, putting one on my head. "I think that will work, just cinch it tight." Then she gave me a pair of boots, gloves and chaps, "So you won't get scratched by the bushes." As I was putting on the chaps and the boots, Caylee was putting a blanket on Casper's back and then lifting the saddle on top of it. I watched her cinch the saddle under his belly.

"You got to cinch it tight, and then just before you mount, cinch it again. Worst thing you want to do is have the saddle turn when you're trying to get on."

She did the same with Rosie, and then put the halter and bridles on. She pushed a small step stool up to the horse. By this time I had boots, chaps, helmet, gloves and backpack on.

"Take the reins in one hand, step up onto the box, grab the saddle horn and throw your leg over." I did as she directed feeling high and very vulnerable. I took the reins in both hands.

"If you want the horse to go right, pull on the right rein, and put your right knee gently into his belly. To go left, do the same thing on the left hand side. You don't have to do it hard, just firmly.

Caspar's a good boy. He just needs to know that you're the boss."

I'm the boss, I thought. *I'm the boss*. Being on top of a horse felt like being at the top of a fully extended ladder truck, with a crazed driver below doing what he damned well pleased. But as the horse began to walk out of the barn into the soft afternoon, I gained confidence.

If you've never seen the world from atop a moving horse, it's a strange sensation. First, you are higher than fences, dogs, sheep, most small bushes and even some trees. You're going a little faster than a human can walk, but slower than riding in a car, so the scenery rolls past you at a human scale. I felt like singing some corny cowboy song "Home on the Range," or "I Ride an Old Paint." I started to sing.

Caylee glared at me. "What are you doing?"

"Singing. Don't you feel like singing when you come out here. The way Gordon MacRae breaks into song when he comes onstage at the beginning of *Oklahoma*. 'Oh what a beautiful morning,'" I sang. "Oh what a beautiful day."

"Shut up," Caylee said.

"I've got a beautiful feeling. Everything's going my way."

She trotted ahead of me and I touched Casper gently so I could catch up.

"Gordon MacRae didn't come out onto the stage on a horse," she said sullenly when we were side by side again. "And cowboys don't sing."

"Gene Autry sang."

"The closest Gene Autry ever got to being a real cowboy, was looking at a picture of one in a bar."

"I thought you wanted to make this fun, Caylee, It's a beautiful afternoon. I'll sing if I feel like it."

"You were the one who wanted to do this, Bernie. Do you think taking some Buckle-Bunny out riding was my idea of a good time?"

"What's a Buckle Bunny?"

"A Concho Whore. A little Yankee gal all duded up, who bats her eyes at a cowboy, hoping to get into his hot roll."

"You were pretty duded up at the dance. What is it with Texas women and their rhinestones?"

"That's different."

"How?"

"I'm a real cowboy. I do it for a living."

We rode for more than forty minutes in silence. I hoped Caylee knew where we were going because if I had to find my way back by myself, I'd be days getting there.

Something cracked loudly, and Caylee yelled, clutching her arm. Rosie, spooked by the sound, danced around and Caylee fell.

"Shit," she said, getting up slowly. I could see blood seeping out through her shirt sleeve. Cautiously I dismounted.

"What happened?"

"Someone shot me. If they're hunters, they're awfully stupid. Do I look like a Javalina to you?"

"What's a Javalina?"

"Like a wild pig. You smell 'em before you see them. Folks around here hunt them for sport." She looked at me. "I'd say it's a hunter." She looked at me. "Unless you know someone who'd want to shoot you."

I thought of Charlie who might or might not still be in jail. I wouldn't put it past him to come to Texas with murder on his mind.

"Well?"

"No one I know of."

"There's a little cabin about a quarter mile from here. We can hole up there for the night. Hopefully by then the shooter will have gotten his hog, or given up trying to bag two women."

"I have to get back. Lupe will be wondering why I'm not there to pick up Miranda."

"Lupe will take care of her. And if we start back now, we'll have to finish the trip in the dark. Do you really want to be exposed to a man with a gun again?"

We walked in silence toward the cabin, which wasn't much more than a bunch of boards nailed together in a box shape. A rude door guarded the entrance, and the roof sagged dejectedly but there was glass in the windows. Inside, a stone fireplace stood against one wall with wood stacked nearby. Two rough beds with blankets stood near another wall. A table and chairs sat in the middle of the room.

"Let me take care of the horses," Caylee said and went outside again. I could hear her moving around, talking softly to Casper and Rosie. I followed her out and helped carry the two saddles into the cabin where we put them on the floor.

"I don't think anyone will try to steal Casper and Rosie," she said. "But if they do, they'll have to ride away bareback."

The desert was cooling off and I could see remnants of a sunset through the open window.

"Christ I'm cold," Caylee said. "Let's have a fire." She went to the fireplace and laid up logs for a fire. After some work, the flames caught, but then smoke was filling the cabin, making my eyes tear. Caylee and I walked outside. It was a clear night, the remnants of the sunset still glowing in the west, but by now, it was too dark to return. When we went back inside the cabin, the fire was burning steadily, giving off some heat. Caylee was holding her wounded arm and swearing softly.

"Let me look at that," I said.

"You a nurse?"

"No, but I could help."

She walked around a little more, muttering to herself. God she was stubborn.

I emptied my backpack onto the table. "Look, I know a real cowboy would run outside, find some plant, chew it up, slap it against the wound and then bind up the whole thing with a sweaty, grease stained bandana."

"You got a better idea?" She was smiling.

I held up the plastic bag that I'd stuffed into my backpack. "Bacitracin and bandages."

"Who brings a First Aid kit on a trail ride?" She asked as I pulled off her jacket and gently tugged away the blood soaked shirt. The bullet had only grazed her skin. She would have a scar but little more. I reached into the plastic bag and pulled out a clean diaper which I used to wipe away the blood, then started applying antiseptic ointment.

"Sponge Bob or Frozen?" I asked.

"What?"

"Do you want a Sponge Bob bandage or a Frozen bandage? Sponge Bob is very popular with the under-three set, but Frozen is more universally desired."

"Do you always carry this stuff with you?"

"I'm a mom," I said, applying the bandages, and wrapping the whole thing with a clean bandana. Caylee pulled her shirt sleeve carefully back down over the wound, and looked at the plastic bag on the table. "What else have you got there?"

I pulled open the bag and up-ended the contents. This was the emergency kit that I usually stuffed into my purse and which I had put into my backpack this afternoon out of habit. On the table was Miranda's favorite book *The Lost Bunny.* "Spoiler alert," I said. "He finds his mommy."

"I think I've read it," Caylee said.

I held up two small containers and pried off the lids. "Cheerios or Goldfish? We could call these hors d'oeuvres." I handed her a granola bar. "And supper."

Caylee grabbed the food and sat down in front of the fire.

"You sleeping with Mike?" she asked.

"That's private," I said prissily.

"Oh come on, Bernie. I know you are. He talks about you all the time. How cute you are, how gutsy you are. It makes me want to heave."

"You and Mike been friends long?" I asked trying to change the subject.

"Since we were kids. Actually, it was Mike and my older brother, Kyle who were the friends. I was just the little sister. They were really tight until Mike was thirteen, then they just stopped talking to each other. After that, Mike and his mom moved away. I never knew what happened."

"Where was his dad?"

"Died when Mike was twelve."

"But you met Mike again," I said. "You knew he was here in Rosalita."

"That was later. I saw him the first time when me and my husband were on the rodeo circuit..."

"Wait. Back up. You were married?"

"Yup. Chet was a good-looking, sumbitch who thought he could make a living getting beat up on the rodeo. I followed him around for three years, watching him get every bone broke, and waiting for the time when he would say, 'enough'. Finally, I realized that wasn't ever going to happen, and I'd just end up hauling bed pans for a butt-sprung cowboy in a wheelchair."

"And Mike?"

"He was riding the circuit too. He'd grown his hair long; was drinking a lot, and seemed to be trying to commit suicide the hard way. When I tried to talk to him, he just ignored me."

Outside something rustled. Javalina? Wild boar? A man with a gun?

I stood up. On the wall was a crude cabinet. I opened a door and found a coffee pot and a canister. "There's coffee here. Want some?"

"Cowboy coffee? You throw some grounds in the bottom of the pot and let 'er boil. No thanks."

I held up a whiskey bottle that had been behind the coffee. "How about this?"

"Now you're talking." I found two cups which I rinsed out with water from my bottle and we poured a generous amount into each. Then I grabbed the blankets from the beds and tossed one to Caylee. Wrapped up, in front of the fire and with the whiskey to warm our innards, we were at least a little bit comfortable.

"Thanks. For the water and the blanket."

"And the granola bar."

"And the First Aid."

"So what happened after you met Mike at the rodeo?"

"I called my brother. Said I'd seen Mike riding the circuit. Kyle hadn't seen him for a long time and I thought my bro would come down and say hi to his old friend, but he didn't. I don't think they've said two words to each other since."

"Did your brother ever say what the disagreement was about?"

"Nope. My brother can be a real asshole." She lay back down on the floor, wrapped in her blanket. "But Mike can be moody, too."

I nodded. I was beginning to know the other Mike.

"One day he can't do enough to make you happy. The next day he's pulled into himself and you can't get through. When he was a kid I loved being around him, he was so much fun. Now, when he's in one of his moods, I stay away."

"Why did you say your brother is an asshole?"

"My father, J.W. wanted two sons, instead of a son and a daughter. He indulged Kyle, and when my brother messed up, Dad patched up his mistakes. My dad gave Kyle a car when he was sixteen, which my brother proceeded to wreck three weeks later when he was drunk. When my brother got his high school girlfriend pregnant, Dad paid for the abortion, and provided 'hush-up' money to the parents. In college, he beat up a classmate during an argument. and Dad made a big donation to the school. That incident made Kyle wake up and after that, he buckled down to work. He was never a great student, but my brother has charm. Charm and my father's political clout. I was as surprised as anyone was when the President put Kyle on his short list for Director of Homeland Security."

"I'll bet you're proud of him."

Caylee rolled over onto her good arm and looked at me.

"He's my brother, but I don't really like him that much."

We sat quietly for a moment. The whiskey and the fire's warmth were making me sleepy, but I didn't want to end our conversation.

"I met Mike again a few years ago. " Caylee said. "This time he was watching the rodeo, not riding. He told me he was going to college, and that he'd bought some land and was starting a business."

"West Texas Fair Trade Coffees."

"I was glad for him. He'd pulled himself out of a bad place, but I kept thinking 'Where'd he get the money?'"

I thought of my own father's generosity. "His dad?"

"Nope. Otis West was just a ranch manager, and Lupe was just the cook. They had some money saved, but nothing like what Mike had when I met him."

I remembered the beautiful house that Mike lived in.

"Maybe he saved up from his rodeo days?"

"Nope again. Cowboys never save. They spend money as soon as it hits their wallet, booze and women mostly." Caylee yawned and stretched her long body flat on the floor. "So why are you in Texas, Bernie?"

Something released itself in me, and I started telling her about the dreams I'd had, and of Dr. Swartz's death and Ellen Maynard's leaving. I didn't tell her about Charlie's friends breaking into the apartment, because I didn't want it to get back to Mike that I'd lied.

"I found my birth mother. She came from Mexico and crossed the border on Christmas day. She wrote a journal about her trip." I looked over at Caylee who was breathing softly, probably asleep.

Outside a coyote howled and I thought of Miranda safe and warm with Lupe, and of Charlie, possibly hiding in the desert outside, waiting for us to emerge. If Charlie were really there, I hoped there were snakes around him and that he was shaking with fear. Let him suffer. Wrapping the blanket more tightly around me, I drifted off into sleep.

The next morning, I helped Caylee saddle the horses, as much as a five-foot woman can help an almost six-foot one. I'd offered to look at her arm again, but she brushed me off, and when we began riding back, she reverted to a frosty silence. I'd been hoping for more warmth between us, even friendship, but I couldn't really blame her for her attitude. If I'd been in love with a guy, I wouldn't want to cozy up to the woman he was sleeping with either. My supper of a single granola bar and some whiskey had left my stomach complaining loudly, and I was sleep-deprived, having been jerked awake the night before by every rustle or howl from the desert outside. The trip back seemed shorter than the trip out, and half way there we met Mike galloping toward us, all in a lather.

"They told me, that you'd gone out riding yesterday afternoon and hadn't come back. I wish they'd said something earlier, I would have come to find you." He was directing all his anxiety toward me, leaving Caylee to digest the truth of our relationship.

"Someone shot at Caylee so we stayed overnight in a small cabin." I said. Mike glanced at her, and she waved her wounded arm at him.

"Are you OK? I'll drive you to the hospital. We should have someone look at it."

"Bernie patched me up. I'll be fine."

Was this just bravado? Stiff upper cowboy lip?

"We'll get it looked at as soon as we get back," Mike said. End of discussion.

Mike and Caylee started off side by side and I followed. Sitting tall in the saddle, they were almost the same height and I wondered if they might patch up their differences. But where would that leave me? Let's face it, I was in love with the guy, but as I knew, there were no guarantees in love. Certainly Caylee had more in common with Mike than I did. When we reached the barn, Mike helped Caylee dismount and then he came to help me down.

"When they said you hadn't come back, I thought the worst," Mike said quietly. Caylee was watching us and I quickly disengaged myself, feeling all the time how nice it was that he had worried.

"I've got to check on Mira," I said. "I hope your arm is better, Caylee."

She gave a grunt but hardly looked my way. I walked to my car and started it. Then I remembered. Charlie.

Quickly I dialed my mother's number on my cell. If anyone could tell me the news, she could, but her phone rang without being answered. I left a message. The second one I'd left in three days. Where were those two? Skinny dipping in a private tropical pool? Romping on the beach in some third world country with no cell coverage? With a sigh I started the car and drove to Lupe's house.

It was about eight thirty in the morning and a Sunday, so the little house was very quiet.

"Mama. Mama," it was Mira coming toward me as I entered the playroom.

"She missed you terrible last night," Lupe said. "I thought you were with Mike, so I just kept her."

"Caylee and I were out riding and someone shot at her. We took shelter in an old shack. Luckily Mike came after us this morning. Mike's taken her to the hospital to get the wound looked at."

"Mama," Mira said grabbing my legs. I picked her up and kissed her, then blew on her belly to make her giggle.

I yawned. "I need to get some sleep, Lupe."

"Go home then. Miranda can stay here, can't you querida?"

I yawned again. Sleep sounded wonderful.

Back in my own house, I took a quick shower, and ate some scrambled eggs. My night without much sleep was beginning to find me, so I lay down thinking I would just nap for a few minutes.

In the dream, I was walking along a road one hand held by a young boy and the other held by my mother. It was hot and dusty and we were very thirsty. Once we stopped and drank from an irrigation ditch, another time, the boy took apples from a tree and gave one to me. I kept feeling that we must hurry, that we must get where we were going because people were waiting for us. Then suddenly our way was blocked by two men wearing black masks.

One of the men beckoned to me and I moved forward. My mother screamed, pulled at my arm, but the man wanted me and I had to go. I went over to him and took his hand. When I looked back everyone was gone, including my mother.

Chapter Twenty Eight

On Monday, I sat at my desk trying to concentrate on the work at hand, but thinking about my birth mother's journal

"You're awfully quiet," Tina said. "Are you fretting over Caylee's accident?"

I shook my head. "Tina, if you were looking for someone who crossed the border more than twenty years ago, where would you look?"

"I guess the ICE keeps records, but you'd have to know someone who works in the department, or an immigration lawyer. Then, again, if they were in the ICE files, they were probably deported."

"I know the state they came from in Mexico. I could call there."

"Good luck with that. Half the time the phone goes dead for no reason, or it is so staticky you can't hear the other person."

Enrique had had a cousin in Miami who'd offered him a job. Maybe the cousin was still there. Or maybe Enrique himself was there. I picked up the phone and dialed information for Miami, Florida.

"I'm looking for a listing for Morales Landscaping or Morales Nurseries." If Enrique had gone to work for his cousin, I assumed the business would be under the family name. The woman put me on hold and I waited for a long time. "We have Gardens by Morales," she said, giving me the number. I dialed it, my heart in my mouth.

"Gardens by Morales," a woman answered. I explained as clearly as I could, that I was looking for a man named Enrique Morales who might be working for the company. There was silence on the other end of a line and then a young man came on. "I am Enrique Morales," he said.

This Enrique Morales sounded much too young to be my uncle. I explained that I was looking for an Enrique Morales who had crossed the border at Laredo, Texas in 1993 on his way to Miami to work for his cousin.

"You want to speak to my father," the young man said. "Let me see if he's available."
Then a deeper, older voice came on the line. "I am Alejandro Morales. My grandson tells me you are looking for Enrique. Who are you, Miss and why are you looking?"

"Enrique Morales was my uncle," I said. "My mother was Lilliana Morales."

"Madre de Dios, you are Graciela."

It took me a moment to realize that yes, indeed, I was that person.

"Si," I said in the unfamiliar language. "I am Graciela Morales."

"Graciela. We searched all over for you. To tell you the truth, we didn't think you were alive. And how is your mother?"

"I don't know. I haven't found her."

"I am sorry. She called us a few times from Texas. We urged her to come to Florida where we would find her work. At first, she didn't have the money for both of you to make the trip and didn't want to take our charity. The last time we talked, she said she'd changed her mind and would come to Florida. We never heard from her again."

I felt again the sadness of my mother's story. I could have had a different name and belonged to a different culture. I would be Graciela Morales, a name as strange to me, as the place where I was born.

"Do you know what happened to my uncle Enrique?"

"He may have crossed the border and gone somewhere else, or changed his mind and returned to Mexico, but when I called his parents, they said that he never appeared."

"He had a new baby. It would be strange for him never to contact his family. And what about the other family, the Guzmans? Did they ever return?"

"I do not know about the other family. Sometimes, when people cross over, they simply disappear," Alejandro said. "You must give me your address and phone number. We have a large family reunion here at Christmas. We would love to have you visit and meet your second cousins."

These were blood relatives I had never met. Even though Miami was a long way away, it would be fun to meet this family.

"I have a little girl named Miranda."

"Wonderful, wonderful," Alejandro crowed. "We will be delighted to meet her."

"One more thing. When you were looking for me, did you ever contact a woman named Beatrice Delgado? She works at Sul Ross University and used to be a nun at the convent in Laredo."

"Beatrice Delgado. No, we never talked with her."

"She had my birth certificate," I said.

"We will be happy to have you here any time," Alejandro said. "And your little *niña*, Miranda. And do you have a husband, Graciela?"

"We're not together " I said. I pictured Alejandro Morales, looking like Fernando Lamas, with white hair and sexy dark eyes. I expected that he was a very proper man and might not approve if he knew I was divorced.

"It is wonderful speaking with you," he said.

When I hung up the phone, Tina looked at me. "Who was that you were talking to."

There could never be any secrets between Tina and me, mainly because we worked in the same small space and each of us could easily overhear the other's phone conversation. Unless you wanted to go outside and talk on a cell phone, there was no privacy.

"My father's cousin," I said. "One I never met."

She nodded. Tina came from a family with second and third cousins up the wazoo. She'd never, like me, been an only child, with parents who were themselves only children.

Mike came into the office and said quietly. "Dance at the Starlight on Friday. I'll pick you up at seven." I floated back to my desk. Things were OK between us. I would buy a new dress for Friday, ask Lupe to babysit, then I would be in Mike's arms, feeling his lips against mine as he kissed me. I had a hard time concentrating on the rest of the day's work

Chapter Twenty Nine

On Friday evening, Mike arrived at my doorstep with Lupe who would babysit. As soon as we got in the car he leaned across the console and kissed me.

We had started away from the house when Mike said. "I forgot my dish. Short ribs with my own special sauce. Can't forget that."

I remembered the great spread of food that had appeared at halftime. Would Mike's special sauce even be noticed among such vast quantities? I would have to make a point to eat his ribs and compliment him on them.

He stopped at house. "It will only take me a minute. I think I left them in the fridge and I have to nuke them. Want to come in?"

I nodded. I liked looking at Mike's house. He was a man who was still a stranger to me in many ways, and looking at his possessions always gave me a clue to who he was. I wandered down the hallway to look at the picture of the bronco buster, and Mike caught up with me there.

"That was me. I was seventeen," he said. "and I had no clue as to what I was doing on that bull, but I was so angry with myself, I needed a way to burn it off."

"You were angry? Why?"

"I'd disappointed the people who believed in me. I was glad my dad wasn't around to see who I'd become."

"Caylee said your father died when you were twelve. That must have been hard."

Mike didn't respond, but led us wordlessly to the front door and then the car.

Mike's barbecued short ribs were wonderful. I made sure at the break to take some on my plate, even though by the time I got to them there were almost none left. We had danced almost every dance. I even tried " The Boot Scooting Boogie," messing up lots of times and laughing at myself. The dancers around me didn't seem to mind. They just smiled and danced along.

It was ten o'clock and I had been dancing for almost two hours. I needed fresh air.

"I'm going to the ladies' room and then outside for a minute," I said. Outside, crowded around the front door were a number of people smoking cigarettes. I moved toward the edge of the building, needing air that was not nicotine clogged.

"Hiya Bernie." The voice was familiar and as he moved into the light, I saw that he had gained weight and wore a beard. It was Charlie.

"Having a good time with your new boyfriend?"

"I thought you were still in jail, Charlie."

"You *hoped* I was still in jail. I got out a while ago, but then I had to do community service which took some time. As soon as I got the chance I decided to pay a little visit to the wife who turned me in to the police."

"I'm not your wife any more, Charlie. We are officially divorced."

He leaned in. I could smell liquor on his breath. I tried to move away but he had me pinned against the wall. "Let's talk about the way a wife ought to behave," he said.

"What are you doing, mister?" I looked up to see Mike. He pulled Charlie away from me, whirling him around so they were face to face, and pushed him hard against the wall.

"I could ask you the same question. This woman is my wife."

"I am not...." I began but Mike was looking at me hard.

"You told me your husband was dead. A car accident you said." His eyes blazed. "You *lied* to me, Bernie." He turned and began marching away.

"Mike," I called, running after him. He was walking fast and I was having a hard time keeping up. "Please listen. I didn't want to lie to you. I just thought you would like me better if I said I was a widow." He was too far away to hear me. I watched as he got into his truck, started the engine, spun it into reverse, and then roared off down the road.

"Seems the man don't like being lied to," Charlie said.

I slapped him hard across the face. "Get out of here. I don't want to see you. You and I are NOT married anymore."

He pushed me hard against the side of the building. "I forgot how pretty you are, Bernie. In jail, a guy gets a lot of time to think, and the person I thought about most was you." He ran his hand down the side of my face, and I flinched, trying to move away from his touch. "I thought about how you double-crossed me." He put a hand on my breast. "I thought about how, when I needed money, you refused to help. I thought about how you got Mira, my own daughter, to hate me. I'll bet she hardly remembers what I look like." He ran a hand down my hip and then lifted my skirt.

"Stop it." I pushed his hand away.

"I'm a lot stronger than you, Bernie. Been lifting weights in jail and working out a lot. What else did I have to do with my time?" He pushed his hand up my thigh.

I lifted my knee and slammed it hard into his privates.

He bent over. "Jesus Christ."

I ran to the entrance of the building and peered inside. There were still people dancing, but all of them were strangers. My home was ten miles away and I couldn't ask a stranger for a lift. Texans are friendly people, but even that seemed too much. I had just enough cash for a taxi, and had taken out my cell to call for one, when Charlie came up again.

"Get away from me. I'm going home."

"I can drive you. You're my wife after all. That way I get to see my daughter."

"Miranda is your daughter, but I AM NOT YOUR WIFE." I was screaming these last words at the top of my lungs. A few men standing near the door, looked over.

"My truck's over there," Charlie said, gesturing toward the familiar red vehicle. I couldn't believe he'd driven that piece of crap all the way to Texas.

I wasn't going to ride with him, so I waited for the cab. Charlie watched as the taxi arrived and when it pulled out with me inside, he was right behind us.

At my house, I paid the taxi, watching as Charlie pulled in and parked. Lupe was peering at us from the window as Charlie came up to me.

"I want to see Mira. Where is she?"

"Inside, asleep. You aren't going to wake her either."

Lupe came out the door and stood watching us.

"Who's that bitch?"

"She's my babysitter." *God, I hated this man.* "You are going to leave now, and I'm going to drive the babysitter home."

"I want to see Miranda."

"If you don't leave now, Charlie. I will call the police. I will tell them that you were in prison in New York state and that you are probably breaking parole. Do you want me to say that?" I took out my cell phone. I had no idea what the number of the local police department was, but I could dial 9 1 1.

"Don't do that, Bernie. All I want is to see Miranda."

"Tomorrow, Charlie. You can see her tomorrow." *I would deal with that problem when it happened.*

Reluctantly, Charlie walked to the truck, got in, started the engine and drove away.

"Who was that man?" Lupe asked. She had come down to the car and was standing beside me.

"My ex-husband, Charlie."

"You said you were a widow. Mike said your husband died in a car accident."

"Yeah, I know. I lied."

"You lied to Miguel? He will not like that."

Tell me about it.

I turned to Lupe. "I have to put the baby in the car seat so I can drive you home. Please don't ask me any more questions. I've had enough for one night."

It was hard waking Miranda from a sound sleep and putting her in the car seat. Once we were in the car, she would sometimes fall back to sleep, but at other times, she would stay awake, and I would spend the remainder of the night trying to sooth an over-tired baby.

Lupe and I said very little to each other on the way back to her house. She had been kind to me, and wonderful with Miranda, but there seemed to be no way around the royal mess I'd made of things. Luckily for me, Miranda fell asleep in the car and when I returned home, I was able to get my still-sleeping child back into bed.

I went into the kitchen and poured myself a glass of wine. I wanted to pick up my cell phone, call Mike and tell him how sorry I was, but I was sure, seeing my number, he would not answer. No candlelight dinner for two was going to fix what I had created. I glanced down at my purse and saw my mother's journal sticking out. In all the drama of the evening, I had forgotten all about it.

Settling myself in my favorite chair, I opened the journal, seeing again my mother's tiny handwriting. It was very possible that I had lost Lupe, my translator, but I might be able to find someone among Mike's employees who would help me read it. I wondered about those people traveling together: Diego Guzman, Adriana Guzman and their brave son Jorge who'd smacked the unscrupulous driver on the back of the head. In addition to these three were "Flaco" Hernandez, his girlfriend, Paloma Rivera, my uncle Enrique Morales, my mother and me. Had these people split up immediately after crossing the border? My mother had gone to The Sacred Heart Children's Home and left me there, but what of the others? Where were they now?

Chapter Thirty

Why had my birth mother abandoned me in Laredo? That was a question for which I had no answer. It seemed impossible that a woman who had taken such tender care of me on the long journey to the U.S. would simply abandon me. My heart would not let me believe that she would do that.

And then I remembered the envelope holding the journal that had been given to me by Beatrice Delgado. Hadn't she said that my mother was living in Rosalita? When I found the envelope, there was a return address written in my birth mother's tiny hand. I could take some time off tomorrow and find the address, and with luck, someone might remember a Latina who'd lived here more than twenty years ago. With even more luck, I might find out where my birth mother was now.

The next morning I got a half day off and drove to the address, which turned out to be a two-story house in a small, unremarkable neighborhood. Painted a dull grey, it had a tiny plot of flowers beside the cement walkway, but the grass needed mowing, and when I got out of the car and started toward the door, I could see peeling paint and cracked wood around the door. I knocked and waited.

I had almost given up hope that anyone was there, when a curtain was pulled back and a woman peered out. I tried to appear non-threatening, and finally she opened the door.

"My name is Bernie Robertson. I'm looking for someone who might have lived here twenty years ago, when it was a boarding house."

The woman nodded. She was in her thirties, too young to have run a boarding house when my birth mother was here.

"You want my mother, Florencia. This was her boarding house, but she's not here. I'm Carmelita, her daughter."

"Where is your mother? I'd really like to talk with her."

The young woman sighed and opened the door wider. "Come in," she said.

I followed her down a narrow hallway with a stairway on one side and a stained, wallpapered wall on the other. I could smell cooked onions and damp. She led me into a living room which had fallen on hard times and settling herself into a straight-back chair, she motioned for me to sit across from her.

"How can I help you?"

"My name is Graciela Morales," I began. It felt strange using my other name, but that was why I was here.

"Didn't you say you were Bernie Robertson?" Carmelita asked.

"I did. Actually I have two names. The name I was born with is Graciela Morales, but when I was adopted my new parents renamed me."

She nodded.

"I'm looking for a woman named Lilliana Morales who might have lived here between March and April of 1994. She had a small child with her. Me."

Carmelita looked at me. "She used to put you in the closet. The only people who came to her room were me or my mother, but if someone even knocked on the door, you were trained to hide."

I had a sudden vision of myself crouched against the back wall of the closet, hearing voices in the room just outside. The voices grew louder, and I heard my mother, pleading, crying. I was trembling, the tears running down my cheeks, but I had been told never to come out when people were in the apartment. Whatever happened I would obey.

"Do you remember what happened to Lilliana? It's a long time ago, I know."

"Would you like a cup of tea?" Carmelita asked, suddenly rising, and without my answer heading toward the kitchen. I followed her into a tiny space, the source of the onion smell and watched as she put a kettle on the stove, took down cups from a shelf and laid out a plate of cookies.

"Do I call you Bernie or Graciela?" Carmelita asked when we were sitting at the table with our tea.

"Most people call me Bernie. It's the name I grew up with."

Carmelita was fiddling with her tea bag, dunking it up and down and staring at it, as though it could help her talk. "I knew someday you would come looking for your mother," she said finally. "And we would have to tell you the story." She looked at me. "Some men came to the rooming house and took her away."

"Took her away?"

"I was just a kid then, but I remember the screaming and crying and then she was gone. We should talk to my mother. She might remember more."

Carmelita reached over and grasped my hand. I could feel the tears starting. "I'm so sorry, Bernie. If you still want to talk to my mother we can. I'm going to visit her this afternoon and you can tag along. She's in a nursing home, and she's not always coherent. You have to promise not to upset her, but she might remember things that I can't."

"I want to see her," I said. I drank my tea in silence, thinking about my birth mother's last sad days in this boarding house. My mother had been afraid of someone, and that person had finally caught up with her. There were plenty of stories in the paper about the Mexican drug cartel and its intimidation and killing of the locals. But my birth mother would never be involved in anything like that. Would she? It was possible that she might have been looking for a way to earn money, but that seemed doubtful. And because my mother was illegal, would the police have even investigated her disappearance?

I had only planned to spend half a day on this quest, but I would not give up the chance to learn something, so I called the office and told Tina that I would be out the whole day. Would she tell Mike that?

When I'd hung up the phone, I looked at Carmelita. "I'm sure my mother had a job. How else could she afford the apartment. What did she do with me when she was working?"

Carmelita shrugged. "I was just a kid then. Maybe my mother will remember."

At two o'clock we went to the Pleasant Rest Nursing Home where we were ushered into a large open foyer with upholstered chairs and occasional tables, looking like the breakfast area of a cheap motel. Further along the corridor was a nurse's station with a woman standing behind it, working on paperwork.

"We're here to see Florencia Gomez, " Carmelita said. "How is she today?"

"This is one of her better days. She might even recognize you." Carmelita led me past a row of doorways to a door, labeled with her mother's name.

"Hola Mama," Carmelita said opening the door, and walking toward a small woman in a wheel chair. She kissed her mother's head and pointed to me. "This is Graciela Morales,"

Florencia squinted at me and then shook her head.

"Do you remember a woman with the little girl. The child who hid in the closet?"

"They took her away" Florencia said. "I saw them do it."

"Who took her away?" I asked.

Florencia shrugged. "They were yelling at her. She was crying, begging them to leave her alone. I watched them take her out of the building. They put her in a car and drove away."

"What happened to her little girl?"

Florencia shrugged. "The girl was hiding in the closet."

"When they took the mother away, did you ever go to see if the child was still in the apartment?" My voice was rising in anger, and I tried to control it.

Carmelita put her hand on my arm. "Mama," she said, sitting down so she was face to face with her mother. "Tell us about the men who took her away? What did they look like?"

Florencia shook her head. "They took her away. She was crying, but they took her away."

How long had I crouched in the closet before I opened the door? An hour? Two hours? And why hadn't the landlady come to look for me? Maybe she was frightened of the men who had taken my mother. Or maybe she thought I'd been taken, too.

Somehow, I'd had the courage to open the door and leave the apartment, thinking I could find my mother in the street. There were so many questions that couldn't be answered because I couldn't remember what happened, and there was no one else who could.

Florencia had begun to rock, rhythmically back and forth. "They took her away," she was saying. "She was crying and begging them..."

"It's OK, Mama," Carmelita said, hugging her mother. "It's all right querida."

"They took her away," Florencia said softly.

"I'm sorry we've upset her," I said.

"It happens. One day when I was visiting she remembered the day my father died, and the next day when I was here, she asked me why he didn't come and visit. In half an hour she won't remember what we talked about."

Florencia had slumped in her chair and Carmelita called for help to put her into bed. When the old woman's eyes were closed, we crept out.

"I hope that helped you," Carmelita said, as we walked away from Florencia's room.

I nodded and thanked her, but I needed more information. Some men had taken my mother but she could still be alive. I drove to the public library, hoping that there might be some news in a local paper. I needed to look at the ones just before or after April 29, 1994, the date I'd been found wandering alone in Laredo.

I scoured the newspapers for Laredo, Texas, and for Rosalita and San Antonio. It was in the April 30 issue of the San Antonio paper that I saw a small news item. *"Unidentified Woman Found Dead in Local Landfill."*

"Police report that a woman was found dead in the county landfill on the morning of April 30.

She had been strangled and her fingers broken, and had bruising about her face and neck. The woman was about five feet tall, one hundred thirty five pounds and had dark hair. She was wearing a uniform that identified her as a domestic and appears to have been Hispanic. For information leading to the identification of this person, please contact the San Antonio Police Department."

I could try to believe that this woman found in the landfill wasn't my mother, but the coincidence was too great. She'd been taken from the rooming house on the 29th and killed some time that night. Oh, my poor mother. I could feel the tears starting and I sat in the library sobbing. All the things I had hoped would happen between us were gone.

That evening, I had just finished getting my sleepy daughter to bed when the phone rang. It was my adoptive mother.

"How are you, honey?" she asked.

""I've been trying to call you for ages, but you're never home."

"I'm sorry. I called to tell you that Charlie's out of jail."

"I know; he's here. I wish they'd tell me these things so I could be prepared."

"Want us to come to Texas?"

"No. It's a long flight from wherever you are. Where are you anyway?"

"Paris. Bernie, I have something else to tell you. Clint and I got married yesterday."

Clint was now my step-father?

"Don't worry. He'll never replace your father, but oh, Bernie, I am very happy."

"Congratulations, Mom."

"You don't sound good, honey."

I unloaded everything. The meeting with Beatrice Delgado, getting the birth certificate and the journal. My discovery that my birth mother had been tortured and killed. "I never even got to know her. We would have been close."

"Of course. She was your mother." There was a touch of something in her voice.

"You'll always be my mother, Mom."

We hung up the phone and I went to my drawer and found the birth certificate and the photograph. On top of the photograph was the newspaper ad from the *Laredo Morning Times*, dated May 21, 1994.

"Looking for my little girl. Has dark curly hair and a heart shaped birthmark on her arm. Goes by name Graciela. If you find, please call L. Morales"

If this ad had been put in the newspaper in May, it had not been put there by my birth mother because my birth mother's body had been discovered in the dump on April 30. Someone else had been looking for me all those years ago, and it had not been my mother. Who had been looking for me and why?

There was a knock on the door. What now? All I wanted was to sit with the reality of my mother's death. I walked to the door and opened it. Mike stood there.

"Can I come in?"

"Sure," I said. "Would you like coffee or a drink?"

"A drink sounds nice. You got any wine?"

"How about a coke?"

He nodded. I knew he hadn't come here to drink Coke. I got the drink from the fridge and put it in front of him. He'd taken a seat on the couch and was looking like he was about to undergo a root canal.

"Bernie, I'm sorry," he said. "I over-reacted. It was just that your husband..."

"My ex-husband, Mike."

"Took me by surprise. I guess I don't expect people to lie to me, especially people that I am close to."

Well, at least he thought we were still close. Was that a good sign?

I sat beside him on the couch. "I don't know why I said what I did. I didn't want you to think that I just moved from one man to the next. In fact, Charlie and I got married when I was seventeen and pregnant, and I don't think I ever really loved him. At least, I'm sure he never loved me. The only reason we stayed together was Mira."

Did he believe me? I couldn't tell. I soldiered on. "Before I met you, I never had a man who really loved me, and who I loved. I know this sounds like I'm a woman with no experience, but that's who I am. If I could do anything to take back the lie, I would, but I can't."

"Where is your ex-husband now?"

"I don't know. He was in jail in New York and I think he's supposed to be on probation. I filed an order of protection against him in New York and I suppose I need to do the same here in Texas, but we have a daughter together and..." I looked at Mike. "It's complicated."

He relaxed against the back of the couch and took a sip of his drink. "You've had a tough life."

My life had been my life, some things bad, some good.

"Bernie, I need to tell you something,"

"OK," I said. "Just let me go pee and I'll be right back."

I went to the bathroom, and then I popped into Miranda's room to see that she was still asleep. When I got back to the living room, Mike had the photograph and the birth certificate in his hand. His expression had changed. "Who are these people?" he asked. "Someone you know?"

"My birth parents," I said. "They came from Tapachula, Mexico. And that is my birth certificate."

"So you found your birth parents?"

"Only my mother. My birth father died before she emigrated." I could feel the tears starting, and I tried to push them away.

"My mother was killed on April 29, 1994 in San Antonio." I said between tears. "After all she'd been through, crossing the border on Christmas Day and leaving me at the orphanage in Laredo, and then coming back for me."

Mike had turned pale while I was telling this. "When did you say your mother crossed the border."

"Christmas Day, 1993. Beatrice Delgado, who was Sister Beatrice, said she remembered the date because it had snowed that night, and my mother was wet from the snow. Your mother has been helping me read her diary because..."

Mike had risen from the chair. "I've got to go, Bernie," he said.

"Got to go? You just arrived. I thought you wanted to tell me something."

He was walking toward the door, shrugging on his jacket. "I remembered something important I've got to finish." His hand was on the doorknob.

"What's going on, Mike?" I asked, moving toward him and touching his arm. "It's late. I thought you were going to stay."

"We'll talk tomorrow," he said and then he was gone.

I sat in the chair, stunned, trying to remember something I'd said that might have turned him away. I went over everything we'd talked about, but nothing came to mind. Maybe he'd decided that he *was* really angry about my lie, but before he left, he seemed to have forgiven me. Mike had been the best thing I'd ever had and now he was gone. Could I beg him to come back? And would my begging do any good? I flipped on the television, but nothing held my attention. Finally I headed to bed, the image of Mike's face still on my mind.

Chapter Thirty One

Mike

Mike drove away from the house, his mind reeling. When he reached the stables, he parked the car. Mouse, his mare, named for the color of her coat, perked her head up when he entered because she loved to be out riding. He took out the brush and began brushing her down, letting his thoughts sort themselves out. People crossed the border from Mexico every day, Christmas day being no exception. A child from Mexico crossing with her mother could be one of many immigrants. But he knew these people. Christmas was a religious holiday, and on Christmas morning, a man or woman would try to get to a church, to say one last prayer for a safe crossing and remember their loved ones at home. They might make a phone call to wish *Feliz Navidad* to someone they hadn't seen for months and hear the relative's answering *Buena Suerte, Ve con Dios.* Even though border guards might be less vigilant on Christmas Eve, many Mexicans would not make the crossing in the snow. There was only one reason someone would attempt that.

How could a woman he was in love with be a woman associated with his most shameful secret? If she didn't know the secret now, she would know eventually, and then she would want nothing to do with him. There was no way he could change the past, no matter how much he might wish it, and he knew that what he'd done would stand, like a shadow, in the doorway to his future. He finished the chore and put the brush away. As much as he cared for Bernie, and though it would hurt, he would keep his distance.

He walked out of the barn, thinking about his father. When his father was alive, they would talk as they headed out on the trail or sat in a duck blind waiting. What would his father say about this situation? His dad had been the most honest man Mike had ever known, sometimes to Mike's frustration. Once when Mike had been given the wrong change on a purchase, his father had made him walk the three miles back to the store to return the overage.

"He'll never miss it, Dad," Mike had tried to argue. "Why should I pay the penalty if he made the mistake?"

"You are the one whose reputation is at stake, not his. People trust us. He may not know who he gave the extra money to, but you know. That means you have to return it."

And so he had walked back to the store, grumbling to himself about the storekeeper, who hadn't been careful in counting out the change, and at himself for not re-counting it when he got it, and finally at his father, who held him to such an impossibly high standard.

He drove to his house, went into the kitchen and made himself a cup of coffee and a sandwich. It was almost ten.

He looked over at the gun cabinet. Some of those weapons were more than sixty years old, originally owned by his grandfather, handed down to him by his father. Mike's father had never killed anything but deer, coyotes, wild pigs and the occasional pheasant. What would he say to the idea that Mike was contemplating? He'd been a coward that night, and he was a coward now? God, he hated himself.

Chapter Thirty Two

Bernie

On Monday when I dropped Miranda off, Lupe seemed the same as usual. I wondered if she had talked to Mike and knew how things were between us. I desperately wanted her to finish reading the story, and right now I had no one else to translate. I gave her the journal, and she smiled. We would continue the story until the end. Thank goodness.

At work, I tried to seek out Mike to ask him what was wrong, but he was staying away. When our paths did cross, he avoided looking at me, and he no longer ate lunch with the rest of us. I felt sad because something was obviously troubling him, and whatever it was, it had to do with our relationship. But if I didn't know what was wrong, I couldn't make things better. Mike's attitude was so obvious that even Tina noticed.

"What's up with Mike?" she asked, looking at me. "I thought you two were tight, but now it's like he goes out of his way to avoid you."

"No doubt one of his moods," I said, hoping it was true.

"I've never seen him like this before." She looked at me. "It sucks. "

That night when I went to pick up Miranda, Lupe met me at the door. She was troubled and I wondered whether she'd heard about Mike and me, and whether she would stop our reading together.

"Bernie," she said. " I have to tell you... the journal is gone. I had it by my favorite chair and when I sat down to read, it wasn't there. Oh Bernie, I'm so sorry."

I gave her a hug. "I'm sure it will turn up, Lupe," I said, though I was disappointed that we wouldn't read tonight.

The next day Mike came into the office and said. "I need to talk with you alone, Bernie."

I followed him into the empty lunch room, hoping that this was going to our the reconciliation, but his face was stony, his manner abrupt.

"I've decided I don't need you anymore," he said.

"Don't need me?" I looked at him. "Are you firing me?"

"The company is losing money, and I can't afford two girls in the office." He wasn't looking at me, just reciting words.

"Mike," I began. I wanted him to look at me, to tell me that I still meant something to him. To say it was all a joke.

"This Friday will be your last day," he said.

I needed to touch his hands, to remind him that we'd once been lovers, but he was tossing me away like so much used clothing.

"You should go back to New York."

"New York? What would I do in New York? I've made a life for myself here and I want to stay, even if you don't want me."

"I'm sorry," he said. "Bernie, it's not safe..."

"Not safe? What do you mean, it's not safe? Even though you've fired me, Miranda and I are staying right where we are until I find something else." I tried to get him to look at me, but he wouldn't. Had he expected that he could simply order me to leave and I would go without a fight? I wasn't that kind of woman. I had been when I was seventeen, but I wasn't now. After this Friday, I would be careful to stay away from the office and the plant, but I was not moving from the house until I was ready. I returned to my desk, but the minute I looked at Tina, I burst into tears.

"What's wrong?"

"Mike fired me."

"Fired you? Why?"

"I don't know. He said the company was losing money, that he couldn't afford two secretaries, and blah, blah, blah. I know it was bullshit."

She came over and gave me a hug. "Oh, Bernie. I'm so sorry. I'm really going to miss you."

That evening when I went to pick up Miranda, I told Lupe what had happened.

"I can't believe my son. He told me what a great secretary you are, how glad he is that he hired you. Did he say why he fired you?"

I told her what I'd told Tina and Lupe didn't believe it, either. She gave me a glass of wine and some sweet pastry, and then she said.

"The journal turned up, right where I had left it. I thought at first I'd made a mistake, and that it was never missing. But now I think someone is messing with my head." She handed me the book. "You'd better take it, just to keep it safe."

I had more to worry about than a missing book. I needed to find a job so I could support myself and my child. If I went back to New York, I might be able to avoid Charlie, who as far as I knew was still in Texas. But could I keep dodging him forever? Staying away from one man, whom I hated, and being rejected by another man, whom I still loved, made my head ache. I needed to find a place that would give me some peace, far from the man my heart still longed for.

I took Miranda and the journal and drove home. After supper, when Miranda was asleep, I went into the kitchen, poured myself a glass of wine and settled myself into the comfortable chair with the journal. Flipping through the book to the end, I realized that something was wrong. There was the entry" December 24." and the words "Tomorrow we will be in *Los Etados Unidos*." I turned the page and there was nothing. Someone had very carefully taken a knife to the last few pages, cutting close to the spine of the book. The job had been done so cleanly that it would not be immediately apparent that pages were missing.

Had they actually crossed the border? Now I had no chance to see how the story ended.

Chapter Thirty Three

A Conversation

"Time is running out, Kyle. Now that you're in line for that job, he's got a magnifying glass on you."

"I know, Dad. I'm doing my best to contain this thing."

"Your best? If you'd been doing your best twenty years ago we wouldn't be in this fix."

"It was an accident, Dad."

"It was NOT an accident. Hitting an animal with your car is an accident. Tripping over a shoe in your living room is an accident. This was not an accident."

There is the sound of liquid being poured into a glass. "I'm drinking too much, my blood pressure's up, and I can't sleep worrying about this thing. It's a wonder you haven't given me a heart attack."

"With all due respect, J.W. We did control things in New York."

"When I want your advice, Sonny. I'll ask. Give me some good news. Tell me there won't be any loose ends popping up to get the police asking questions."

"No loose ends."

"Did you ever find the doctor's notes?"

"Nope. But it doesn't matter. If no one's around to testify, the notes will be irrelevant."

"What about Mike, Dad?"

"Mike won't say a word. He's got as much to lose as we do and we've paid him off well."

"You know he and the girl are sleeping together."

"I'm not worried about Mike. Whatever happens, he's on our side."

"Why not just get rid of the girl now, sir. Then the President can nose around as much as he wants and he won't find anything."

"I need to know what she remembers. Then we'll take care of her. I know you're not happy with this, Sonny, but we'll do it my way."

"But soon, sir. We need to do it soon."

Chapter Thirty Four

The evening of the day Mike fired me I wasn't just worried about how I would support myself, I was thinking how to avoid Charlie. He could show up at any time, try to snatch Miranda as I was walking from the house to my car or steal my vehicle and leave me stranded. He could put a snake in my living room, and then cut the telephone lines so I couldn't call for help. I was sorry now that Mike and I had cleared away the brush piles where snakes might make their home. It would be nice to see Charlie writing in agony from a snake bite, while Miranda and I watched through a window.

To give myself a feeling that I was fighting back, I went down to the local police station and filed an Order of Protection. I called Charlie's parole officer in New York, but the man never returned my calls. Detective Anders, the person who'd advised me to move away and call whenever I needed help, was on vacation. I was on my own.

I called a locksmith and asked him to make a special house call to put new locks on the doors and windows, remembering even as I did so, how poorly new locks had protected me in New York. When I picked up Miranda at the day care center, Lupe was in another room and didn't even come forward to say hello and the next day when I dropped Miranda off, she was in another part of the daycare center so I had no chance to tell her about the missing pages. It seemed that a woman who had been my friend was now against me too.

When I got to the office, I learned that Mike had left on a on a business trip, maybe to avoid the whole awkwardness of firing a woman he'd once been sleeping with. It would have been nice to talk to him again, but we didn't even have a détente. On this, my last week at work, I'd begun to think that maybe I should leave Texas and go somewhere where Charlie couldn't find me. No one, except Tina, was talking to me. I was in a lonely bubble that no one could touch.

At lunch time I went outside to eat my sandwich. I needed a break from the jollity in the lunchroom that excluded me. I took a seat at a deserted picnic table under a ramada. I had eaten half my sandwich, thinking that perhaps it really was too hot to sit here like a mad Englishman, when I looked up. There was Charlie, leaning against his red truck looking at me.

I froze, prepared to bolt back into the building. I had just gathered up my things to make a run for it, when Charlie moved. He was faster than I was, and stronger and he blocked my way to the door.

"I'm not going to hurt you, Bernie. I just want to talk."

I moved away from him. "Talk from there," I said.

"What's going to happen with my daughter? You and I have joint custody, but I never see her."

"You've been in jail, Charlie. I'm not going to bring her into jail."

"Instead you move to God-damned Texas."

As far away from you as I could get.

"Let's go for a ride, Bernie."

"Not on your life. I'm not getting in that piece of crap with you."

"Let's go inside then It's too damned hot out here. I need somewhere cooler."

"I'm not taking you inside the building. You're a stranger to these people and I don't want them to know we used to be related."

He gestured toward a path that led away from the buildings to a second picnic table perched under some trees beside a small artificial pond. The trees promised shade and the pond some coolness. We walked down the path, sat at the picnic table, and looked at the water.

"I have a right to see Miranda," Charlie said.

"If you want to be in Miranda's life, you need to help support her."

"I'll take you to court again."

"Be my guest."

He stood up, took off his shoes, and waded into the pond until the water was almost to his knees. He reached down and cupped his hands, bringing the water to his lips. I was hot and thirsty, and wanted this discussion to be over so I could go back to my nice air-conditioned office. Charlie held something up in the air. It was my cell phone. The one that had been on the picnic table beside me as I was eating my lunch.

"You want it?"

It wasn't the phone itself, but all the numbers in it that I had nowhere else.

"Charlie please. Just give it back."

He dangled the phone close to the water. "Come on in, Bernie. The water's great."

I took off my shoes and stepped gingerly into the water, slipping on the rocks. Slowly I made my way toward Charlie who held the phone high over his head. Just as I reached him, he grabbed my arm hard and began pulling me down, forcing my head to the water. I struggled against him, slipping and sliding, but I couldn't get purchase and fell head first into the water. He was pushing my head under, and I struggled to get a breath. I kicked and thrashed, fighting for air and feeling things starting to go black, but trying to hang on, because giving up would mean that Miranda would not have her mother. I was losing energy, when suddenly the pressure stopped.

Groggily I lifted my head. Charlie and some man were punching each other in the middle of the pond. Then the man was pushing Charlie down, pounding his head into the rocks. I couldn't watch. Struggling to stand, I made my way gingerly to the edge of the water, and turning my back on the two men, tried to catch my breath. I didn't care what was happening to Charlie; I was only relieved that I was alive. Grabbing my shoes I struggled back along the path toward the office.

I was half way there when I heard footsteps behind me.

"Bernie," the man called. I turned. He was balding, with Asian features and seemed vaguely familiar. Had I met him before? He began to walk beside me.

"What happened to Charlie?" I asked.

"Don't worry. Not bother you again. "

"Thank you for saving me."

"You welcome."

"Have I met you before?"

"Don't think so. Name is Sonny."

"How did you happen to be there at the right time?"

He shrugged and kept walking beside me. I didn't know everyone who worked for Mike, and this guy could be perfectly innocent, but his appearance spooked me.

We had reached the area of the picnic table when I remembered my phone.

"I have to go back," I said. "Charlie has my cell."

I turned and that's when I felt the handkerchief over my mouth and the smell of chloroform. Then everything went black.

Chapter Thirty Five

Mike

On Thursday Mike went to have supper with his mother. He'd come back from Mexico the day before, but the trip, which he'd hoped would help him distance himself from Bernie, had done the opposite. He was hurt that Bernie had lied to him, but that annoyance paled in comparison to the fear that she was now in danger. Being fired hadn't convinced her to move back to New York, just the opposite. He needed to sit down and tell her everything from the beginning and let her make her own decision.

He could smell his mother's enchiladas as soon as he walked in the door. At home he had a good housekeeper who doubled as a cook, but no one could cook like his mom.

They were almost done with the meal when his mother said "I wonder when Bernie is coming back."

"Coming back? Where did she go?"

"You're still angry at her aren't you?"

"I guess so," he said. "I've been too busy to think about it," which was a lie because all he'd done while lying on his bed in his hotel room had been to think about Bernie.

"Caylee told me that she and Bernie were going to Goliad. They were having a girls' week out and would be back in a few days. At least that's what she said when she picked Miranda up yesterday."

"Did Bernie tell you about the trip?"

Lupe shook her head, and returned with a piece of paper which she handed to Mike. "Caylee gave me this. You think I did wrong, Mike, giving Caylee the baby?" Mike looked at the note, giving permission for Caylee to pick up the baby. It didn't look like Bernie's handwriting.

"I didn't think they liked each other," he said aloud. "After that horse riding trip where Caylee got shot, they didn't talk much." He felt fear rising in his belly. *Why would Caylee pick up Miranda from day care?*

"I think I'll call Caylee," he said, dialing the number. It rang and rang and finally the voice mail came on and he left his message. "Caylee, this is Mike West. If you're around, please call me. It's important."

"You could go to Bernie's house, Mike. See if she's there. It's possible that the two of them got back tonight."

He jumped up from the chair.

"I'll wait dessert," Lupe said.

He drove to Bernie's house which was dark, the front door locked. He took out his flashlight and began walking around the building, shining the light in through the window. From what he could see of the kitchen, it looked like the normal clutter of a busy woman, who might be returning that evening. He couldn't see into the bedroom, so he had no chance to see evidence of clothes being packed. Everything looked ordinary, and that, more than anything, made him worry. He drove back to his mother's house.

"What did you find?"

"The house looked as though she's gone for the day. I was tempted to break in, to see if she'd really left, but I don't think she'd appreciate that.

How did Miranda react when Caylee picked her up?"

"She wasn't happy. The baby doesn't know Caylee, so there was a lot of crying and fussing while Caylee got her into the car seat. I tried to calm Mira down, but she wanted none of it. If anything happens to that child..."

They sat in silence for a moment, each imagining the worst.

Mike remembered when he and Caylee were dating, and had talked casually of getting married. Caylee had been firm on the idea of no kids. Now he realized that this was probably why their relationship had tapered off. He wanted more than a wife. He wanted a family.

"I'm driving to Caylee's house," he said.

"Tonight? It's twenty miles one way."

"I can't just sit here and wait for something to happen. And Mom, can I borrow the note from Bernie?"

The trip to Caylee's house yielded nothing. The house was as dark and as closed up as Bernie's had been. He performed the same ritual, walking the perimeter, shining a flashlight in through the windows. Caylee's car was missing and, that alone, told him she'd gone somewhere. Had she and Bernie really gone to Goliad?

He drove back to his own home and phoned his mother, though it was already close to eleven o'clock. Then he undressed and lay down in the bed, his mind whirling. Had Bernie gone to Goliad against her will? What reason would Caylee have to take her? He knew the two women weren't friends, and he was probably responsible for that, but he hadn't expected jealousy to erupt into violence. At about three o'clock he fell into a fitful sleep, where he was running after a figure he assumed to be

Bernie, but she kept disappearing around the corner.

The next day, Friday, he went into the office, just as Tina was sitting down to work. Perhaps it had all been a mistake and in a few minutes Bernie would breeze in and take her seat at the computer.

"Where's Bernie?" he asked.

Tina shook her head. "I don't know Mike. On Wednesday she went outside to eat and never returned. About one-thirty, Caylee came in with a note from Bernie, saying you'd given her permission to take some time off. Caylee said the two of them were going away."

"The two of them? Not Miranda?"

"She didn't mention Miranda. Is something wrong?"

"Can I see the note? And do you have something that she's written?"

"Sure. What's going on, Mike? I'm getting worried."

Bernie had been missing since Wednesday and it was now Friday. If he'd given Bernie permission to take time off during her last week of work, he would have remembered. He put the note from Bernie next to the handwriting sample Tina supplied. Definitely a different writer. Then he took out the note his mother had received. It was the same writer as Tina's note, but the script wasn't Bernie's.

"I'm going to scour the grounds," he said. "Maybe she's had an accident."

He went outside where the employee picnic table stood. It was just too hot to eat and the place was deserted. Pulling the chairs away from the table, he studied the area underneath and then he saw it. A purse. He didn't pay much attention to women's purses, but this one looked like Bernie's.

He unzipped it and looked inside. There was a wallet with about twenty dollars and a New York State driver's license with Bernie's name and picture. No woman would go on a trip and leave her purse sitting under a picnic table. His heart clenched.

He looked at the path leading toward the pond, trying not to imagine what he might see. It had been days since anyone had seen Bernie and the heat had kept people away. He walked down the path, and was within sight of the pond when he saw it. There, in the middle of the water was the body of a man, lying face down. At first Mike thought it might be an employee, but no one had been reported missing. That didn't prove anything. Bernie had been missing since Wednesday and he hadn't known about it.

He walked closer and saw that some creature had begun feeding on the bloated body. He could smell decomposition too. My God. This was the backyard of his business. He took out his cell phone and dialed 9 1 1 and asked to be connected to the local police. He would be waiting for them in the parking lot. At least the body wasn't Bernie's he thought as he walked slowly back up the path. Thank God it wasn't Bernie.

When the police and the ambulance arrived, he walked the men back down the path to where the body lay. A man, whom Mike assumed to be the coroner, waded out into the pond to turn the body over and prod and poke at it. Another man in plain clothes, no doubt a detective, was going through the pockets, looking for identification. A photographer came and took pictures, then paramedics loaded the body on a stretcher and hauled it down the path. When Mike got back to picnic area, they were loading the body into an ambulance, and people were stringing yellow police tape across the entrance to the path.

He was sitting at the picnic table when one of the detectives came over.

"The dead man is Charles Robertson, do you know him?"

Mike nodded. "I was dating his ex-wife," he said. "I didn't know she was married at the time. He showed up here about a week ago and we had a few words. But *she's* the one who's missing. The reason I came out here was to try and find where she might have gone."

The detective, whose name was Shryer was looking at him sharply. Was he himself now a suspect? "I didn't know Bernie was married until this dude showed up at a dance. That was the only time we had contact."

"Where was the dance?"

"The Starlight Café here in Rosalita."

The detective had taken out a notebook and was writing in it. "I'm worried about Bernie Robertson," Mike said. "She's disappeared and no one has heard from her since Wednesday."

"Did she tell you where she was going?"

"She left a note with the other secretary, but the handwriting isn't hers."

"It doesn't mean she didn't decide to go somewhere, Mr. West. Did you have a handwriting expert analyze the note?"

"No."

"I wouldn't worry too much about it. Sometimes when we write in a hurry, we write sloppily."

"I found her purse under the picnic table. What woman would go on a trip and forget her purse?"

"Anything in it?"

"Her wallet. And her car's still in the parking lot, along with her husband's truck."

The detective looked at him for a minute. "If you're really worried, go down to the station and fill out a missing person's report. But keep in mind, if they think she's just taken a trip, they may not do anything. You'll just have to be patient. How many people work here, Mr. West?"

"Twenty five, including myself."

"We're going to have to close down everything. My colleague and I want to interview every single person who might have walked through this area. I'm sorry for the inconvenience, but that's the way it is."

Mike tried not to think about how some of his employees would react to being interviewed by the police. Most of them were legal, but there were always a few who had relatives or friends who had been deported after an interview. He was careful who he hired, but he paid more attention to a man or woman's work ethics than to where they were born.

"Let me talk to my people first," Mike said.

"I want to speak with *everyone*," Shryer said.

Chapter Thirty Six

Mike

Three days later, Mike got a call from Shryer again. "We have just a few more questions for you, Mr. West. Can we meet at your office?"

He'd gone to the police station and filled out a missing person's report. He'd put up posters with Bernie's picture on them in every public place he could think of. He'd put an ad in the local paper offering a reward for information about her whereabouts, but so far no one knew what had happened. He had been trying to concentrate on his work, but the thought of Bernie as someone's prisoner haunted him. He was getting very little work done at the office, so he might as well talk to the police.

He invited the detectives into his home office, and Maria brought them all coffee. When they'd settled into their chairs he said. "What can I do for you?"

Detective Shryer gestured toward the other man. "This is Detective Young. We're here to talk to you about the evening at The Starlight Cafe."

"Do you have a quick temper, Mr. West?" Young asked.

"No, not generally."

"People outside the bar remember you threatening a man. From their description, that man was Charles Robertson."

"Maybe I pushed Charlie against the wall. I thought he was bothering Bernie."

"You just called him Charlie. You told us you'd only met the man once."

Marguerite Mooers

"That was what Bernie called him."

"Bernie is?"

"Charles Robertson's wife. The woman I was dating. The woman who is missing." *Hadn't these guys been listening to anything he was saying?*

"It must have been inconvenient for the woman you were dating to have a husband."

"I didn't know about Charlie. Well, I knew about him, but she told me he was dead."

"Why did Mrs. Robertson tell you that?"

Mike got up and walked over to the coffee urn and poured himself another cup of coffee. All this questioning wasn't helping him find Bernie. That's what the police should have been working on.

"Mr. West, why did Mrs. Robertson tell you her husband was dead?"

"I don't know. I guess she wanted me to think she was free to date."

"Let's go back to the afternoon when you found the body. Why did you walk down that path behind your property? "

"I was looking for Bernie. On Wednesday, she went out for lunch and didn't come back to work. Some time Wednesday afternoon, Caylee Harder came into the office and told Bernie's co-worker, that she and Bernie were going on a trip and would be gone for a few days. Then Caylee went to the daycare center and picked up Bernie's daughter, Miranda, telling my mother, that she and Bernie and Miranda would be away for a while."

"So maybe she *did* go on a trip."

"I don't think so. She never asked for time off. I went over to her house. It was locked and there was no evidence of packing. She left her purse under the picnic table and her car in the

266

parking lot. Why would she go without telling anyone?"

"Had you been getting along well with Mrs. Robertson?"

Mike sighed. *Could he adequately describe their up and down relationship to these guys?*

"We'd been getting along fine."

"You are her employer, Mr. West. Mrs. Robertson was living in a house on your property. Maybe it was just too much closeness? Perhaps she was trying to get away from you?"

Mike shook his head. "I would have backed off if that was what she wanted."

"Where were you on the day Charles Robertson was killed?

"I was returning from a buying trip to Mexico."

"What time did you return to Rosalita?"

"About one. I got home, threw my bags on the floor and went to bed. I didn't even go to the office. "

"Did you contact anyone after you got home?"

"Nope."

"And you're sure you didn't see or talk to Charles Robertson that day?"

"I'm sure. What's this about? " He looked at the two men.

"Charlie Robertson was killed sometime in the early afternoon on Wednesday. We're trying to determine who might have motive and means to kill him."

"I did not kill Charlie Robertson. Hell, I hardly knew the man."

"But you were dating his wife. That might give you a motive to get him out of the way. Do you have a temper, Mr. West?"

"No, I don't think so. I'm fair to my workers."

"Tell us about Marcus Phillips."

"Phillips?" *It took him a minute. Yeah that was the bastard he'd caught stealing. The guy was brazenly loading coffee into the trunk of his car, right in the parking lot. It was only by accident that Mike had walked by and seen him and asked what he was doing.*

"He was stealing from me. I fired him."

"After you beat him up?"

"I didn't beat him up. OK, I threw a punch at him."

"You broke his nose. And then what happened? You walked down the path to the pond?"

Had he? Yeah, he guessed so. "I wanted to talk to the man in private. I was so mad I couldn't see straight. I had given this guy a job and paid him well. Why did he steal from me?"

"What happened on that walk?"

"Nothing much. We argued. He told me I didn't pay him enough, and he felt entitled, *entitled* to help himself to the product."

"So you pushed him into the water and tried to drown him?"

"It wasn't like that. We fought, I admit that. I pushed him down, or maybe he slipped on the rocks. Then I walked back up the path, retrieved the coffee he'd stolen and got security to escort him off the property."

"Mr. Phillips tried to sue you, didn't he?"

Mike nodded. "Said I'd tried to kill him."

"Did you?"

"What?"

"Try to kill him?"

"Hell no. I'll admit I get a little hot under the collar when I find a man stealing from me, but he deserved what he got. You know what? I don't give a flying fuck about Charlie Robertson. The person I care about is Bernie. She's the one who's gone missing. I've done everything I can to try and find her, and you guys aren't doing a damned thing."

"We don't deal with missing persons," White said sourly. "Did you file a report?"

"Of course I did. Not a single member of the police has come out here to ask about her. No one. What does that say about your priorities?"

Shryer folded the notebook and shoved it into his pocket. "Thanks for the coffee," he said and then he and White were gone.

He should return to work, and try to push all of this out of his mind, but the thoughts kept whirling around. Would anyone believe that he'd fired Bernie to protect her? Not a chance. Would anyone, having seen Charlie's body on his property, believe that he was innocent of murder? The police didn't believe him. Bernie was gone, and he could only suspect that the worst had happened.

Two days later Shryer and White were back. Reluctantly he invited them into his office. He hated the sons of bitches. They were doing nothing to find Bernie.

Detective Shryer leaned forward. "Let me give you my scenario, Mr. West. You and Mrs. Robertson had a fight. She'd decided she wanted to break up with you, and you didn't want that. When you left for Mexico, she got a friend to take the baby from the daycare center and the two women and the baby go somewhere where you can't find her. She's afraid of you. Afraid of your temper."

"I never..." Mike began.

"Hear me out. When you get back from your trip, Charles Robertson comes calling. He's learned that you're dating his wife, and he wants her back. He parks his truck in your parking lot and comes to find you. The two of you walk down to the pond and argue about whether Mrs. Robertson is going to stay with you or return to her husband. The argument escalates, he throws a punch, you throw a punch. He lands in the water and smashes his head against a stone. An accident, but now Charles Robertson is dead on your land."

"Why would I call the police about a man I killed?"

White shrugged

"I DID NOT KILL CHARLIE ROBERTSON." Mike shouted.

"Duly noted. After you killed Mr. Robertson you went home, leaving the body where you hoped nobody would find it."

Mike jumped up from his chair. "I DID NOT KILL CHARLIE ROBERTSON."

"So you have said. Tell me, if you didn't kill Mr. Robertson. Who did?"

"I don't have any idea."

"And if you didn't kill him, why would he be dead on your property?"

Mike shook his head. They sat in silence for a moment.

Detective Shryer pulled out a plastic bag from his pocket. Inside was a cell phone. He handed the bag to Mike. "We found this near the body. Is it yours?"

He took the bag and looked at the phone. It was Bernie's. Something terrible had happened to her and he was helpless to do anything.

"It's Bernie's. I'm sure of it."

Shryer and White both stood up. "Mr. West there is no such thing as coincidence. We believe that you tried to kill Marcus Phillips, and you did kill Charles Robertson. We're taking you into custody for his murder."

"This is all wrong," he said. "I'm not the person you should be arresting. You need to find out where Bernie Robertson has gone."

"Mr. West," said Shryer. "If you'll just come with us."

"No," Mike shouted. "I've been trying to tell you..."

Shryer was close, reaching out with the cuffs, when Mike hauled off and decked him. Shryer went down, hit his head on a table and lay still.

Shit, I've killed him, Mike thought.

White was looking on in horror. Mike could make a run for it, but that would get him into worse trouble. White knelt by his partner, and Mike watched in relief as Shryer groaned and then roused himself.

"Assaulting an officer is a serious crime," White said. He helped Shryer to a couch. Mike ran to a sink and got a towel and held it out to White, who put it on Shryer's head. Then he sat and watched as White called for an ambulance.

"You're coming with me," White said after Shryer had been loaded into the ambulance, "And no more funny business."

He was cuffed and loaded into the police car and taken to the station where he was booked into jail.

Chapter Thirty Seven

Mike

He had been sitting in the lockup for a few days when Shryer came in. The detective sat down beside Mike as though they were best buds. Mike moved away. It was all he could do not to punch the bastard again.

"The charges have been dropped," he said. "Though if it had been up to me, I'd of left you here to rot."

Mike looked toward the cell door which now stood open. Standing there were Kyle Harder and a balding Asian man Mike didn't know. He supposed that he owed these men his freedom, though he'd hoped never to see Kyle again in his life.

"You're coming with us, Mike," Kyle said.

"I have a business to run. I've been away too long already."

Kyle moved forward and took Mike firmly by one arm and the Asian man took the other. He had no choice. They hustled him out of the jail and to a waiting limousine. They drove to San Antonio where a private jet was waiting, and he was escorted aboard. When they were airborne, a stewardess came around offering them drinks. Mike took a coke. He needed to keep his wits about him.

Kyle gestured toward the Asian man. "I'd like to introduce my bodyguard, Sonny"

Mike reached forward to shake the man's hand and his own was gripped in a vice so hard he thought his fingers would be broken. Trying to extricate himself without being too wussy, he looked up to see the man smiling. The bastard was enjoying this.

"Sonny saved me from a black kid who was trying to rob me," Kyle said.

"Boss carry too much money." Sonny said softly. "*Baah Kwai.*"

Kyle nodded. "He's saying I wasn't smart. Anyway, Sonny comes to my rescue, beats the guy up, offers his service as my bodyguard. Did you know Sonny was born in Thailand?"

He should have stayed there, Mike thought.

"Nice place to vacation" Sonny said. "No good if you born poor."

"But you learned some useful skills there, didn't you," Kyle said, looking at Sonny.

Sonny nodded. Kyle seemed proud of this jerk, as though Sonny had taught him everything.

"Why am I here, Kyle?" Mike asked. "You've sprung me from jail and now you're flying me somewhere. What is it you want?"

"We've heard that this woman, Bernie, has a journal her mother wrote. The mother talked about crossing the border on Christmas Day, 1993. How could this have come out, Mike? We paid you a lot of money to keep things quiet."

"I did keep things quiet." *Why had he ever agreed to be involved in this? It had ruined his life, destroyed any self-respect he'd ever felt. He looked at Kyle and this other man. He hated them.*

"What does she know, Mike?"

He sat, arms crossed staring at the two men.

"Come on, Mike. We're waiting. How did Bernie get hold of the journal and what does she know? "

"She doesn't know anything."

"I think she does," Kyle said.

"Is that why you kidnapped her?" he asked. "You've taken her because you think she's going to reveal your dirty little secret. I'm telling you she's innocent."

"We could make her talk." Sonny said, flexing his fingers. "Should have done it long ago. Save lot of trouble."

Kyle looked at Mike. "I should have taken care of you that night, Mike. I could have made up something --accident with the gun, got run over by a drunk Mexican, fell into the Rio Grande and drowned. Everything would have been so much simpler."

Mike felt a sharp pang of anxiety. They could do it here, and no one would be the wiser. If they'd already killed Bernie and Miranda, one more body wouldn't make any difference.

"How did you find Bernie?" he asked.

"Boss very smart," Sonny said, "but J.W. rich."

"A couple of months after the event, I realized that there was someone we had forgotten so I hired a couple of detectives to find her." Kyle said. "If you have nowhere else to go in Laredo, the nuns can always find you a place. Eventually we found the mother."

"Lilliana Morales?"

"A little jingle always loosens people's tongues. We took care of that problem."

"And Bernie?"

"We knew who her adoptive parents were, but not where she'd gone. We even put an ad in the local paper, hoping to lure her out. Then her father published a book, with his kid's picture in it, and we had a name and where she lived."

"And this," Kyle handed him a newspaper cutting. It announced the wedding of Bernice

Sorengard to Charles Robertson. The address of the couple's new home was highlighted in pink.

Kyle took out a small silver tape recorder and set it on a table, then he took a sip of his drink. "This is an edited version of Bernie talking with her mother on September 21." Kyle pushed a button and Bernie's voice filled the cabin.

"I'm just so tired of the same dream where someone is chasing me through the desert..."

"When are you going to see Dr. Swartz?"

"Next Wednesday."

"You bugged her cell phone?" Mike asked.

Kyle laughed. "Don't you just love modern technology? You can listen in without even touching the phone."

"So you found Bernie in New York."

"And the therapist who hypnotized her." Kyle said. "Unfortunately he died, but then the secretary was suspicious about her boss' death." He pressed the button again.

"Did you find the files, Ellen?"

"Nope, but I found where your files should have been. Your file was the only one missing. Bernie, I have something I want to show you. but I don't want to tell you over the phone. Can you meet me at Fancy Beans tomorrow at three o'clock?"

"What happened to the secretary?" Mike asked.

"Bad accident," Sonny said.

"You killed these people so Bernie wouldn't learn what happened that night?"

"Insurance, my friend. When I become Director, none of this will matter, but right now we need to minimize the damage. Tell me she doesn't remember anything."

"She doesn't remember anything," he said aloud. He thought of the papers in his pocket.

There was one person who would testify about the crime, and he would lend his own voice to hers. First, though, he had to survive this plane trip with two killers.

Chapter Thirty Eight

Bernie

I woke in the dark, feeling dizzy and sick to my stomach. I was lying on a cot with something was sticking into my arm. Clumsily I reached over and felt the needle, held in place with tape. Damn, they had drugged me. I had no idea how long I'd been here. It could have been hours, days, weeks, even months. And where was Miranda? If I'd been gone a month, would Lupe still be caring for her? Of course. The thought made my panicky heart slow to something that seemed to be normal. At least my daughter was safe.

I hated the thought of the drugs. If I were going to leave this place, I needed my grey matter to be functional, so I fumbled with the tape and painfully pulled out the needle. Sitting up was going to be the next challenge. Slowly I raised myself from the bed, feeling a wave of dizziness wash over me. My stomach roiled and I bent over and dry-heaved on the floor. I was terribly thirsty, and now that my stomach was empty, hungry.

Mainly I needed to move. Whoever had drugged me and kept me here would be coming back soon. I listened carefully for the sounds of anyone outside, but all was silence. The only illumination came from a small window, high up on the wall which showed a pale pink light, either sunrise or sunset. I stood up, breathing hard. *I can do this. I can do this. Think of the little train.* Getting myself upright, I shuffled across the room, noticing what had been shadows resolving themselves into a wall of stacked cardboard boxes.

277

I knew Caylee's dad had a ranch somewhere in West Texas. Is this where I'd been taken but why? That was a question for which I had no answer.

I looked again at the pile of boxes. It was possible, with a lot of tugging and moving that I could make a sort of ladder up to the window. When I tried to move a single box, though, it was very heavy. and having been drugged and immobile for a long period of time hadn't left me in the best of shape. What the heck was in them? I pried one open and was looking into a carton of expensive tequila. Hopefully all of these cartons did not hold booze. I put four boxes side by side as a base, then lifted three, then two to get up to the window. Some of the boxes were lighter. Clothes, maybe? Watches? Purses? Would Prada purses or Patek Philippe timepieces carry my weight better than good Mexican tequila? The work was slow, and I was getting anxious that someone would come in and catch me in the act. I drew in a deep breath, remembering the Lamaze class I'd taken before my first baby. Breathe in. Concentrate. Lift a box. Breathe out. Concentrate. Put it in place. You can do this. Think of the little train.

In about half an hour I had a stack of boxes, like stair steps leading to the window that was high in the room. The sky that had been a pale rose color when I woke was now turning brighter. Just as I was moving the last box in place, I heard a rattle in the door. There was no more time. I bolted up the 'stairs' and tucked myself under the window.

The door pushed open, someone came in and flipped on the light. Nothing happened. "Damn," a woman's voice said.

She went over to the bed and peered down. Then she took out a flashlight and held it over the bed.

"Shit," she said, pulling out a cell phone and dialing a number. I pushed hard against the window. *Come on. Open.* The woman finished her call and began playing her flashlight around the room. I pushed again. The window protested loudly. The woman looked up and then shone her flashlight directly on me.

"Don't move," she said. *In your dreams, lady.* I pushed against the window, thinking that it hadn't been opened in a hundred years and probably never will. Then I felt it give. I threw my body hard against the window and heard the glass crack and then I was out, tumbling down into the cool morning air and landing on the grass.

My overwhelming instinct was to run as fast as I could, but I couldn't get my legs and feet to understand that concept. I could hear the woman crashing around the corner of the building, calling for me to stay, but I was like a robot with a new handler. *OK feet you have to be under me.* I pressed myself hard against the building hoping that the shadows would hide me, talking to my body at the same time. *Come on feet, move. Right leg up. Left leg up.* I was tottering like a new colt. At last, my body seemed to remember how it was supposed to work, and with some effort I began to run.

What I thought was grass was actually rough pasture, dotted with small scrub bushes and cacti, the kind of pasture that in Texas harbors poisonous snakes, scorpions, spiders, fire ants, chiggers, fleas, and ticks. And that was just the biting or stinging things. There were also Mesquite bushes, Prickly Pear, Horse Crippler, Cholla, and other cacti.

I soldiered on, trying not to think about the clothes I was wearing. Many days or weeks ago, I'd gone to work wearing a nice silk blouse, polyester trousers and sandals. Had I known I would be traveling through all this stuff, I would have worn army boots and leather chaps. I hit a rock and fell, striking my knee sharply.

I could hear people behind me calling to each other as they ran. My only consolation was that they were dealing with the same difficult terrain I was. Someone cried out. Maybe they'd even found the same rock. I stopped and crouched down. I could hear voices circling around, and then moving away. I held my breath praying that they were, like me, out of shape and unused to running through Texas pasture.

When it seemed that the people behind me had given up, I rose and began to walk. It was now full light, but storm clouds had moved in and it looked like rain. In the distance loomed a large house, brightly lit and right out of *Dallas*.

I drew closer to the house which had a long driveway running up toward it. Across the driveway at the entrance, was an iron archway, with an image of cowboys herding cattle cut into the metal, and the words Rocking J underneath. I left the scrub land and began walking up the driveway toward the house. Suddenly a dog bounded toward me, barking. I backed up close to the fence which I saw now, was electrified.

The dog kept his distance, but didn't stop barking. "Don't come any closer," I said. "Or I'll..." What could I do against a homicidal canine, call the dog warden on my cell?

"Ridley? Come here baby," a woman called.

Baby? I would never have characterized this threatening animal as 'baby.'

"Come on Ridley. Come on home."

The woman had spotted me cowering near the fence.

"Don't be afraid of him," she said. "He's really a pussycat. He was abused as a puppy and so he's a little afraid of strangers. Especially men."

A little afraid? This dog needed serious therapy.

"Come on sweetie," the woman said, and Ridley, a changed dog, went placidly over to her. She put her hand on the dog's head and I waited for the dog to eliminate her fingers. Instead she snapped the leash onto his collar. "I wouldn't get too close to that fence," she said. "The electrician who wired it, did a poor job. It could give you quite a jolt. We're going to have him come back tomorrow and fix it."

I heard thunder and saw distant lightning. The threat of rain was serious.

"We'd better get in before we get drenched," the woman said. "By the way, I'm Hannah Grimes, the housekeeper. And who are you?"

"I'm Bernie Robertson."

"You must be Caylee's friend. the one who's here for the weekend. Where are you sleeping?"

In a storage shed on your property. I've had better accommodations. I pointed to the house. "I went for a walk. The place is so big that I forgot how to get back to the room."

"I'll show you," she said, leading the way.

Chapter Thirty Nine

I walked with her up the steps, through the front door and into the lobby. Hannah directed me toward the upstairs bedrooms and then disappeared. When I started up the stairs, someone grabbed me by the arm and marched me backward.

"You come with me," a voice said.

I looked at the man who was gripping me tightly by the arm, the same guy who'd pushed the chloroformed handkerchief in my face. I struggled against him, but he was stronger, bulldozing me down the hallway ahead of him.

"Let me go."

"Not on you life. We work hard to get you here. Now you talk."

He hustled me toward a closed door. I got the fleeing impression of high ceilings, yellow walls, and Texas ancestors in gold frames. A man in a white shirt and dark pants, carrying drinks passed us, entered a room and we followed.

Here it was all dark wood, leather chairs, walls lined with books and paintings of Longhorns grazing in fields of bluebonnets. In addition to the Asian man called Sonny who'd brought me, there were three men in chairs in the room: a man in his fifties, and an older man with thinning hair and Mike.

Mike and I looked at each other in surprise. He stood up and moved toward me. "Where've you been, Bernie."

Sonny held up his hand to prevent Mike from getting closer, and shoved me roughly into a chair, then the older man began to talk.

"I'm glad we're all here. I would have issued a formal invitation, Mrs. Robertson, but you might have refused. Time is getting short, so I'd like to nip things in the bud before they get out of hand."

"Where is my daughter?" I asked.

"Can't you control her?" The older man asked, and Sonny came over to my chair and pulled me up so I was standing. He took my arms and twisted them hard behind my back. "Shut up," he said.

"You're hurting her," Mike said. "J.W. you told me nothing would happen to Bernie."

"You haven't held up your end of the bargain, Mike," J.W. said.

"She doesn't know anything," Mike said.

What was he talking about? What didn't I know? I looked at the man I thought I had loved. In the time since I'd last seen him he'd morphed into a dangerous stranger.

J.W. looked at me. "Tell me about your mother's journal."

"I don't have it. It's at home. If you let me go, I'll be happy to get it for you." If all they wanted was the journal, I'd be glad to retrieve it, though I had no idea how far away from home I was. Then I would hop the first plane back to New York.

"I don't want to see the journal. I want you to tell me what you remember from the journal."

"She doesn't know anything," Mike repeated.

"SHUT UP," J.W. bellowed. "I'm talking to Bernie. What do you remember?"

"My mother left Mexico with her brother- in-law, Enrique and another couple, the Guzmans and their son Jorge. When they were close to

Mexico City, they paid a man to drive them, and he abandoned them after..."

"Yes. Yes. What happened when they crossed over to the U.S.? What did they say about Christmas Day, 1993?"

"I don't know. I didn't read it."

"Why not?"

"The journal was written in Spanish and I needed Lupe to translate, and then the journal was stolen and when I got it back, some pages were cut out."

I looked at Mike who was nodding. *What did he know about this?*

"I told you that there's no problem," Mike said.

"Shut up," J.W. said casually. He turned to Mike. "You seem to know something about this. What happened to those pages?"

Mike reached into his pocket and pulled out the missing pages and handed them over.

J.W. looked at them quickly. "Who the hell can read this. It's in Spanish." He handed the pages back to Mike.

"Look Dad," the younger man said. "We're going overboard with this. Mike's not going to say anything and Bernie doesn't know anything. I don't know why you don't let us take care of it."

"TAKE CARE OF IT?" J.W. bellowed jumping up from his chair. "When you were six and looking up the skirt of the downstairs maid, I was the one giving her extra money so she wouldn't quit. When you shot the neighbor's dog; when you drove my new jeep into the fence; when you cheated on the finals in high school math, who do you think went to the trouble to keep things quiet? You have cost me a lot, Kyle, not just in money but in time and effort. But, I said to myself, he's my son, he's worth it."

"What happened in the desert was self-defense," Kyle said. "They came after me with knives."

"That's not true, Kyle," Mike said.

"You promised."

"I made a mistake in not telling the truth then, but I'm going to tell it now. You shot those people, Kyle. They were defenseless and you shot them."

"The kid had a knife, Mike."

"Yeah, maybe he did. He didn't like you messing with his woman. But what of the others? You killed them in cold blood."

"That's not what you told me," J.W. said, looking at Kyle.

Kyle shrugged. "What's the big deal? They were illegals. They were gonna come over here and take jobs from Americans who pay taxes. They use the schools, the hospitals, the social service system. Why do we need them?"

"Did you kill them in cold blood, Kyle?"

"Have you read the papers lately? Do you know what happens in the border towns of Mexico?"

"Did you murder those people, Kyle?"

Kyle reached over to the table and took a gulp of his drink. J.W. was watching him.

"I'm sorry you are my son," he said quietly. "I have always been proud of our family name. It means something. I was thrilled when they tapped you for public office, thinking that what I'd done for you was justified, because you'd only been a kid. Now I realize that I have squandered not just money, but our good name on a man who has no moral fiber."

"You think I don't care about the repercussions of this thing?" Kyle asked. "It impacts me more than anyone. But we've taken care of it." He looked at Bernie. "Well, most of it."

"What do you mean?" J.W. asked.

"Just like I said. Anyone who might have known something is no longer an issue. It has been contained."

"You killed Dr. Swartz," I said, looking at Sonny. "And Ellen Maynard."

Sonny said nothing.

"You killed my mother because you thought she would tell the whole story."

"And Charlie Robertson," Mike said looking at Sonny. "This isn't going away. I'm telling the police everything I know, especially about the murder of Charlie Robertson."

"No police," Sonny said, reaching toward me and hooking his arm around my neck. I could feel something cold against my temple. A gun.

"Don't do it, Sonny. Please." Mike said.

"It don matter," Sonny said. "I'm already fucked." He pushed me forward. "Walk," he said.

"Sonny, don't do this," Kyle said, but we kept walking.

"You think you know me *Khum* Kyle. You think because you give me job, you my best friend." We were walking toward the glass doors that filled one wall of the library. It was raining hard and beyond the fence I could see Longhorns grazing. I tried to breathe and not think about my child who might soon be an orphan.

"Sonny," Mike said. "Think about this." He moved toward us. I thought he was going to try and take the gun, but Sonny pushed him away, slid the glass door open and we were outside in the rain.

We moved toward the fence and at that moment, Ridley came bounding toward us. He stopped, surprised. I was someone he knew but this other person, this MAN was a stranger. He started barking loudly, showing his teeth, and growling.

"*Bai loi, Maa,*" Sonny cried. The dog held his ground, moving us inch by inch toward the fence.

"*Bai loi. Bai loi,*" Sonny was screaming, genuinely panicked. He moved the gun around, trying to shoot the dog, but his hand was shaking. I felt hands pulling me away and then I was on the grass with Mike on top. Ridley was moving toward Sonny, growling and snapping, inching Sonny inexorably toward the fence. *Come on Ridley. Good boy.*

Sonny's back hit the fence and I could hear the electricity crackle. Sonny stiffened, jerked and then fell forward.

Mike knelt beside me. "Oh God, Bernie. I'm so sorry I ever got you into this," he said.

I was numb. Mike helped me to my feet and I looked over at Kyle down on the ground by Sonny's body. "I think he's dead," Kyle said.

"This isn't going away, Kyle," Mike said. "I've sent the pages from Lilliana's journal to every newspaper that will print it. By tomorrow, everyone will know what kind of man you really are."

"Who will believe a crazy Mexican woman?"

"I'm going to add my voice to hers. And I will request a police investigation into the deaths of Dr. Swartz, Ellen Maynard and Charlie Robertson. You're finished Kyle."

"You wouldn't do that, Mike. We've been friends for a long time."

"I don't think we were ever friends."

I had other issues on my mind. "Is Miranda with your mother, Mike?" He shook his head.

"Where is she?"

"Inside, upstairs." he said, "but..." Before he'd finished I'd already started running toward the house. "Wait, Bernie," Mike called. "We need to talk."

I raced up the stairs and dashed down a corridor that seemed endless, pulling open doors and then slamming them shut. Unless they had her in a shed out in the pasture, she had to be here.

Then I heard it, Miranda's wailing. It was the cry she uses when she is very angry or very tired. I dashed toward the door and pushed it open. Caylee was sitting in a chair and Miranda was standing in the middle of the room, crying.

"Oh baby," I said, rushing toward her and cradling her in my arms. She pushed her face into my chest, hiccupping.

"I know how it looks, Bernie," Caylee said. "But I was never going to hurt her, I promise you."

I wanted to punch Caylee, to tear her hair out, but I had my arms full of my daughter. Instead I walked over and stomped my foot hard on her sandaled toes.

"Ow. That wasn't fair."

"What was going to happen to her, Caylee? Did you ever think of that? They kidnapped me, and if they thought I knew anything they would have killed me. Did you have orders to kill the baby too?"

"No, Bernie. Of course not. I would have taken her with me, protected her, though to tell you the truth I'm not that fond of children." My anger was winding down. I stroked Miranda's fine hair, feeling the weight of her in my arms. I sat down in a chair and put her in my lap. She snuggled against me.

"I need to say something." It was Mike, standing in the doorway.

Caylee jumped up. "I've got to go see my dad."

I didn't tell her about Sonny's death, or Kyle's admission to being a murderer. She'd find out soon enough. Caylee fled and Mike sat down.

Miranda was falling asleep in my arms.

"I can't ask you to forgive me," Mike said. "I've done some terrible things. But I'd appreciate it if you'd hear me out."

Miranda had her thumb in her mouth and was breathing loudly as she settled into sleep. "Go ahead, I'm listening."

"I'll start at the beginning." He took a deep breath. "I grew up on this ranch, the Rocking J. My father was the foreman and my mother was the cook. I didn't have any brothers or sisters, so Kyle and Caylee filled that role. Especially Kyle. Caylee was just a girl, and younger than we were."

"Anyway, Kyle and I did everything together. We rode horses all over the place, learned to smoke, stole whiskey from J.W.'s liquor cabinet, talked about girls and stuff. He was kind of wild, willing to try anything, and I was three years younger, a kid who looked up to him. Once we put a penny on the railroad track and waited while the train went over it to flatten it. I remember the vibration of the train as it went by, thinking that I all I wanted was that power. Kyle represented that power to me. He was like an older brother who could teach me the ropes, show me how to be a grown up. When my dad died, I had no other man in my life. Kyle became that man."

"Anyway on the day before Christmas, 1993, Kyle and I decided we would go down to Nuevo Laredo and have some fun. He was sixteen, almost drinking age. I was only thirteen, but I was tall, and I was sure no one would question my age. At any rate we drove down, bummed around the town, had a lot of drinks and ended up in a little bar with a pool table. It was Christmas Eve, people were getting drunk or just having a good time. Kyle was playing pool and this little, dark haired Mexican girl came up to flirt. She didn't speak any English, but I spoke Spanish and anyway, what she wanted didn't need any translation. Her name was Paloma, I think."

"Paloma Rivera. She was going to be a movie star."

"She was flirty and fun and Kyle warmed up to her. I was too shy. Kyle taught her to play pool. Then he started putting his hands all over her and she pulled away. A guy came up, her boyfriend I think, and asked Kyle to stop bothering her."

"'Flaco' Hernandez. Skinny guy?"

"It's like you know these people. I wasn't paying much attention to him. I was watching Kyle. The thing about Kyle is that no one ever tells him *no*. All his life, he's had anything he's ever wanted, and if he makes a mistake, so what? He doesn't have to pay the consequences. The girl went back to a table where a bunch of other people were sitting and I tried to talk him into letting the whole thing ride."

I thought about the scene. The bar would have been decorated for Christmas and there would have been Anglos and Latinos crowded together, all eating, drinking and talking in their own language. My uncle Enrique would have been there, and the Guzmans. Where was I in all this?

Maybe sitting on my mother's lap, eating refried beans with chicken and yawning with weariness. 'Flaco' and Paloma were teenagers. They had great dreams of life in America. For the others, especially the adults, there might have been anxiety mingled with some relief that the trip was almost over.

"One of the men, who seemed to be the leader, paid the bill and then all of them stood up and left. Kyle was watching them go. The girl never looked back and I think Kyle felt this was a contest that he had lost. One thing Kyle does not do well is lose."

"I went to the men's room and when I came back, Kyle had disappeared. I waited for a while, thinking he might have gone to have a smoke, or he might be using the men's room himself."

"Finally I went outside. He had pulled the car out of the parking lot and was gunning it toward the street and the desert beyond. I got him to slow down and let me in. He was driving crazily. I asked him what was wrong, but he said nothing. Then I saw them. The group of people from the bar, walking fast away from town, into the desert."

"It had started to snow, just lightly and I thought the car would get stuck if we went out into the desert, but I couldn't convince Kyle to turn around and go back. We caught up with the group and stopped the car. They huddled together. I tried to say something, to tell them not to be afraid, when suddenly Kyle pulled out a gun."

"No," I said. "No." He turned the gun toward me. He would have shot me right there.

Then he turned to the oldest man and shot him. The people started screaming, crying, begging for their lives, but he continued to shoot until every single one was dead."

I thought of my uncle, who'd lost his wife in childbirth, his friends Adriana and Diego Guzman and their son Jorge. Antonio "Flaco" Hernandez and his girlfriend Paloma Rivera. All of them lying dead in the desert, with the snow falling over them.

"It wasn't until you mentioned to me that your mother arrived at the orphanage on Christmas Day covered with snow that I remembered there had been two other people sitting at the table in the bar, a mother and her little girl who had not been killed by Kyle, but who had been witnesses."

I don't know how my mother had the foresight to hide as Kyle and Mike drove up. Maybe it was just the luck of having to pee behind a rock or maybe it was something else. Six people had been shot, and only two of us had survived. I closed my eyes, imaging the gunshots, and seeing my mother's grim face as we struggled away from the scene into the desert.

"I was a kid, Bernie. I had no power to stop Kyle from shooting those people. When we got back to the ranch, I didn't even have the courage to tell J.W. what had really happened. A month later, I convinced my mother that she and I should leave the ranch. My father was already dead, so it was easier. I didn't explain the real reason why I wanted to leave, I just said I needed a change of scene. It took me a long time to come to terms with my own cowardice, and I haven't forgiven myself today. When I was twenty-seven, J.W. contacted me. He wanted to give me some money, he said, to help me set myself up in business. He didn't pretend that it was anything other than hush money. But I was grateful to get it. I can't return that money, but I did use some of it, to try and make amends to the people of Tapachula for what happened in the desert."

Miranda was now fully asleep and I set her carefully down on the bed.

"One more thing. You heard me say that Charlie is dead. Sonny killed him." He reached over to take my hands, but I pulled away from him. "I am so sorry for all of this."

"Charlie and I were already divorced when I came here, Mike. He only said we were married because he wanted to hurt me."

"Why didn't you tell me the truth, Bernie. I would have accepted it."

"It seemed too sordid. Would you really have had any regard for me if I'd said, I was a divorced woman whose husband was in jail? I wanted to make a clean start here and I wanted you to like me."

So much had happened that was surprising and sad. I thought about the bodies of the six people I had grown to know, lying un-mourned in the desert. Few, including the relatives left behind, could know what happened.

Mike was looking at me. "I can't deny what I've done, Bernie. Can you forgive me?"

"I want to go home," I said.

He nodded. "We're a long way from Rosalita, but I can get us there."

Chapter Forty

Two days later the article appeared in the New York Times. In it were quotes from my birth mother's diary and from Mike. I don't know what the President said to Kyle Harder, but there was also an announcement saying that Kyle had withdrawn his name from the short list of nominees "for personal reasons."

Of course, the story was all over television too. "Though the information is still sketchy," one television announcer said, "the author of the article Harold Barrenger has said that he received a handwritten document, from a witness to the massacre, accompanied by a statement from another. The first witness is apparently deceased, but the second witness, whose name shall be kept secret, is still alive and willing to testify in court against Kyle Harder . A criminal investigation has begun."

Mike had done everything he threatened to do. I didn't know yet how I felt about the revelations. As secret as Mike's identity might be now, people would find out. It was just too hot a story. J.W., Caylee and Kyle were still alive. How did Caylee feel now that her brother was known as a killer?   How would Guadalupe feel when she learned that Mike had been at the site of the killing and kept it secret all these years? I had little sympathy for Caylee, she had snatched Miranda and put her in danger. But Guadalupe had been good to both us. I needed to talk with her.

I put Miranda in the car seat and drove over to Lupe's house. It was the middle of the day, but I heard no sounds of children as I knocked. Finally,

Lupe came to the door. She was wearing a dark dress, and when she got closer, I could see her eyes were red from weeping.

When she saw it was me, she almost closed the door in my face.

"Lupe, please. We need to talk."

She nodded and I followed her into the house, carrying Miranda. I had never been here when there weren't children around, and it seemed not just quiet, but terribly lonely. I suddenly understood why she had decided to open the day care center.

"Where are all the kids?" I asked.

"I am taking a vacation," she said. "Sooner or later it will come out that Mike was involved in all of this and then no-one will bring their children here."

"But you aren't responsible for what happened in the desert."

She nodded. "Tell that to the parents of these children. Many of them are the children or grand-children of immigrants. They trusted me, Bernie. Now, because Mike is my son, they will not."

"Mike was just an innocent bystander, Lupe. He couldn't stop Kyle from killing those people and I think he did everything to make amends. Do you know he built a school in Chiapas that he supports by himself? He is your son, Lupe. Can't you forgive him?"

She sat down hard in a chair, put her head in her hands and started to cry. I sat down beside her with Miranda in my lap and put my arm around her shoulder. Miranda patted her arm. "Sometimes people get caught up in terrible things, and through no fault of their own, become sinners too."

She raised her face from her hands. "Do you love him, Bernice?"

Did I? He was much better than anyone I'd ever had in my life. I nodded.

"You should tell him that. Right now he needs a friend."

I got into the car and Miranda and I went to the plant, where after some searching, we found Mike in the sheds, inspecting the product. He looked tired and I wondered if he'd gotten any sleep.

"Can we talk, Mike?" I asked.

He nodded and without a word, we walked to the picnic table where I had encountered Charlie, and sat.

"Mike. I came to tell you that ...if you need a friend, I'm here."

"It could get nasty," Mike said. "At some point people will know that I sent that stuff to the papers. Kyle was popular. Some people will say I should have kept that secret to myself."

"I can't believe it."

"The person who blows the whistle isn't always a hero."

"But you did the right thing, Mike."

"I was wrong in not doing it years ago." He looked at me. "Is that all you came to tell me, that you want to be my friend?"

I nodded.

He looked at Miranda, who held out her arms to him. He took her into his arms and she hugged him hard. When she was sitting on his lap, he said. "I don't want to be just your friend, Bernie, I want to be your lover. I want to be your husband."

I loved him, too, but was I ready to be his wife? My daughter had already made up her mind, and I knew she was a gal with very strong opinions.

He took my hand across the table. "I've never asked anyone to marry me, Bernie, but I'm asking you. Will you marry me, flaws and all?"

I thought for a minute and then shook my head.

His face fell. "I thought you cared for me?"

"I do, Mike. I love you. I have never loved anyone the way I love you."

"But why?"

"Let me try to explain." I got up and went around the table so we were sitting side by side. I took his hand, and we sat there silently for a minute. Then I said, "I have been married since I was seventeen, so for about a third of my life I've been someone's wife. I've only been single since November, and to tell you the truth, I like the feeling."

He withdrew his arm and moved away from me. "So you won't marry me?"

"I didn't say never, Mike, just not right now."

"I could be a good husband to you, and a good father to Miranda."

"I know that. You're the best man I've ever known."

"And this has nothing to do with what happened in the desert?"

"I'm sorry you didn't tell me everything. If you had, I might have been able to protect myself and Miranda from J.W., Kyle and Caylee and Sonny. But I've forgiven you for that."

"I wish I had trusted you enough to tell you."

"Mike, all that is past. We can't change it. We need to go on."

He reached forward and kissed me, drawing me to him, with Miranda between us. "I love you, Bernie. I want you and Miranda for my family. I will do everything in my power to keep you safe. You believe that don't you?"

"I do," I said.

"But you won't marry me."

We drew apart and I looked at him. "I said I wouldn't marry you now, Mike. I didn't say I'd never marry you."

He looked crestfallen and I needed to cheer him up, because this was a man I loved, and would one day marry. "Let's go to Mexico on our honeymoon," I said. "I'd like to see the area that my birth mother came from."

"It's a beautiful part of the country with mountains and coffee plantations. Wait a minute, you said our honeymoon."

"Uh huh. Our honeymoon, in about a year or so, when we've gotten so used to each other that we know each other's teeniest, tinyest secrets. When that happens, I promise. I will marry you."

The End

Did you like the book?

Think of writing a review recommending a book to a friend. You are not only helping the author, but you are helping other readers find a book they might like. To review the book, click on my name and the title, and then click on the line of stars Write what you honestly feel about the book. And thank you for being a reader and for helping me write the best books I can.

A word to my readers

Every novel begins somewhere. It may be another book, it may be a whispered story at a party or a magazine article that catches your attention. This book began with a dream of a woman running through a snowy landscape, pursued by a man with a gun. Why was she running? Who was chasing her? Who was with her? In this case her daughter. From its shadowy inception a novel blooms and many of the questions contained in the original premise are answered. And since I like to put love stories in my murder mysteries, there is one here. And a happy ending. I'm a sucker for happy endings.

Thank you for choosing this book. You, my reader, are the reason I write. You can contact me through my Facebook page or e-mail me at funstories043@gmail.com

Made in the USA
Middletown, DE
07 September 2019